DEADLY ORDEAL

DEADLY ORDEAL

Miles Tripp

This first world edition published in Great Britain 1999 by
SEVERN HOUSE PUBLISHERS LTD of
9–15 High Street, Sutton, Surrey SM1 1DF.
This first world edition published in the U.S.A. 2000 by
SEVERN HOUSE PUBLISHERS INC of
595 Madison Avenue, New York, N.Y. 10022.

British Library Cataloguing in Publication Data

Tripp,   Miles,   1923-
        Deadly ordeal
        1.Detective and mystery stories
        I. Title
        823.9'14 [F]

        ISBN 0-7278-5474-7

Printed and bound in Great Britain by
MPG Books Ltd, Bodmin, Cornwall.

One

Sylvester Manley hurried along a residential road that ended in a cul-de-sac, beyond which was a small wood consisting of a dense growth of bushes and trees. It was early on a cold November morning and the eastern sky was beginning to lighten with the sickly pallor of someone with a hangover, who is reluctant to rise from bed. Once past a weak glow of street lights, Sylvester switched on a torch and entered the wood on a track which ran through it. Although the track provided a shortcut to the railway station, it was seldom used at this time of day, and never by women on their own at any time. The wood was said to be the haunt of bag-snatchers and of sexual deviants; more than one case of indecent exposure had been reported.

On his way to work a shift at a large supermarket, Sylvester wasn't deterred by the reputation of the wood. As a black eighteen-year-old in an area of high unemployment he felt himself lucky to have a job which paid reasonable wages. Today, although slightly late, he reckoned he had time to relieve himself and to catch the early train. Half-way along the track he went through a gap in the vegetation to the shelter of some bushes close to a small clearing. He put away his torch, unzipped his trousers and urinated on to a carpet of sweetly pungent leaves which had fallen from an overhanging tree.

1

It was as he was about to rejoin the track that he heard shouts and running footsteps. A fierce note of anger in the raised voices sent Sylvester back to hide behind the nearest thick bush. He sensed danger and would wait out of sight until the runners had passed. Peeping out from his hiding place, he saw a girl, illuminated by torchlight from behind, who was obviously being pursued. She was almost level with him when she stumbled and fell forward. He watched in horror as three males appeared.

"Gotcher, you little fooker," said the first, and he stamped his foot on the girl's back to prevent her from turning over.

"Why did you do a runner?" asked the second man. "We wasn't going to do you no harm."

The third, who looked more like a boy than a man, hung back as if reluctant to be associated with the others.

Sylvester remained motionless as the two men spoke to each other in lowered voices. The girl made no effort to free herself from the pinioning foot and he wondered if the fall had stunned her. He knew he should shout 'Stop!', but his vocal cords seemed paralysed. His mind became numb at the sight of a flash of steel from the blade of a knife held by the second man who, he realised with a shock, was someone he knew.

It was Jason Marchant who had been a senior boy when Sylvester was new at the school which both had attended. Marchant had been expelled for selling drugs to other boys and eighteen months later had been sent to prison in Brixton after a conviction for aggravated assault. Like Sylvester, he was black. The other two appeared, in the dim light, to be white.

The man who had the girl pinned to the ground turned to the young-looking one. "Gimme yer scarf," he demanded.

"What?"

"Yer fookin' scarf, yer stoopid git. And be quick about it."

He grabbed at the scarf and crouched beside the girl to tie it tightly round her head so that she was blindfolded.

"You made one big mistake," said Marchant as the girl was roughly rolled over to lie on her back. "You done yourself no favours by doin' a runner. So you gotta learn some manners."

"And we'll fookin' well learn you, by fook." The speaker turned once more to the youngest of the trio. "You stay here and keep watch."

"Where you going?

"You'll see."

The girl was dragged out of sight into the small clearing, almost brushing the bush where Sylvester was sheltering. The grunting and heavy breathing while the girl was being pulled across uneven ground covered the slight noise made by Sylvester as he shifted his stance so that he couldn't be seen from the clearing but was himself able to see it through a tangle of vegetation. His vision of the track was now totally obscured and he had no idea where the youngster on guard was stationed. With anxiety increasing with every second that passed, he wondered whether to try to make a break and run for it, thereby risking capture and knifing, or to stay until the girl's ordeal was over, thereby being late for work and facing the wrath of the supervisor.

The girl had not uttered a sound; no screams, no pleas for mercy. It was as if she had accepted what was happening to her. Her camel-coloured topcoat was flung wide open, its belt untied; she resembled a huge light-brown moth, its wings outspread, transfixed ready to be added to a collection. Her legs, pressed tightly together, gave the impression of a long, tapering body.

"Now then. Get them fookin' jeans off."

The girl, her face almost covered by the scarf, made no movement.

"A'reet. We'll take 'em off for yer."

She was unable to protect herself because the men, in kneeling beside her, kept her arms trapped in the sleeves of the topcoat. The jeans were wrenched off and tossed to one side together with a shoe. Then her pants were savagely ripped off and thrown away. They landed on an offshoot of the bush where Sylvester was hiding and dangled there, a limp white flag of surrender.

With a fearful fascination he watched the girl's legs being prised apart, and she spoke for the first time. "Please don't," she begged softly. "I'm a virgin."

"Time you wasn't then," said Marchant.

The double rape witnessed by Sylvester was quickly over, but not before he felt an involuntary reaction, a hardening, in part of his own body. He hated what he was obliged to see and closed his eyes before the acts were finished.

As the men left their victim, Marchant called out, "You wasn't no virgin, girl."

Sylvester waited until the sound of footsteps was no longer audible and moved out of hiding. He needed to move fast if he was still to catch the early train, and yet not so fast that he caught up with the trio. As he hesitated, the girl, who had removed her blindfold, seized a torch lying on the ground and shone it full at him. He was caught in its glare a split-second before he could raise his hands to cover his face. Moments later he was on the track once more hurrying, but not too quickly, after the departing men.

In his panic to get away Sylvester had knocked the panties from the shoot into the middle of the bush. When the girl, shocked, bruised and shivering, staggered to her feet, they were not visible. It didn't matter; her jeans lay in a crumpled heap nearby and she slipped these on. Before tying the belt of the topcoat she felt for an inside pocket to check that the little bag of cosmetics and cash was there. It was a relief to find that the humiliation of rape had not been compounded by the insult of robbery.

She continued to shiver as she put on her shoes and tried to get her bearings. As she stood looking around, she slowly brushed damp leaves and bits of soil from the topcoat, her hands sweeping and picking as if operated by remote control.

The sound of approaching male voices made her freeze with the fear that her violators might return. A few seconds later, she glimpsed two early-morning commuters, both carrying brief-cases, as they passed by. She now knew the whereabouts of the track and was about to go to it when she noticed a brownish-grey scarf, its dull colour merging with the ground where she lay. Realising it could be a useful piece of evidence, she picked it up and stuffed it inside her topcoat.

As she left the wood and entered the cul-de-sac her pace slowed. Her home was in a road which ran to the south of the wood, and she needed to collect her thoughts before facing her parents. They would want to know why, when they had expressly forbidden her ever to use the shortcut, she had come home that way, and why had she arrived at such an early hour in the morning from a small party for schoolgirls held the night before.

It was school half-term and Kimberley, a sixteen-year-old, was on holiday. Like many in her peer group, when out of uniform she could, with lipstick and a touch of eye-shadow, look three or four years older. Her friend Sharon had invited her and other girls in their form to a party. She had asked her parents for permission to go and had promised to be home by midnight, if the party lasted that long.

"If it's midnight you'd better take a taxi," said her father.

"Will her parents be there?" her mother asked.

"Of course. They'll be around but they'll stay out of sight."

This was a lie. Sharon's parents were attending the funeral of a close relative in Scotland and would be staying there overnight. Taking advantage of their absence Sharon had invited Kimberley and three other girls round for the evening. One of the girls had a good-looking brother who might drop in later with some pals.

"It's a single-sex party? No boys will be there?" Kimberley's mother persisted.

"Mum, this isn't a rave. Drugs and all that. It's just a half-term get-together. Don't be so suspicious."

She nearly added, 'Don't bring your job home!' – a reference to Samson Associates, the detective agency where her mother worked. But that would have been unfair: her mother often overcompensated for her devotion to her career, paying special attention to all Kimberley's practical needs and giving in to some of her whims. It was her father who would give her a hug and a kiss when she was upset.

"I'm not being suspicious, Kim dear; just cautious. If you assure me it's strictly a hen party – if the expression doesn't sound offensively old-fashioned – then I accept, and I hope you have a good time."

At its start, the party had gone with a swing. Girls at the school had been forbidden to display any form of piercing, with the exception of their ear lobes. In defiance, Kelly, one of the five present, had recently acquired a ring through her navel. "I reckon I'll charge boys a pound to look at my belly-button," she said amid admiring laughter. Kelly had also borrowed one of her mother's vibrators and a couple of rubber sex toys to bring to the party. A gang of youths had arrived shortly after ten at night.

At about eleven thirty, when she expected her mother was in bed and hoped that her father was watching a late-night movie, Kimberley phoned home.

"It's only me, Dad. Look, the others have all gone home and I'm staying behind to give Sharon a hand with the washing-up and tidying. I'm pretty tired already and Sharon's parents have said I can stay the night. Will that be all right? I won't if you don't want me to, I'll get a taxi when we've finished, but I'd quite like to stay."

A pause. Then, "OK, sweetheart. See you tomorrow. Take care."

A slightly slurred note in his voice indicated that he had been drinking. As she replaced the handset Kimberley gave a thumbs-up to Sharon, who burst into giggles. Sharon was still laughing as she rejoined the party, which had now grown to about twenty people, including three or four gatecrashers. The sweet reek of smoked cannabis permeated the atmosphere; a heated argument was simmering about a football club's chances of winning any trophies this season; Kelly had taken her toys and vibrator to the spare bedroom where she was entertaining a couple of youths; heavy rock music with an amplified string base was resonating through the house; a drunken boy was trying to dance with a kitchen chair, and someone was demanding of an Asian lad, "Why can't you go and fetch us a bloody curry?"

A year or so ago Kimberley might have happily taken part in the chaotic scene, but she prided herself that she had now grown up a bit and began instead to suffer the slow strangulation of boredom. When she was eight years old, a headmistress had said of her, 'She has a remarkable old head on young shoulders.' The

6

correlation between age and intellect was not the glittering pinchbeck coin of passing precocity; it was the solid gold of wisdom beyond her years. She preferred to stay on the sidelines of childish exhibitionism. By three in the morning she was tired and bored and ready to go home, but she had promised Sharon to help her to clear up. Periodically she had to fend off crude, fumbling advances from one fellow who called her 'a stuck-up bitch' after she had repulsed him for the fifth time. Most of the other girls had shrieked with attention-grabbing excitement when they were groped.

Sharon's house was close to Streatham Common and the high street. A crowd of youths spilling out of a nightclub were attracted by the noise and gatecrashed. Rooms were now packed with teeming, squirming bodies. If it hadn't been for her promise to Sharon, Kimberley would have gone home. And then, at about five in the morning, Sharon herself gave her a pretext to leave. She reeled over to the corner where Kimberley was sitting and said aggressively, "For Christ's sake, what's the matter with you? You're sat there looking all fed up and disapproving. Get a man. Have a ball, or get out."

"Right. I'll leave you to it," replied Kimberley, and without rancour or regret left the noise and smoke-filled room with its debris of crumpled cans, spilling ashtrays, littered carpet, scattered cushions and one smashed china shepherdess. On her way out of the house she picked up a small torch, which someone had left on the hallstand, opened the front door and stepped into the dark night. Nobody saw her leaving.

Her home was situated more than two miles away, but less if she took the shortcut through the wood. She paused to check that she had a front-door key in the small bag inside her topcoat. Probing fingers failed to find it and so she shone the torch on to the interior lining of the bag. The key was missing. Then she remembered. She had left it on her dressing table at home. "Damn!" she said aloud. She had intended to sneak quietly indoors and go straight to her bedroom, but now she would have to rouse her parents and think of a good reason why she should have left the party when she had said on the telephone she was staying the night. She was still searching for a reason as near as possible to the truth without telling too many outright lies when she neared the wood.

During her journey she had seen only one other pedestrian and three or four cars, but suddenly a car came swooping down the road and with a screech of brakes pulled up alongside her.

"Give you a lift, darling?" the driver asked as the window was lowered.

She glanced to her left and saw a black man. A white youth was sitting beside him in the passenger seat. There appeared to be someone else, possibly two people, in the back of the car.

"No, thanks." She quickened her steps. The car drifted in low gear beside her.

"Hold it, darling. We won't give you no aggro. Where you going?"

She made no reply.

"Come on," the driver wheedled. "Tell us where you going. It ain't safe for a bird to be out on her own. We'll look after you. Take you where you wanna go."

She was now almost running to what she hoped would be the sanctuary of the wood.

"Fooking cow," said the white man. "Let's get her."

As she started to run she heard shouting and car doors slamming behind her.

Frightened, she ran into the wood and along the track. Her pursuers seemed to be gaining on her. Looking quickly over her shoulder she saw that they too had torches, but in glancing back she lost her footing, stumbled and fell heavily forward. Already breathless, the impact on the ground winded her completely.

As she was dragged into the clearing she knew she would be raped. This was a fearful enough prospect, but having raped they might kill. This could happen if she screamed and struggled; it would be best simply to let them get on with it and hope that once satisfied, they'd leave. As her legs were prised open she made the single plea to their collective conscience – if there was one. "Please don't. I'm a virgin."

It was a useless appeal.

The first entry was painful. The second less so, but the man's body smell was stronger. As he climbed off she waited for the third and a possible fourth, but the ordeal was over. She heard a man call out that she wasn't a virgin and the sound of footsteps receding. While the men had been changing position she had managed to loosen the tightly knotted scarf. She tore it off and threw it to one side. She had clung on to the torch most of the time and found it beside her. A noise nearby sent a new wave of panic through her. Had one of the men stayed behind to have his turn? She switched on the torch and its beam fell on the features of a black man, who instantly covered his face with his hands before running away. It was a face she vaguely recognised; someone she had seen somewhere before. But it was his hands which could provide a positive identification. The index finger of his left hand was little more than a stump; it was less than a half-finger. Bruised and shivering she staggered to her feet.

Now, as she neared home, her mind was in a turmoil. She had lied to her mother and father and pretended that Sharon's parents would be in the house and that it was an all-girl party which should finish before midnight. She had lied to her father on the telephone, and she had broken the taboo against ever taking the shortcut through the wood.

It was as she walked up to the front door that she broke down, sobbing and crying. She had managed to remain cool in spite of the ordeal, but the pressure of reality broke through her defences and she was engulfed in an enormous wave of self-pity. She felt dirty and used. All she now wanted was a bath to wash away the residues of a horrific experience. Why worry about what her mother and father might think of her deceptions? She was the one who had suffered a traumatic experience she would never be able to forget.

She reached out and pushed hard at the doorbell.

Two

Although the sky had lightened, the front of the house and its porch remained in shadow. Kimberley's father, who wasn't expecting her home, did not recognise her at first and called out from an upstairs window, "Who's there? What do you want?"

"It's me, Dad," she wailed.

"Kimmy! I'll be right down." And then on opening the front door, "Why are you..." The sentence was unfinished as she pushed past him and ran to her mother who had just come down the stairs in bare feet, her undone housecoat flapping behind.

Sobbing miserably, she was ushered into the nearby sitting-room where she sat down and nestled in her mother's arms.

"Darling, what's happened. You look in a mess. Your hair! Your coat! Let's have that off... Paul, make some tea, will you."

"Brandy might be more appropriate by the look of her. Would you like a brandy, sweetheart?"

Kimberley shook her head.

"Paul, please! Put on the kettle."

The corners of his mouth dipped in resentment. "I will. First, I'd like to know what's going on."

"I don't know any more than you do. But she's freezing cold and needs a warm drink."

11

"Brandy would be better."

The sobbing became heaving sighs and between shudders Kimberley managed to say, "I don't want either. I want a bath. I've been raped."

A stunned silence was broken by both parents speaking simultaneously.

Her father, Paul, exclaimed in disbelief, "Raped? Raped!"

Her mother, Shandy, said, "Tell us about it. In your own time, darling." And as she spoke she folded her arms even tighter around the girl's shivering body. They were on a settee and Paul, who had been standing close by, started striding up and down the room. When he paused, his face was distorted with the rage of someone whose most precious thing in life has been wantonly smashed in front of him by a stranger. "Who?" he shouted. "Who? I'll kill the bastard!"

"For God's sake, Paul. Don't bellow at her. Go and put the kettle on. Please!"

"All right. I'll put the bloody kettle on but" – he pointed a finger at his wife – "I don't want her to say anything until I come back. OK? I want to hear it all."

As soon as he had left the room Kimberley began, almost inaudibly and punctuated by breathless pauses, to tell what had happened. Shandy listened, holding her daughter close in a way that hadn't happened for some years. Kimberley had inherited her mother's blonde hair, blue eyes and high cheekbones. As a young woman, Shandy had once or twice been mistaken for a Scandinavian film star. Now in her forties she was still a very attractive woman.

Kimberley began by apologising for having misled her parents about the sort of party she wanted to join but went on to say in the event it hadn't been quite what she had expected. It had become so dreadful with the thumping din of over-amplified rock music, the stink of cannabis and sweaty bodies, the obscene propositioning to any girl on her own, the coarse and aggressive gatecrashers from a notoriously rough housing estate, and finally Sharon's rudeness, that Kimberley had left, so full of suppressed anger that she hadn't even thought of telephoning for a taxi, and once the front door had slammed behind her she couldn't bear the thought of going back and, anyway, the walk would cool her down.

"I thought I'd got my key with me but I hadn't. I didn't want to wake you up. That was before those men—"

Paul entered carrying a tray with three mugs of tea. "What men?" he asked. "I specifically told you not to talk about it until I came back." He slammed down the tray and some tea spilled. "That's fine, that is. I don't count for anything round here any more."

Shandy, who had been listening to her daughter in silence, spoke up: "She needed to talk and so I let her. When she is finished, we must ring the police."

"We'll do nothing of the sort. Not until the thing has been properly discussed."

"Discussed! There's nothing to discuss. Our daughter has been raped. That is a criminal offence. The police should be informed as soon as possible. There's a chance the culprits might still be around."

A warning finger was again pointed at her. "Before anything else I want to know exactly what happened. We'll argue later about police intervention. Let's hear what she has to say before jumping the gun."

"Go on, darling," Shandy whispered. No response. "Go on please."

Between sips of tea Kimberley haltingly gave a bare outline of what she had suffered.

Paul, who had been waiting impatiently for her to finish, asked, "How many of these bastards were there?"

"Three, I think, maybe four, I couldn't tell. They blindfolded me, but I heard at least three different voices."

"Were they local men, by their accents?"

"One wasn't. I think he came from the North somewhere."

"And all three or four did it to you?"

Shandy intervened. "That's enough! It's for the police to question her. They have trained officers for cases like this. They don't charge in like a bull in a china shop."

13

"Oh, right. So that's what I am now, is it? A bull in a china shop. That's proof of how little I count for these days. Because I'm out of work and you've got a job in a tinpot detective agency – oh, sorry, as *head* of a tinpot agency from today – you think you can treat me like some clumsy fool."

"Paul, this isn't the time or place to be talking like this."

"No? But there never is the right time, is there? I tried the other night to explain what it was like for me and what did you do? You fell asleep!"

Suddenly Kimberley tore herself from the arms of her mother. "Stop it! I can't bear it!" She faced her father, her face disfigured with fury, smudged make-up under her eyes, her hair a tousled mess, and screamed, "It's your fault. I hate you!"

Before either parent could react she had run away, upstairs and into the bathroom. Paul's face, which had reddened with his tirade, became a pale mask of bewilderment, confusion and hurt. "What does she mean by that?"

He wasn't speaking to Shandy so much as thinking aloud. But she replied, "It's your fault that she's so upset," before herself running upstairs.

Half a minute later she came down. "It's no use. Kim's locked herself in. She's having a bath. We'll wait until she comes out. I don't want to call the police behind her back."

"I bet you'd call them behind my back, if you could."

"I shall, and not necessarily behind your back."

The bickering and arguing continued, but it hadn't always been like this. For much of their time together it had been a loving relationship. Shandy had once referred to marriage as 'a beautifully elaborate game calling for lots of skill and bluff and a very strict observance of the ground rules'. High among these rules were fidelity and loyalty, but neither she nor Paul realised the devastation that could be caused by outside forces beyond their control.

For some years Paul had been an assessor for an insurance company, but when the company failed to spread its risks and became insolvent he was for a short while out of a job. His CV, personable appearance, and an impressive performance when interviewed, gained him the preference above fourteen other candidates for a position in the estimates and tenders division of a large building and construction firm. However, through no fault of his, the company had lost millions of pounds on a huge contract deal at the same time that a recession had hit the building trade, and he had been made redundant and given a golden handshake. In the ten months since then, despite very many applications, he had failed to find suitable work. He had become depressed.

As his star fell, so Shandy's had risen. Except for a time when she had borne Kimberley, and a short while after, she had all her adult life been the principal employee of a private investigator. With hard work, clever detection and, most importantly, a handful of influential clients (word of mouth brought others), they had become a formidable team. When their premises was totally gutted by fire Samson took a chance on prosperity continuing and acquired the lease on an office development in a prestigious part of London's West End. Situated in the clubland area of St James's, and with a core of satisfied clients some of whom were members of these clubs, Samson Associates went from strength to strength, and its founder earned the reputation of being the highest-paid private detective in London.

Years of unremittingly hard work had paid off for Samson, but at the price of his health. Shandy was now due to take his place in the firm, and her fortune contrasted sharply with that of her out-of-work husband. In the space of months their marriage had changed from a relatively happy one to a failing union.

Paul was making bitter comparisons when he paused to say, "What's Kimmy doing up there? The water has been running for ages." Without waiting a reply he hurried upstairs. From the landing he called down to Shandy, "The bathroom's empty with the taps still running!"

Kimberley had pulled out the plug so that there would be no overflow and locked herself in her bedroom.

Paul knocked on the door. "Let me in, sweetheart."

The appeal was met with a muffled "Go away!"

15

Shandy joined him and added her voice, "Please, darling. We only want to help."

Her plea received a somewhat softer "Leave me alone, Mum. I'll come out when I'm ready."

Her parents looked at each other askance. Shandy broke the silence. "I'm calling the police," she said.

"I thought you didn't want to call them behind her back."

"I don't. But you want the guys who did that dreadful thing caught, don't you?"

"Christ in heaven! What a silly, fatuous question. Of course I do, but I want to hear the full story from her first."

Downstairs the argument continued like the rollers from an implacable ocean breaking against uncompromising rocks. Whenever Shandy moved towards the telephone Paul barred her way.

"At least let me call the office and tell them I shall be in late."

"Of course, I nearly forgot. It's your big day. The day you become *supremo*, commander-in-chief of Samson's little empire, and he becomes *El Presidente*! Big deal!"

The venom in his voice brought a twitch to her face, as if she'd been struck by a poisoned dart.

"I *must* phone the office."

"Why? They can manage a few hours without you. Nobody, or so I was told when I got the boot, is indispensable."

"Paul, I have to take in his present."

"What present? Are you giving him a present? This is the first I've heard of that."

"It's a present we have all subscribed to. A farewell gift."

"I thought he wasn't leaving but staying on as a consultant."

With a great effort Shandy controlled the anger which had risen within her. At last, she told him that the present was a computerised chess set and that it was gift-wrapped and in the back of her car.

"But he's already got a computerised chess set. What's he want another one for?"

Wearily she replied, "Because it's old and some of its pieces are missing. He told us about it that night we had him for dinner after he came back from that holiday in France."

"*He's* old and, if you ask me, some of *his* pieces are missing. He made himself a right idiot over that Greek girl. Stupid old fool."

"That stupid old fool is Kimberley's godfather!"

"So he is, and that's a pity. I don't want you bleating to him about what's happened to Kimmy. I can deal with it. I don't want him interfering."

Although her anger had reached boiling point Shandy managed to say calmly, and for the second time. "I must phone the office."

"All right," he grudgingly gave consent. "Just tell them you'll be late. Nothing more. Make sure you do."

Three

John Samson didn't much care for self-analysis. In his opinion, prolonged examination of one's thoughts and feelings could lead to depression which, in turn, could lead to lack of motivation, and an unmotivated human being wasn't of use to himself or anyone else. And yet, on the day of his retirement he found it almost impossible not to think back on the credits and debits of his career, even of his whole life.

For a few moments after shaving he stared at himself in the mirror. He saw thinning hair, a pallid, pitted complexion and hooded, sleepy eyes. What the mirror did not reveal was that a large head was set on a big frame, but that his legs were short. It looked as if his maker had become bored with his construction and had skimped on the lower half of his body, preferring to start work on plans for a more aesthetic being.

After shaving he went through a routine of limbering-up exercises before getting dressed to go out, if the weather permitted, for an early-morning walk in St James's Park. Exercise, his doctor had told him, was good for his heart, provided it wasn't excessive or prolonged. However, it wasn't his heart condition which had finally precipitated retirement; it was a malady common among men of his age: an enlarged prostate gland.

A prostatic specific antigen count was abnormally high, and a biopsy had revealed the presence of cancer cells. His urologist had informed him that invasive surgery would be necessary. He slept badly during the night following this news but by the morning had decided to go into partial retirement, hand over control of the firm to his junior partner, Shandy, and continue to be involved to a limited extent as a consultant. "I may be getting old and ready for the knackers' yard," he said, "but I want to die in harness." His name would still appear on the firm's letterhead but he would no longer be concerned with the day to day running of the office or in decision making. Like the figurehead president of a club, or a king without a crown, he would receive lip-service but have no power.

As he stepped out on to the street from the building where his flat was situated, he thought briefly of the day ahead. He had been warned that there would be a small presentation ceremony during the lunch hour by the office staff – "And I'm only telling you this so that you won't skive off," Shandy had said.

He wished fervently that the day was over.

There weren't many people around at this time during November: no tourists posing for camera shots standing beside a wooden-faced, bearskin-headed soldier standing guard outside St James's Palace, nobody hanging about hoping for a glimpse of royalty at Clarence House close by, and only a few early-morning commuters scurrying like treadmill work-mice to their place of employment.

The sky, a pale uniform grey, hung over town like a burial shroud waiting to be used; at least, that was how Samson felt as he lengthened his stride towards the Mall. Road traffic was comparatively light, and once he had crossed the famous avenue leading to the sovereign's London residence and entered the park, his pace slowed. November had never been a favourite month for Samson; it was the time when the dead of two world wars were remembered, a time when his mother had died, a time when russet and brown leaves still clung tenuously to trees waiting for a chill wind to bring them to earth for collection and disposal by a mechanised sweeper; it was a month imprinted with death and ghosts from the past. And now it was the time of his retirement after nearly thirty years during which time he had built up a run-down debt-collecting agency in south London to a prosperous private investigation agency in the most exclusive part of town.

On this day, of all days, it was difficult to keep his mind from introspection. As he walked towards the bridge spanning a lake where wildfowl congregated, later to be joined by pigeons hoping for crumbs from sturdy bird-lovers who braved all weathers to see them fed, some of his thoughts were tinged with melancholy, a feeling he never usually allowed. Today he permitted himself the rare luxury of a fleeting nostalgic sadness.

He had, as the saying goes, come up from nothing. His birth certificate stated bleakly 'Father unknown'. His mother had told him that while a maid servant at a gentleman's club she had been seduced by 'one of the nobility'. When questioned, she was vague about the man's name and Samson had to be content with 'I dunno. Lord Something-or-other. But a real gent. Got himself killed in a hunting accident, or so I heard.'

In retrospect it seemed his mother was always ailing with some illness. On occasions when there was a little spare money, he would be sent out to buy a bottle of health tonic from the chemist's shop. There was always food available but it was of the stomach-filling, appetite-quelling kind – potatoes, suet dumplings, bread puddings and nearly everything was flavoured with streaky bacon. At school his girth earned him the nickname 'Jumbo'. For a while he was made miserable by teasing but a kindly sports master taught him the art of boxing and, when he was ready, he took on the school bully and thrashed him in front of sycophant supporters. From that time, he was spared taunts about his size. Visits to Southend and Clacton during school holidays, financed by earnings from newspaper delivery rounds, fired him with the notion of life of the ocean wave and as soon as it was possible he joined the Royal Navy where he served as a rating without distinction for a few years.

By a rare stroke of luck he left the navy just before the death of an uncle whom he hardly knew, but who, in his will, had left

Samson a small private inquiry business which was effectively nothing more than an agency for process serving and debt collecting. In later years he suspected that Uncle Tommy was an intimate friend of his mother's – he was someone who had always 'just left' when Samson arrived home from school – but he could never be sure. His mother had died without ever saying more than, "He's really more a distant relation than an uncle but it's polite to call him 'uncle'." His mother had suffered from so many complaints, her lumbago being the most common, it was hard to imagine her and Uncle Tommy misbehaving.

Shandy had come into his life after answering his advertisement, posted on a shop board in Streatham, for a part-time secretary. Some women are born organisers; they find fulfilment in organising everything around them. Shandy was an Organiser Supreme. First, she brought order to the chaos of his office, and then she dealt with him. "I'm not going to work for a boss who wears clothes that look as if they'd been pinched off a scarecrow," she announced. "You need taking in hand, and," she added with a twinkle in her eyes, "I mean that in the acceptable sense, not the vulgar."

It was a new experience for Samson to be told what to do by a woman young enough to be his daughter and, because it only happened when both were aware of its necessity – she never spoke to him in this way in front of clients – he tolerated her strictures with a weary grin. By degrees Samson had been transformed from a fat, untidy man into someone well built, almost dapper; and from a philistine into a limited appreciator of the aesthetic. Thanks to Shandy's influence, life began to have a purpose beyond existing from day to day, and it didn't matter that the purpose was the mundane one of building up a successful private inquiry agency.

Their relationship was asexual. Samson had never had a libido bursting for generation of the species, or even for scoring, and it was no yearning hardship to spend several hours a day in the company of an attractive young woman. Even in the Navy, where there was a red-light district in every port, he would usually opt out of visiting brothels with shipmates. He had had some moments of consummated desire but, on the whole, he regarded sexual peccadilloes as a recreational dead-end. Anyway, there was always available a mature lady with a Mayfair flat willing to entertain him; and once, leaving him to ruminate – 'There's no fool like an old fool' – a hot-blooded Greek-Cypriot girl had given him something to regret and relish in retrospect. He thought of her as his Delilah.

Shandy had insisted that it was essential to put a good price on his services. "Value yourself highly and others will do the same," she had said. "We aren't a cheap firm." Samson had taken this advice while allowing himself the latitude of not following it if a case interested him and the client was unable to meet the full tariff. Politically he was to the left of centre and as one-time underdog had never forgotten his humble roots and the despair of having insufficient money to pay for something which others took for granted.

Until now he hadn't realised how much a part of his life Shandy had become. He had been a signatory witness at her marriage to Paul Bullivant many years before, had become godfather to her only child, Kimberley, and had spent nearly every Christmas as a guest at her house. He had already been invited for this Christmas, but with the bonds of a common employment loosened, he wondered if it would be the same. He and Paul had never quite hit it off; sometimes he felt his presence was barely tolerated in the house in Streatham. It had puzzled Samson why they still lived in what he considered to be an insalubrious outpost of town when they could afford something better – until Shandy had explained that Paul had been born and brought up in this area and didn't want to move and so she had instead bought a mobile home in the south of France and, more recently, an apartment near Puerto Pollensa in Majorca.

The early years of marriage had appeared idyllic but, although loyal to him, Shandy had let slip on one occasion that she feared Paul had a drink problem which had been exacerbated when he was made redundant. Once or twice she had arrived at the office unduly late and looking careworn in spite of liberal make-up.

Samson was so preoccupied with thoughts of Shandy and of the day ahead that he arrived back at his apartment feeling he had hardly been away. He could scarcely remember anything of the slightest significance during the early-morning walk. He had almost forgotten to call in for his regular cup of coffee at the cafeteria in Crown Passage. Absent-mindedness was so uncharacteristic that it worried him slightly. The prospect of retirement, albeit only partial, weighed on him. He had seen too many contemporaries go swiftly downhill once they had retired from an active life. They had not prepared for the sudden slackness which comes from not having a settled purpose, and found that their own resources when tested were inadequate. One should never, he reflected sadly as he took an egg from its carton to boil for breakfast, put all one's eggs in one basket.

Two members of Samson's staff, Martine and Kennedy, were studying law in the hope of one day qualifying as solicitors. Normally, Kennedy was first to arrive at the office, but today Samson wanted to be alone for a short while before the working day began and after his light breakfast he opened up the office and went to his room.

Seated in a battered old swivel captain's chair at his desk, he looked around. Oil paintings of harbour scenes hung on the walls. In the Navy he had always enjoyed berthing in harbour. It marked the end of a voyage; and now his voyage was ending. Everything in the room had a personal connection. The swivel chair had been his first purchase when taking over the debt-collecting agency. The hour-glass standing on his desk was used for initial appointments. He would tip it up, thereby activating a tape recorder concealed in a desk drawer and when, after half an hour, the sands had run into the bottom bowl he would terminate the interview. Today, he idly tipped the hour-glass as he continued to survey the contents of the room – the chairs for clients mostly taken from his former office and none so comfortable as to encourage a prolonged period of sitting, the box in one corner where he had kept private papers (now empty), and the bookcase filled with reference books.

As he contemplated the trickle of sand he thought of Time. In so far as he had a religion, Time was God. Time, the aged Chronos of Greek myth, came before everything, even before space and matter. It was the alpha and omega of all things. For many years he had collected rare clocks – until he realised that clocks were not Time but merely representatives, just as crucifixes with tiny impaled figures of Christ were icons of the Christian religion. The collection had been sold at Christie's, just down the road, at a good profit.

Shandy would be taking over this room. She had told him she would leave it exactly as it was – 'For you to occupy when you're here.' It was a kind thought on her part, but he knew that he would not be called upon very often; eventually the decor would be changed, feminine touches added, the pictures and other objects carefully stored away until he claimed them. It was then that he remembered one item that he should take away. It was a miscellany of facts and hypotheses. Opening the book at random, he came across a reference to heretical Zoroastrians who considered Time to have religious significance, references to Hipparchus who invented the astrolabe in about 150 BC, and the motto '*Tempus fugit*', beside which he had written: 'Time is immutable, it is we who fly; we exist for approximately seventy chronological years, a blink in the eyelash of Time, before disappearing for ever'; and the query, 'Is Eternity cyclic and endlessly repetitive, or is it linear and infinitely continuous?'

Perhaps, he thought, a book about Time using all the notes might be a retirement occupation.

The door of his room was slowly prised open and a black face appeared peering cautiously around its edge. "Oh, it's you, Mr Samson. I found the outer door unlocked and I wondered if there had been a break-in during the night."

"Come in, Brian," said Samson affably. "Come in and take a seat."

Brian Kennedy – known as Kenco by other staff members due to his liking for coffee – went uncertainly to the nearest chair, a hard upright piece of furniture, and sat down uneasily. He hero-worshipped Samson, who had once saved his life. He held him in a sort of high esteem that left him in constant fear of ever upsetting his idol.

Samson began reading from the volume on Time.

"'There is a theory that Time has an atomic or granular structure and its minimum spatial displacement corresponds to the diameter of a proton, and the minimum time to cross this infinitesimal distance is called a chronon.'" Samson looked up. "Does this theory of atomised Time make sense to you?"

Kennedy hesitated, riven with the uncertainty of the best answer to give to this incomprehensible piece of quasi-scientific jargon. In the end, he shook his head. "Don't think so, Mr Samson. Should it?"

"No. Human imagination could never grasp that a chronon is a million millionth part of a million millionth part of one second. For the purpose of this theory I find it easier to think of Time as chronons strung together like pearls on a necklace."

To Kennedy's evident relief, Samson closed the volume. "Was that all?" he asked.

"Not quite. As you know, this is my last day as an active partner here. If I don't get the opportunity later on, I'd like to wish you now all the very best for the Law Society's finals next year." Samson stood up and extended a hand. "Good luck."

Kennedy leapt to his feet and grasped the outstretched hand. A few moments later he was out of the room. "Pearls on a necklace," he muttered to himself as he went down a short corridor. Inside the room Samson sat down. I must pull myself together, he thought. Can't have them thinking I've gone soft in my old age.

Georgia, Samson's pert and perky receptionist, took Shandy's call.

"I shall be in late today. Thought I should let you know. No need to panic."

"Everything all right? You sound a bit out of breath."

"Do I? It's nothing I can't handle. Tell you about it when—"

The phone went dead. Georgia looked at her handset as if it were responsible for the abrupt ending to the conversation, and then keyed Samson's extension.

"I've just had a call from Shandy, Mr Samson. She rang to say she'd be late in today. She didn't sound herself, and the call stopped while she was still speaking."

"The line went dead?"

"Yes, but not dead like a sudden disconnection, if you know what I mean. There was a funny sort of noise a split second before it went dead."

"Call her back... No, I'll call her."

Using a phone with a direct outside line Samson keyed Shandy's home number. Then he went back to Georgia. "All I'm getting is an engaged signal. Either someone else is on the line or the phone's off the hook. Keep trying, and if you get her, put the call through to me."

Kennedy, who was standing close to Georgia as he sorted incoming mail into piles of three, asked, "What was that all about?"

"You heard. Shandy'll be late."

"I meant, what was the funny sort of noise you heard?"

Georgia looked at him through narrowed eyes. She and Kennedy often sparred with each other in verbal contest which she, Cockney and streetwise as an alley-cat, nearly always won. His stance was studiedly casual and his question sounded a shade too off-hand. Georgia suspected a trap.

"Don't be daft. Kenco. If I knew exactly what it was I'd say so, wouldn't I? It was like I say, a funny sort of noise. All right?"

Kennedy continued to peruse the envelopes before placing them carefully on one of the piles. "It's just that you went on to say this funny noise happened a 'split second' before the line went dead."

"So, what you trying to say, Kenco?"

Kennedy put a final letter in place before replying. "It's just that me and the Old Man were having an interesting chat about Time a little while ago. About atomic time. String of pearls and all that."

Georgia gave a short laugh of disbelief. "You and Samson talking about what? Atomic time? Do me a favour! The only Time you're interested in is going-home-time."

"That's where you're wrong, Georgie girl. I was actually wondering what you meant by 'split second'. How many chronons were there in this split second of yours?"

Georgia wrinkled her forehead. "You what?"

He gave a stage sigh and repeated slowly, "How many chronons were there in the split second?"

"I don't know what you're on about." Georgia turned away her head and began keying Shandy's number.

"I wouldn't expect you to know about the theory of atomic time," said Kennedy. "It's way above your head," and before Georgia could think of a riposte he'd gathered up a small pile of letters. "I'll take these and leave them on Shandy's desk for when she comes in."

He was grinning broadly as he made a quick exit.

Paul had snatched the handset from Shandy.

"What the hell do you think you're doing," she demanded angrily. "I was in the middle of speaking to Georgia."

"And you were saying you'd tell her when you got to the office. I presume you were going to talk about our daughter's rape. Well, I think some things are private, not for office gossip."

"Office gossip! There won't be any gossip. The office will have to know sometime and it's better I tell them now before they read about it in a newspaper. Now give me back that phone."

"No way," he replied, keeping the instrument just out of reach of her grasping hand. "Nobody hears about this until we've talked it over with Kimmy."

"There's nothing to talk about. She's been raped. The police must be told. She'll need counselling. And I have to get in touch with my office."

"So it's *your* office now, is it? Not *the* office any more."

With an effort of self-restraint Shandy said, "Look, I do know how badly you've taken your redundancy, and I do understand. But please don't take it out on me, or Kim. Now, of all times, she needs our support. A show of unity and backing."

"And I want to know exactly what happened before we do anything more."

"She's told us. She was raped."

"I don't know what she said to you while I was making the tea—"

"Nothing much," Shandy interrupted. "The only bit you missed was that it had been a rotten party. Sharon had been rude to her and she was so fed up all she wanted to do was to come home. She didn't think about getting a taxi until it was too late. She'd already left the house. Then you brought in the tea. You heard the rest."

"Only part of the rest. There were three or four of the bastards, she was blindfolded, and one of the rapists had a northern accent. That's not enough. There must be more she could tell us."

"What more do you want? All the nasty details?"

"Don't shout at me," he replied, raising his own voice. "There must be other details. I'd like to know what they are before we get the police here."

"Such as what? Did she recognise the after-shave one was using? Whether they said 'Please' and 'Thank you'?"

Her sarcasm brought a flush to his cheeks. He half raised an arm and for a moment it seemed he was about to hit her, but he lowered it slowly and said, "I should like to know whether contraceptives were used. If not, it's as important to get her to a doctor as to call the police. I should have expected you, as her mother, to be worried about that. Some mother!" he added bitterly.

She opened her mouth to say something, thought better of it, and a brief silence fell between them.

It was broken when he went on, "I want to know the full story. Everything."

Recovering her poise Shandy said, "Why? What good will that do? Or do you intend to go macho; look for the men who did it and take your revenge."

"You've got it in one."

She looked at her husband incredulously. "I've never heard of anything so absurd."

"Absurd?" He gave a short, unamused laugh. "What's absurd about wanting to punish men who've committed a crime against one's own daughter?"

"It's absurd because you've no idea who they are or where to find them. Apart from that, it'll be for the court to convict and punish them if they're caught."

"If they are caught. *If* is the operative word. We all know how the police are overstretched and underfunded round here. For them it'll be just another case of a teenager getting herself into trouble walking in a place which has a bad reputation already. They'll say, 'She probably deserved what she got. High-heeled shoes. Make-up. Looks older than sixteen.' I know what men are like, and I'll bet the police have a liking for filthy innuendoes."

"She was going to a party, for God's sake. What do you expect? That she should go in fancy dress as a nun! Get real, Paul. Our daughter dresses like all the other girls in her age group."

"As bait for rapists."

Shandy moved away from him and he replaced the handset in its cradle. Turning round she spat, "You make me sick!"

"Ah, now we're getting to the nitty-gritty," he retorted with an air of satisfaction. "I make you sick, do I? Well, *you* make *me* sick. You can think of nothing, talk of nothing, but 'the office' and bloody Samson. He's an ugly old sod but he's got it made. From bastard to boss-man in easy stages. He sees more of you than I do." He paused as if struck by a tangential thought. "That might be dead right. He may see *more* of you. I see little enough these days, or nights should I say."

"What is that supposed to mean?" The question was delivered with an icy calm, which contrasted with the earlier heat of anger. "What are you implying?"

He made no reply.

"Don't ever let me hear you imply anything like that again or we are finished. I shall petition for divorce. I've had enough of your whining self-pity and..." She broke off in mid-sentence.

Kimberley, wearing a white bathrobe and looking like a pale ghost of herself was standing in the doorway.

*   *   *

30

Sylvester's shift at the supermarket ended shortly after two p.m. He returned to his home, where he lived with his parents and younger sister, by the same route that he had taken to go to work. Entering the wood he experienced a flutter of trepidation. The wood had become tainted with evil, it was a place to be shunned in future, and yet it would be chicken to take the longer walk home simply because of what he'd seen earlier in the day. He certainly wouldn't tell anyone about it, least of all his parents. His father would say, 'You were a witness, son, to a wicked act. You should go to the police and tell it like it was,' and his mother, round-eyed as a cartoon Negress, would throw up her hands and say, 'We are God-fearing folks, Sylvester. You do as your daddy says'.

No way, he thought. He hadn't told anyone at the super-market although he had been tempted to say something to Madhu who worked at a checkout. He fancied Madhu a lot but hadn't yet plucked up the courage to ask her out, although once or twice she had given him encouraging smiles. She was more gentle than the other girls and kept herself to herself; she was the sort who could be trusted with a secret. But it troubled him that he had had an erection when the girl's pants were torn off and her legs forced apart. He wouldn't tell Madhu this.

At this time in the afternoon there was nobody else in the small wood and as he approached the spot where the rape had occurred his pace slowed. He stopped altogether when the clearing could be glimpsed and, as he stared at the place where a crime had been committed, his eye caught sight of a white patch almost obscured by the growth of a bush where it hung. He stepped forward and, after furtively looking around, he reached inside the bush and carefully extracted a pair of white pants. After stuffing them in a coat pocket he hurried from the scene like a thief making a quick getaway.

A feeling of guilt mingled with shame came back, but not as strongly as before, and it was overpowered by a sense of excitement which he had no doubt his God-fearing mother would describe as 'sinful'. And then he thought of his little sister, Coral, aged ten, who called female pants 'knick-knacks'. If he had not by this time entered the cul-de-sac he would have chucked them away. But it seemed ridiculous to go back to the wood simply because an unwanted thought had passed through his mind. He resolved to be very careful when he reached home not to reveal the crumpled piece of cotton in his pocket. He'd go straight to his bedroom and look for a suitable hiding place.

After he went to bed that night he found it difficult to get to sleep. During the evening, it had occurred to him that the police might regard the panties as evidence and if he was found to have them in his possession... The consequences were too dire to contemplate. He decided that after work the next day he'd go to the police station, hand them in and make a statement. He'd seen enough police procedurals on the telly to know this was the form. Soon after making this decision he fell asleep.

But a cold grey dawn brought cold grey reality with it. What if the police didn't believe him and accused him of being a rapist himself, or of being involved by default? The telly, that invaluable guide to what was wrong with the world, had shown enough cases of mistrials and wrongful convictions to put anyone off being, as his mother might say, a decent God-fearing citizen. And anyway, racial prejudice was a live issue in this area. Statistics showed that a disproportionate number of blacks were arrested on minor charges. No, I won't fall for that one, Sylvester thought, as he checked under the mattress of his bed to make sure the pants were still there.

Four

Samson knew it would be a long morning. During the previous week he had been shedding case-work in readiness for the take-over by Shandy. It was unlike her to be late and particularly on this his last day. After pacing around his room and working on a short speech of thanks for the unavoidable presentation of a leaving gift – which, in spite of his pleas for no fuss, he knew the staff were determined he should accept – he called Georgia on the intercom. "No, nothing yet," was the reply he received, "and her phone is still engaged."

Then his telephone rang. He rushed to his desk. A disappointment. It was Bernard, a friend from New Scotland Yard, to wish him a happy retirement. This call was followed almost at once by Bob Broadbent, the custody sergeant from the police station near where he had worked in south London, with a similar message. Unlike some other inquiry agents, Samson had made it his business to overcome the professional hostility which was apt to exist between the differing public and private sectors by, amongst other things, making regular contributions to a police benevolent fund. 'It may seem like crawling,' he had once said, 'but I prefer to think of it cross-pollination.'

Other calls followed. One was from Cyril Huntington-Winstanley, a very rich, ageing queen, whose time was largely occupied in round-the-world cruises. He was a former client and whenever back in England would ask Samson out for a meal, an invitation once easily refused on spurious grounds of pressure of work but now accepted. After years spent in building up his practice, he was now aware of having neglected anything like a social life. Changes must be made.

The morning post had also brought a wedding invitation from another former client, Mary Lewis, a woman of conscience if ever there was one, who had finally accepted a marriage proposal from a man who she had at one time wrongly suspected of having been involved in the murder of her husband. She and Samson had met while on holiday in Funchal, and this had led to a mission to Florence. At the foot of the invitation Mary had written, 'You were there at the beginning; please do come to a happy ending'. Right, thought Samson, I will.

Georgia, whom Samson had commissioned to provide a buffet for the farewell, came to his room. While Samson watched fretfully, she cleared his desk, pulled up a folding leaf table, and spread a cloth. Plates of sausage rolls, smoked-salmon sandwiches, cheese sticks, and other foodstuffs followed.

"Who's going to eat all that?" Samson asked.

Kennedy, who had just brought in bottles of red and white wine, answered. "Don't worry about that, Mr Samson. We've all got healthy appetites around here."

All except me, Samson thought. He had been in tight and tough spots before, but none had made him as nervous and as lacking in appetite as he was now.

His telephone, now on the floor, rang. In his haste to answer it Samson nearly tripped over the cord.

All the staff except for Maunder, a pensionable odd-job man to whom Samson had charitably given fresh employment, were in the room. Maunder had been left in charge of the outside phone lines. A silence fell as Samson exclaimed. "Shandy. Where are you?"

"Good news," he said replacing the handset. "She'll be with us in a quarter or an hour or so. To a barrage of questions which followed this announcement he could only reply, "She didn't say."

He looked at the table laden with food and his appetite returned. He would never have admitted it, even to himself, but Shandy's non-appearance had worried him.

As if she were a professional actress, Shandy's persona changed the moment she entered the office. She wore a mask of brightness and, with Maunder trailing like a dinghy bobbing in the wake of a yacht under full sail, entered Samson's room.

"Sorry I'm late, everybody. Explanations later." She put down two gift-wrapped parcels and asked, "Where is the man of the moment?" although Samson was clearly visible.

He made a pretence of cowering out of sight, which, on account of his bulk and ungainly pose, was faintly comic. Georgia laughed, a merry tinkle, and while Kennedy poured out wine Samson played fake clumsiness for laughs. It was a charade in which he, a key player, took charge. Before the presentation he insisted on a formal enthronement of Shandy by steering her to the swivel chair and making her sit down to cheers and hand clapping.

"We've always been a happy ship here," said Samson, gazing fondly around at Martine, Georgia, Kennedy, Maunder, and the latest staff member, Julian, an hon. by birth, whose speciality was genealogical research. Julian was a sprig on a family tree, which had begun with the Norman invasion in the eleventh century. Samson had been of service to his father in a messy divorce case in which the detective had acted as an anti-publicist and managed to keep sordid facts from tabloid publicity by cleverly planted misinformation. He had not only been well paid for the deception but had been given a large gratuity to take on Julian, described by his father as 'queer as a coot'. Samson gave the young man an interview, liked the way he had said honestly, "I'm gay, Mr Samson", discovered he had a penchant for research, and took him on as an assistant in the booming agency side of genealogy under Shandy's surveillance.

Before handing him the gifts, Shandy made a short speech in which she paid tribute to her former boss and emphasised that it wasn't goodbye but only *au revoir*. Before replying, Samson unwrapped the parcels and his normally sleepy eyes opened with gratified surprise. The first was a soft-touch sensory chessboard, and the second a satinwood box containing chess pieces.

"You can keep the pieces in a compartment under the board," said Shandy, "but the box was such a bargain we decided to get that too."

After thanking them for the chess set Samson took the white queen out of the box and placed it in front of Shandy. That's you," he said, and then he put a black knight beside it, turned to Kennedy and said, "And that's you. Brian, protecting the queen."

"What about the rest of us?" Georgia asked. "I suppose we're all pawns."

Samson wished he had not made the quixotic gesture but, thinking fast, took out a castle. "This is you," he said to Maunder. "Guardian of the keep and very valuable in the end game."

He fished in the box and pulled out a white bishop. "How about this for you, Julian?"

"Very apropos," the young man drawled. "No end of the family took holy orders in the past. It's said that Chaucer based his Pardoner's Tale on one of the earlier Halbequeurs; another was defrocked for being naughty with choirboys. Well, why not a bishop for me?" As he spoke he looked challengingly around at the others.

"Don't push it," Georgia began, and was about to say something else but Samson intervened with, "That leaves Georgia and Martine." He took a black and a white pawn from the box. Placing the black pawn next to the knight he went on, "This can be you, Martine, keeping the knight company."

Martine, a shy woman whose family originated in Malta, shot a quick glance at Kennedy. Although they tried to keep it concealed, theirs was a budding office romance.

"Finally you, Georgia." He placed the white pawn on a chess square.

"I knew I'd be a pawn."

"Ah, but every pawn carries a gem-encrusted crown in her holdall," Samson replied. "If she can get to the eighth square without being taken she becomes a queen."

"Without being taken? Big deal. It's just my luck to be taken!"

Kennedy couldn't resist a risqué play on words. "Don't tell us you wouldn't like to be taken, Georgie girl."

"Depends who the taker is."

"A nice guy, naturally. Not some brute who'd take you by force."

"Enough of that!" This intervention from Shandy brought a startled look to Kennedy's face. The others seemed surprised at the sharpness of her rebuke. In an attempt to cover up, Shandy went on: "Sorry, didn't mean to snap at you, Brian, but I've had rather a bad morning. Anyway it's time for all of you to finish your wine and start clearing up." She glanced towards Samson in mute appeal for support.

"That's right," he said, "and once more, I am very touched by your thoughtful presents. I shall take them with me when I go for my op. Nothing like concentration on a game of chess to take one's mind off unpleasant things."

It was in subdued mood that the remains of food and drink were taken away. When the door had closed Shandy turned to Samson and said, "That was a bad start. Being bossy like that."

"Don't worry about it."

"It started so well too," she continued. "We both hammed it up like mad, didn't we? I don't think anyone suspected anything was wrong. Except you. You guessed. All the fooling around was to take the spotlight off me. Thanks. Sorry I lost my bottle at the end."

"Tell me about the problem."

She rose from the swivel chair. "Here, you have this. You've been standing long enough. I'll sit on the side of the desk. Just like I used to in the old days when there were just the two of us."

They switched places and she began her account of Kimberley's rape with the disastrous party at Sharon's house. Samson only interrupted the flow of narration when it was necessary to clarify a point.

"That's all Kimberley's side of the story," she said, "at least, the hearsay part. The rest is more like direct evidence, so far as I can recall details."

Samson's face had remained expressionless throughout, except for when Shandy first mentioned the rape, with the same stark suddenness she had felt at Kimberley's first outburst. His eyes had closed for a few moments, and his lips had drawn down at the corners; these small indicators were enough to show the revulsion he felt.

"Any questions so far?" Shandy asked.

"Two. I hope she doesn't become pregnant."

"She should be all right. Paul insisted on her having a morning-after pill. He didn't know she was already on the pill and still doesn't. I was coming to that. In context."

"Fair enough. The other point is this: from what I remember of the district, it's a built-up residential area on each side of the wood. Respectable without being too affluent." A gleam came to his eyes. "I have to be careful – you live there…"

"Paul's wish, not mine. I'd like to live more up-market, as you know."

"But Sharon's house is in a small, slightly better area. Too close to the high street, but quite some distance from the wood. What perplexes me is why a car of men bent on doing no good should be cruising a relatively quiet area looking for lonely women. I assume the police have been called?"

"Eventually they were, yes. Paul was difficult about it at first, but they came. Why?"

"Did they remark on the oddness of cruisers being in such a quiet suburb?"

Shandy frowned thoughtfully. "I don't recall that they did."

"No matter. Carry on."

"After she'd told us what had happened, Paul began hassling her with questions. I told him it was for the police to find out details. You know, they have trained WPCs for the job. He blew his top and Kim just couldn't take it. She screamed that it was all his fault, that she hated him, and ran off upstairs to lock herself in the bathroom."

"What did she mean – his fault?" Samson asked.

"His fault that we were arguing. We were still going hammer and tongs when she reappeared. She was standing in the

38

doorway. I don't know how much she'd overheard." As she spoke, Shandy looked directly at Samson. "Paul had just implied that ours, yours and mine, was something more than a platonic relationship."

Samson gave a wry smile. "That's ridiculous. No man could be jealous of me. So what happened next? How was Kimberley?"

A slight frown creased Shandy's forehead and she paused before replying. "She seemed almost unnaturally calm. Self-possessed. Completely different from the child who had screamed at her father and—"

"Child?" Samson interrupted.

"Yes, child. I still regard her as a child. She's only just sixteen."

"Out of school uniform she looks a young woman. That's what I thought the last time I saw her... Sorry, I interrupted you. What were you going to say?"

"That she was so self-possessed and calm that I wondered if she was all right. It was almost as if she was in a sort of trance. When Paul said, 'Your Mum wants to report this to the police, how do you feel about that?' she looked me straight in the eye and said, 'There's no need, Mum, I'm OK now.' I just was so taken aback I couldn't think what to say. In the end, I managed something like, 'Of course they must be told. You don't want those bloody men to get away with it, do you?'"

"How did she react to that?"

"Coolly. Calmly. And with some logic she said she couldn't be sure they were old enough to be men. They might just have been lads of her age. She only saw one, very briefly, after the event, when she tore off the blindfold. He looked like a black lad. Paul pounced on this and wanted to know exactly what he looked like. She said she wouldn't recognise him because, quick as a flash, he covered his face with his hands – which, in my opinion, is something only someone guilty would do. But she said that she noticed an index finger on one hand, the left she thought, was missing. It was just a stump. Paul got very excited about that. Told her she was brilliant to have noticed this and it would make identification easy. He said the northerner was probably white and the black bastard was probably from Brixton or nearby and shouldn't be too difficult for him to find."

"For *him* to find?" Samson asked. "Is he intending a one-man vendetta?"

"That's what it sounded like. It made me more determined than ever to get the police. Paul and I may not be on very good terms, but I don't want him to go looking for trouble in the back streets of Brixton. He wouldn't last long."

Samson nodded his head. "He's a bit racist, isn't he? I noticed at the office party last Christmas how he cold-shouldered Brian."

"That's right."

"But you managed to get the police?"

"Only after a physical struggle with Paul for the phone and Kim saying, 'Oh, let her have her own way Dad. It'll be all right. I can cope.'"

"What a strange attitude," Samson commented. "Do you think it possible that she felt a sort of guilt. That she deserved to be raped. Was she wearing a short skirt?"

"She may have taken one to wear at the party, but out of doors she was certainly in jeans. It's far too cold for anything else."

"Can you find out whether she did take a skirt to wear at the party?" Samson asked.

Shandy gave him a lingering look of curiosity. "You aren't thinking of getting involved? Do I have to remind you that you have an operation on Friday and you won't be fit for investigation for a while?"

"And do I have to remind you," he retorted, "that I am this firm's consultant and that you are in the process of consulting me? Anyway, it's only Tuesday and I'm not due for admission to hospital until late on Thursday."

An impasse created by opposing views was dissolved, as it often is between good friends, by laughter from both.

"True," Shandy agreed. "I suppose I do want your advice and that amounts to consultation."

"A consultation between consenting adults. We mustn't omit 'consenting adults'."

"OK, so you want to be involved, and I'm very grateful you do. You asked whether she felt that in some way she deserved to be raped. I'll have to think about that one. As for whether she took a skirt to wear, I can find that out."

"Good. Let me know. I'd like to speak to her myself. Do you think you could arrange that for tomorrow?"

Shandy thought for a moment. "It might be difficult to invite you to our place with Paul in his present mood, and I don't know whether she'd be willing to come here, especially if he didn't want her to."

Samson began playing with a paper knife which lay beside the hour-glass on his desk.

"What's troubling you?" Shandy asked.

"Well, I know it's none of my business really, but did you say that you were coming to why Kimberley is on the pill?"

"Because it's you, I'll tell you. Nobody else but the doctor knows it, but she's like Paul" – Shandy paused before uttering the words as if they were alien – "she is quite highly sexed. One night, Paul and I went up to town for a meal and a night at the opera, but when we got there he found he'd left his wallet behind and I had no money with me. So we raced back home and he stayed in the car while I ran indoors to get some cash. I'd left Kim doing her homework, but there was no one downstairs and the light was on in her bedroom. I went upstairs, burst into her room and found her stark naked about to get into bed with a boy. He looked absolutely terrified when he saw me. I told him to get dressed and get out of the house. Kim begged me not to tell her dad. I said I wouldn't if she'd promise that the boy wouldn't come back, and I said I'd speak to her in the morning. Half her classmates were doing it. You weren't one of the gang unless you'd lost your virginity." Shandy sighed. "I may have been wrong but I thought it best she went on the pill. Kim has always been a determined girl when she really wants her own way."

Although she had been sitting erectly on the side of the desk, Shandy's body slumped once she had made this admission and she looked away from Samson as if fearing to see reproof in his face.

He said, "I understand."

41

"I didn't like having to tell you of all people, her godfather, that my darling daughter, always top of the class at school, captain of the netball team, every teacher's pet, has a weakness."

"I can understand that too."

She faced him once more. "Bless you."

"Glad of your blessing," he replied. "I need all the blessings I can get if things go awry and I go to that bourne from which no man returns. Who knows what lies on the other side?"

"Are you nervous?" she asked.

"Of course I am. What human being, particularly one with a dodgy heart, looks forward to being out for the count under a surgeon's knife."

"That's the first time I've ever heard you admit to being nervous of anything."

"Let's hope it's the last," he said, adding quickly, "and let's change the subject before I get morbid. Try to bring Kimberley up here to see me tomorrow. Bring her to my flat, not the office."

"Will do," Shandy replied sliding off the desk. "Now I must get home. Can you hold the fort for the rest of the day? I know it's a bit much to ask on your retirement day, but I'd be ever so grateful."

He gave her a fond smile. "Any time you want me, you can have me," he said, "but don't quote me on that to your husband."

Five

The set expression on Shandy's face relaxed into a half-smile as she approached the front door of her home. Even from outside she could hear the noise from her daughter's CD player reverberating from a back bedroom. The ear-splitting volume meant firstly that Kimberley was, in one sense, back to normal; it also meant that Paul must have gone out. Although he was inclined to spoil his little girl, and would do almost anything to please her, he couldn't tolerate loud pop music. Moreover, he couldn't bear the CD which was playing, entitled *Ladies & Gentlemen*, not because the vocalist sang badly, but because he had read that George Michael was gay. To Paul Bullivant, homosexuality was a repugnant perversion. In his mind, homosexuals and black men were consigned to the waste-bin of humanity.

As she turned the key in the lock it flashed through Shandy's mind that she had once committed auditory mayhem with the early records of Cliff Richard, just as her mother before her had done the same with Frank Sinatra. Perhaps all fathers were like this when they felt excluded from their daughters by the powerful lungs of an invisible, alien, male presence. With Paul she suspected there was also a hint of jealousy.

Kimberley didn't hear her mother's knock on the door. It was only when Shandy had gone into the bedroom and shouted, "I'm home, Kim," that she turned from where she had been sitting rocking to the rhythm on the side of the bed.

"Oh, hello, Mum." Kimberley reached out and turned down the volume.

Shandy asked, "Are you feeling all right, dear?"

"Yes, thanks. Fine."

Nobody would have guessed that some twelve hours earlier Kimberley had been violently raped. Shandy's amazement at the sang-froid of her daughter was tempered by discomfort that she had recovered so quickly. She went and sat beside Kimberley. "Are you really all right?"

"Well, it's no use feeling sorry for myself, is it? I'll survive. It's Dad who's taken it all very badly."

"Where is he? I guessed he wasn't at home when I heard George Michael."

Kimberley shrugged. "I don't know. He said he was going for a walk and left about ten minutes ago. I reckon that he can't be cross with me today of all days, even if I play his favourite hate."

"Did he say where he was going?"

"No. But I can guess. You remember when the police came they bagged up all the clothes I'd been wearing for examination by forensics, and the WPC had asked where my panties were, and I said I didn't know but I thought they must have been left in the wood, and they said they'd look. I think Dad phoned the police station to see if they'd been found. I was listening from the top of the stairs and heard him say something about the perverts having taken them or else the search hadn't been thorough enough. Honestly, Mum, I can do without his interference. He might think he's protecting me, but I want to get on with my life."

Shandy put an arm round her daughter's shoulders. "Of course you do, but something as nasty as that won't just go away."

A pause followed while Kimberley considered this statement. "I suppose not," she said grudgingly. "Anyway, I think that's where Dad's gone ... to look for my panties." There was a touch of disdain in her voice as if the thought of her father's search was somehow repellent.

For a while they talked of other things; Christmas was still a few weeks away, yet stores had been celebrating the so-called festive season since the end of summer. The chore of sending Christmas cards lay ahead, some with the never to be fulfilled message 'We must meet in the New Year', and they agreed that already Christmas fatigue, like charity fatigue, became counter-productive to the spirit of giving.

Suddenly Kimberley switched the line of conversation. "Sharon gave me a call after you'd left. To say how sorry she was at what had happened." Releasing herself from her mother's protective arm, Kimberley swivelled round to look her full in the face. "How did she know?"

"I assume the police must have called at her house after they left here."

"It's really upset her, I can tell you. Not what happened to me, but because her parents aren't back yet and she'll have a hell of a lot of explaining to do." Kimberley's lips twitched in a smirk of satisfaction. "Serves her right."

"Do you know what she told the police?"

"Not much, I imagine. How could she? She was pretty far gone by the time I left the party. I think she tried to make out it was all above board. No gatecrashers. Just a few friends together."

"You told them differently," Shandy interrupted.

"I know. But she didn't say anything, so they must have let that go. And it sounds like they ignored the state of the house, which must have looked a total wreck. In fact, I don't know what she was beefing about. The cops only stayed about ten minutes."

"Didn't she show any concern about you?"

Kimberley hesitated. "A bit, but it was token concern. Anyone can fake sympathy. Empathy is different, and there was no empathy. She was more interested in learning the sordid details than in putting herself in my shoes ... meta-phorically speaking," she added with a short unamused laugh. "But I wasn't having any of that and said so. Then she asked if I'd be back at school next week and I hung up on her."

A quavering note had entered Kimberley's voice as she spoke the final words and a moment later tears flooded out of her eyes as the dam of self-control was breached. She flung herself into Shandy's arms. "Oh, Mum! I can't face going back there. Everyone will know…"

"Don't worry, darling. No one's going to make you."

"Dad might try. Not out of nastiness, but he might think it's the best way to get over it all. Face the music and the tune will change for the better."

"Leave your father to me," said Shandy grimly, squeezing her daughter in a comforting hug. "There won't be any school until you're ready for it."

A tear-stained face looked up at Shandy. "Oh Mum, you are lovely. Thanks so much." Kimberley eased herself from the embrace and went to the dressing table. After wiping her face with a tissue and blowing her nose, she peered into the mirror. "I look terrible," she exclaimed. "If he comes in now, Dad will know I've been crying."

"Does that matter?"

"Before he went out he was beside himself. Swearing he'd castrate and then kill the bastards when he caught them, and swearing to God he *would* catch them. I don't want him to end up in prison. He was a bit calmer when he left, but if he noticed I'd been crying it would start him up again."

While she had been speaking, Kimberley had taken a cotton-wool ball from a white china jar ornamented with blue-birds and, having added a few drops of witch hazel from one of an assortment of bottles, was dabbing at the puffy flesh under each eye.

Shandy watched for a few moments before saying, "I'll go down and make us a pot of tea. If Dad comes in, I'll keep him talking until you're ready to come down."

Kimberley turned her head to look at her mother's reflection in a side panel of the triptych mirror. "Thank you, Mum," she whispered. The reflection smiled at her before it disappeared and left the room.

She had decided that the subject of taking her daughter to see Samson in his flat must wait until the exact right moment arrived. Too soon or too late, and Kimberley's reaction could be a stubborn refusal or an apathetic reluctance.

It would be necessary to raise the matter without Paul there. As she made the tea, Shandy prayed he wouldn't come home before she'd broached it.

Kimberley walked into the kitchen just as a tray was being prepared. "Shall we have it down here, Kim?"

"Why not?" As her mother poured out two cups of tea, she went on, "Mum, I'm sorry for the things I've said about you spending so much time at your office and not enough at home. I guess it was selfish of me."

"But natural enough. I tried to make it up to you whenever I could."

"I know, and you have. I wish I could do something for you."

There would never be a better time. Appearing to concentrate on milk and sugar for tea, Shandy said, "There is something you could do."

"What's that?"

"You might not like the idea, but it would mean a great deal to me."

"Go on."

Shandy took a deep breath. "Tomorrow, I'd like you to come with me to see Uncle John in his flat. He goes into hospital the next day and he said he'd love to see you."

She looked quickly at Kimberley who was smiling as if the suggestion was a relief, something much better than she had expected. "That's no problem, Mum. I love Uncle John. What on earth makes you think..." Her voice trailed away and the smile vanished, wiped away by the realisation that this wasn't to be simply a goodwill visit to her godfather. "Oh, no. Not that! I can't be interrogated by him of all people!"

"He won't interrogate you."

"Not much! I suppose you told him the ugly facts."

"I had to, darling. I was late at the office for his party and when we were alone I told him. He's the only one who knows."

"I don't know why you *had* to," said Kimberley peevishly. "It could have waited until after his operation."

"John's a close friend, as well as a very special colleague. Besides which, he is an excellent private detective. He may not be able to second guess the police in their inquiry, but he may have some useful ideas. We all know how stretched the police are in this area, and they may not have the time or resources to follow up the case adequately. The fact that they only spent ten minutes interviewing Sharon says it all."

"I don't see what he can do from a hospital bed," said Kimberley sulkily.

"Probably nothing much. Maybe nothing at all. But you do want these men caught, don't you?"

"Of course I do. Especially if it stops Dad doing his nut."

"So you will come with me tomorrow?"

Shandy looked at her daughter, willing her to say yes.

A few seconds elapsed before, almost inaudibly, the words, "I suppose so," crept out of Kimberley's mouth. "But Dad mustn't know," she added.

"He won't. I shall say I'm taking you out on a shopping spree to cheer you up. If he asks about the office I'll say I'm taking the morning off."

Kimberley brightened. "That's brilliant. He hates shopping. Especially when he might have to blow the dust from his wallet."

"Now then," Shandy admonished. "He's not a mean man, and certainly not with you. And these days he has to be sensitive about money. He's not bringing much in."

"I know. It's just that…" Kimberley broke off at the sound of a key being inserted in the front door. Waiting until her father was indoors, Kimberley continued in a louder voice, "That would be great, Mum. It'll cheer me up a lot." As he entered the kitchen, her tone changed from false excitement to false surprise.

"Hello, Dad. I didn't hear you come in. Did you have a nice walk?"

"What would cheer you up a lot?" he asked.

"Mum's taking me shopping."

Paul touched the teapot, "Still warm. I think I'll join you, if I may."

"I'll make some fresh," said Shandy rising to her feet as her husband went to a cupboard to get his favourite mug, which had been given to him as a birthday present from Kimberley when aged five and which no one else was allowed to use. "No need to," he said over his shoulder.

"It's no trouble. Of course you can join us."

He reached out for the birthday mug and, still without looking at them, replied, "I didn't mean join you for tea. I meant join you tomorrow when you go shopping." He didn't see the horrified dismay which clouded the two faces; the dismay of crime plotters whose carefully laid plan has been torn open by the sudden appearance of law enforcers.

They only just managed to wipe away the evidence of shock as he turned around, but he must have sensed a change of atmosphere. Shandy was frozen to the spot with a teapot in her hand and Kimberley had shifted in her seat. "Is that all right with you?" he asked. "If I come shopping with you?" He relieved Shandy of the pot and began pouring tea into the mug.

It was Kimberley who broke a tense silence.

"Of course it is, Dad. We'd love you to come, wouldn't we Mum?"

"Yes ... of course," Shandy confirmed.

"Thought you would have to be at your office," said Paul, pulling up a chair to the table.

"I'm taking the morning off."

"Starting as you mean to go on?" he asked with heavy irony.

Shandy made no reply and again Kimberley took charge. "As a matter of fact, we'd discussed asking you to join us, but we thought you wouldn't want to go round looking at dresses and make-up and things. But if you're sure you won't be bored... In a way, it's a good idea. Get you out of the house. Change of scene, and all that."

He stirred sugar into the tea, slowly, as if the action helped concentration. "Maybe you're right," he said at length. "I could get bored, and I have other things to do."

Without warning Kimberley got to her feet and hurried out of the kitchen. As they heard the patter of her feet going upstairs Paul asked in bewilderment, "What's up with her? Was it something I said?"

49

Her self-possession now restored, Shandy replied, "No. She's been very brave, but every so often she needs to be alone to have a little weep."

"Shouldn't we be with her?"

"No. That's the last thing she'd want. She needs space to come to terms with what happened. Where have you been?"

"Where do you think? The wood. I support our police force in most things. But this is personal, and I'm not sure they'll be thorough enough in their search."

"Search?"

"For Kimmy's pants. I've combed the place where the bastards put her through it and there's nothing there. Tomorrow I'll go through the rest of the wood. Can't do it now as there won't be enough daylight. I'll be lucky if I find anything. I'll bet they took the pants as some sort of trophy. Some men are like that." He paused to allow a dark insinuation to sink in before continuing. "God, I'd just love to catch one of them with her pants in his pocket!"

"Paul, you mustn't get too obsessive about this."

"What? Obsessive!" he shouted. "My daughter has been raped and you have the bloody nerve to call me obsessive. Watch what you say, Shandy. I'm in no mood to be told what to be or not to be. You're not in your office now, and I'm not an employee. OK?"

She shot him a look which, had it been a flame-thrower, would have reduced him to ashes, before leaving the kitchen. He didn't follow but cradled the mug between his hands as if it were a precious and living thing, deserving of the comfort he would have liked to have given to his daughter.

Six

It had been a hot summer's day in August, he remembered, and she had been fourteen at the time. He had come home early, showered and changed into shorts and an open-necked shirt; Shandy was busy working at Samson Associates. He had been about to go into the back garden to catch some late afternoon sunshine when she had called out, "Dad, a wasp's got in!"

It was an anguished appeal for help; he raced up to her room and found her cowering beside the bed clutching a pillow as protection. The insect was swiftly killed with a rolled-up magazine. He picked it up gingerly by a wing and tossed it out of the window.

"Thanks, Dad. You're ever so brave!" She lowered the pillow and he saw she was wearing nothing more than a pale blue bikini. As she sat down on the bed she went on: "I can't bear them near me. Not like this, anyway. Might get stung."

He couldn't think why he did it, but he had gone and sat beside her. "Had a nice day?" he'd asked.

She had snuggled up against him. "Not bad. Tennis practice this morning. I would have been with Sandra this afternoon but she had to be at the dentist's at four, so I came home. I've been in the garden but it got too hot." She leaned sideways so that her head rested against his shoulder and it seemed natural enough to slide his right arm round her. He wasn't sure what was said next, but he remembered her saying, "I love you so much."

It was strange that he could recall the tennis practice and Sandra's dental appointment at four, but subsequently, try as he might, he couldn't remember what had been said immediately prior to her 'I love you so much'.

He wasn't sure whether she'd added the word 'Dad'. Perhaps she hadn't. Perhaps a false memory had been created by a sense of guilt.

He knew his response to her declaration of love had been "And I love you too, sweetie," although the endearment had never before been used to her.

She had wriggled close and lifted her head to look up at him. At the same moment, to keep his balance – to keep his balance? – he had put his free left hand against her body and, by chance, on her right breast which was round and firm enough to cup with his hand. Suddenly, shocked by an awful pleasure at the placement of his hand, he was about to remove it when her hand, half the size of his, came up and clamped his hand against her breast. She shifted her body, twisted her neck sideways and back and kissed him full on the lips.

Later, he realised he should have pulled away at once, but he had lingered on the kiss – for how long? One second? Three? With his heart hammering against his breastbone, and almost overwhelmed by a surge of sexual desire, he forced himself from her. He whispered, "We mustn't, Kimmy darling, we mustn't!"

She had flopped back on to the bed, eyes closed, thighs parted. Not another word was spoken by either as he managed to stumble from the room. Nor was the incident ever referred to, and nothing like it had happened ever again. Indeed, it might never have occurred. But it had, and it left him with a residue of guilt in bad moments; and, in good moments, a deep gratitude to the man he had once been to resist a temptation so powerful that it had almost overcome a primal taboo.

As he sat in the kitchen, nursing the mug of cold tea, he was in the throes of self-criticism. He wondered if in some obscure way she held him partly responsible for her apparent lack of resistance to the rape. She had told the woman police constable, "I didn't struggle or scream because I was afraid if I did they might kill me. One of them, I think it was the black one, whispered that if I made a squeak he'd cut my face to ribbons." The WPC had replied soothingly, "You did absolutely right to keep quiet."

But what had she meant when, not long after arriving home, she had run from the room shouting, "It's your fault. I hate you!" Shandy had said it was his fault that she was so upset, and had left to follow her daughter. He wasn't so sure. Her 'I hate you!' had knifed him and brought the hound of guilt snapping at his heels once more.

As he rose wearily from the kitchen table he said to himself, "I didn't do anything wrong. I stopped in time." But he knew the desire had been present, and was still with him, and that this was why he wanted to mete out rough justice to men who had carelessly taken what he had, with a great effort of will, resisted.

Seven

Whenever he had flirted with thoughts of retirement Samson had, in the past, always found an excuse to avoid being married to the idea; but after prostate cancer had been diagnosed, he found himself walking up the aisle like a man who has finally succumbed to the blandishments of a bride whose wedding dress could ultimately serve as a burial shroud. During periods of such flirtations he had fantasised about moving his living quarters from a third-floor apartment in the St James's area to somewhere with a warm climate near the sea. But the creeping crab of cancer had clawed away the flesh of fantasy and left a bare-boned reality.

Although he knew nothing about his antecedents on his father's side, his mother, who seemed to revel grimly in tales of sickness, hospitals and death, had mentioned more than once that her father and her grandfather had both died 'under the knife' during an operation to remove a prostatic tumour. With ill-concealed glee she would invariably add that the prostate was 'a trouble all men suffer from', as if the exclusively male condition were retributive justice for women's gynaecological problems. For Samson, the information imparted by his mother put his own mortality into sharp focus, and the prospect of death was a formidable barrier against dreams of sandy beaches and a turquoise sea glittering under the noonday sun.

His urological consultant, Mr Timson, had assured him that the operation was routine and nothing to worry about, and that his first patient had lived for ten years after the initial diagnosis, before dying from a heart attack.

Samson had taken an instant liking to Mr Timson, whose rounded belly testified a love of good food and wine and whose consultations were lightened by chuckles of laughter. "Yes, I know of your heart condition (chuckle). Your GP told me in his letter of referral. You've been on beta-blockers, I understand. No problem there. The anaesthetist will be informed and there's no reason why you shouldn't last a good time. No need to rush home and make a will (chuckle) and no need to worry."

The chuckles had been more sparse when Samson had confessed that during most nights he was obliged to visit the bathroom three or four times and, though at bursting point, could only relieve himself by a feeble trickle. It had been after a look at his swollen ankles that Mr Timson had said, "We must get you a hospital bed soon. There's a lot of water to get rid of before I operate."

He was due to be admitted to hospital on Thursday. Today, Wednesday, was a day to be got through. In an effort to avoid brooding on what lay ahead while waiting for the arrival of Shandy and Kimberley, Samson went to a large box in his bedroom which contained a number of scrapbooks containing newspaper and magazine cuttings. Whenever he read something bizarre or arcane which might conceivably be of use one day, he would cut it out and paste it in a scrapbook.

He took a book to the living-room where a CD of Chopin's studies was playing softly and sat down in an armchair to read. Under the heading 'Rape' he found the report of a ruling by Italy's Supreme Court of Appeal whereby it had been held that a woman cannot claim to have been raped if she was wearing jeans at the time of the alleged offence. The reason given for the ruling – which had aroused Italian feminists to unprecedented heights of fury – was that 'jeans cannot be partly removed without the effective help of the person wearing them ... and it is impossible if the woman is struggling with all her force'. No allowance was made for a victim too terrified to struggle. Samson put away the scrapbook. A mere ten minutes had passed, and not for the first time he reflected on the irreconcilable difference between psychological and chronological time.

His visitors arrived carrying shopping bags marked 'Harvey Nichols'. They accepted his offer of coffee and for a short while he and Shandy talked of generalities concerning the office, before he gently led into the reason for Kimberley's presence.

"I know you've had a bad time, Kim, and if you don't want to tell me about it that's all right with me."

She swallowed. "I don't know what you can do," she said in a strained voice.

"Neither do I. Probably nothing. But we must do all we can to put these men behind bars. They may be serial rapists. Anyway, I'd like to hear your account of what must have been a horrendous experience. Tell me in your own time and stop when you've had enough."

He sat back and closed his eyes. Every so often during a halting narrative he nodded his head to indicate that he wasn't asleep and interrupted only when it was necessary to clarify an ambiguity or to make sense of her faltering account. For her, it was much more difficult to speak to someone she loved and respected than to a police officer who was a stranger. At last she concluded her story.

Samson opened his eyes. "There are one or two questions I'd like to ask, if that's all right," and without waiting for her comment, he went ahead. "Did you see everyone who gate-crashed the party?"

"I saw everyone who came into the room where I was, but some were in other rooms, I think, and some went upstairs." She turned to Shandy and uttered the single word, "Kelly."

"Kelly?" Samson asked.

Shandy explained. "Kelly is one of Sharon's friends who is sex-mad and took over an upstairs bedroom to indulge herself."

"And so," Samson continued, "the villains could have been at the party but not seen by you."

"I suppose so."

"And one of them might have seen you leaving and tipped off the others to follow you?"

Kimberley thought about the possibility. "I suppose so," she said once more.

"Did the police raise this point?"

"No."

"Do you know what kind of car it was?"

"It was a BMW. I told them that."

"And did you by any chance see the number-plate?"

"They asked that as well. I said I thought it began with an 'H' but I couldn't remember anything else, and I only knew that because when I hurried away they drove a little way after me and passed me before stopping and I saw the 'H'."

"An H-reg BMW," Samson spoke to himself, making a mental note. Then, to Shandy, "There have been so many changes of staff since we were south of the river that, so far as I know, only Bob Broadbent is still at the nick there. I'd like to know who owns the BMW."

"I could ask him. Off the record. He's got a soft spot for me."

"What about Kim's statement? Might be worth getting a copy."

"I doubt it. I read it through before Kim signed, and there's nothing in it she hasn't told you."

He turned to Kimberley. "When you left Sharon's house you didn't notice a BMW lurking nearby?"

She shook her head. "I was so fed up with Sharon I didn't notice anything in particular. Cars were parked in the drive and on the road, that's all I can remember."

"Never mind." Samson smiled to lessen the impact of his next question. "I'm sorry to have to ask you this, but am I right in thinking you didn't shout for help when you were assaulted?"

Kimberley sat up as if a firecracker had exploded beneath her and with its flame in her voice she said, "Dead right. When they took off my jeans the driver whispered in my ear that he'd got something which would cut my face to ribbons if I made a squeak or put up a struggle. And when the other one said, 'Lift your bum, you bitch', I did."

"Did you tell the police this?"

"I told them about the knife, but not about having to lift up."

"I was thinking that if they do get caught, a defence lawyer might assert that you willingly participated, although it's quite clear that you risked having your face badly scarred unless you did as you were told. And you were blindfolded too. That must have added to the terror of what was happening. The police have the scarf for forensic evidence I believe."

Shandy spoke. "I was in touch with CID earlier. The scarf is obviously home-made with ordinary knitting wool, but they want to see if there are any hairs on it which might be evidence if it comes to a DNA test."

Samson resumed his questioning. "The man you saw after pulling off the scarf – the index finger of his left hand was a stump?"

"That's right."

"And very useful as a means of identification. But are you sure he was one of the men?"

"I can't swear to it, of course, but he could hardly have been an innocent bystander, could he? Dad reckons the scarf belonged to him and he was coming back to get it when I flashed the torch on him. He panicked and ran off."

"That sounds plausible," said Samson. With a smile he added, "And that's the end of the inquisition. I hope it wasn't too traumatic."

For the first time Kimberley smiled in accord. "Not traumatic at all."

"Mention of your dad reminds me. I gather he takes the matter extremely seriously."

"He's gone over the top," said Kimberley bluntly. "I think if he could lay his hands on anyone in the gang he'd murder them."

Samson turned his head towards Shandy as if seeking confirmation.

"Over the top and very obsessive," she said. "He's going to comb through the wood today in a search for Kim's knickers. He doesn't really expect to find them, but it's the 'no stone unturned' philosophy. He thinks one of them took the knickers as a sort of trophy. He says it's the sort of sick thing they would do."

Kimberley, full of adolescent poise and worldly-wise knowledge spoke up in a firm voice. "If he carries on like this he'll be the sick one. The way he's behaving now sickens me, anyway." Without warning, the teenage bravado vanished and tears sprang to her eyes. "It all makes me feel dirty, soiled, used..."

As Shandy comforted her daughter she said, "I think we'll leave soon, John. I need to go to the office and Kim is going to a friend's place until I get home."

From a tear-stained face pressed against a maternal bosom came a defiant, "I'm not going home to spend the afternoon with him asking me things he already knows the answer to."

"You don't have to, darling," said Shandy soothingly. "You can go straight from here to Sandra's." To Samson she said, "Good luck tomorrow. I know you'll be all right. I'll come and see you. By the way, if you're stuck for a name when they ask for your next-of-kin, feel free to use mine."

As executrix and chief beneficiary under the terms of his will she was already effectively his next-of-kin, but he expressed gratitude for permission to do something he had fully intended to with or without her consent.

When the time came for them to leave, Kimberley pecked him on the cheek and said, "Thank you, Uncle John."

"Considering everything, I think you're bearing up wonderfully. By the way, I feel you're old enough to dispense with the 'uncle' bit. Just call me 'John'."

A quick smile came to her lips and eyes. "Thanks, John."

When the door had closed behind them he considered the situation. There was little he could do except give support and encouragement. Seeking his opinion hadn't been altogether a waste, although he would have preferred to spend the time talking with Shandy about cases she had taken over from him.

For a few moments he thought of the uncertainties ahead. His presentation chess computer was ready for use on a reproduction French secretaire on the far side of the room. For Samson, concentration on a game of chess was an excellent means of staving off oppressive thoughts. He went to the computer and switched it on. Recently, on his old inferior computer, he had been playing black and the computer white. Normally whether he was playing as black or white, he liked to attack, but his strategy had changed to one of defence. He was experimenting with what he thought of as a 'double fianchetto' in which white played conventional openings to which he would respond by four moves which would result in each bishop occupying a square vacated by a knight's pawn, thereby giving them diagonal command of the board's centre.

Determined to win this last game before admittance to hospital he played slowly, thoughtfully, consuming the hours until it was time to prepare an evening meal.

Before he retired to bed, he reflected that the defensive ploy had started the day after hearing Mr Timson's diagnosis. He wondered whether his change from being an aggressive player to a stonewall defender, one who waited for the enemy to run out of steam, had subconsciously been dictated by cancer. And then he had ticked himself off for morbid self-absorption.

Tossing and turning in bed, fitful sleep was plagued by fragmentary but vivid dreams in which he was travelling through a strange and hostile country sometimes on foot, sometimes on horse, and once in a howdah on an elephant's back.

Eight

Resentment at his wife's successful business life had contributed to the bitterness he already felt at the near-breakdown of the sexual relationship. He was a prideful man and none of his previous colleagues would have described him as easy-going or laid-back. 'Ambitious' and 'self-seeking' were more likely epithets, and yet in spite of his desire to climb the ladder of personal achievement he had never been one to move upwards by crawling from rung to rung. Pride forbade that he should ever be a brown-nose yes-man. Perhaps if he had been a trifle more deferential to senior management, he wouldn't have been made redundant while a more flexible man managed to cling on to his post despite being less efficient. Paul Bullivant was a copybook example of someone who is his own worst enemy, an archetypal self-defeater.

Although he could not have admitted it, resentment – combined with a quick temper and an increasingly heavy consumption of alcohol – had combined to make fertile ground for obsessive behaviour. The furnace of anger at Kimberley's rape was cooling into an iron-hard determination to find and punish the rapists and their associates one by one. Nor could he have admitted that his intention to mete out retribution was in any way connected with incestuous thoughts which he had striven to suppress, or that the fury he had experienced was in part due to the rapists having taken by force what he by a supreme effort had declined. Matters had been made worse, if that was possible, by the colour of the skin of one of the rapists.

As he began a more detailed search of the wood for the missing underwear, he started to plan a means of revenge. First he went to the clearing where the offence had taken place – not that he expected to discover anything after his own search as well as one by the police; but he had a belief in the untrustworthy adage that a criminal always returns to the scene of his crime. He lingered there a long while, just out of sight of the footpath, but himself able to see whoever passed by. In spite of the wood's reputation as the haunt of flashers and perverts a surprising number of women used it. They were white; as were the few men who possibly, like himself, had no workplace to go to, or were of pensionable age. It was a chilly day and many passers-by wore overcoats and scarves. In some cases, particularly among the older ones, gloves were also worn. It occurred to Paul that if a black man appeared wearing gloves, he could not demand that the left glove be removed. Then, on the assumption that a young black wouldn't be seen dead wearing gloves, he dismissed the idea.

At length, feeling as though he was stepping out of a refrig-erator, he began a wider search, systematically crossing and re-crossing the wood. By the time he had finished pushing past bushes and gazing up at the lower branches of trees it was obvious that the garment was not to be found and he was now convinced that it had become a trophy of one of the rapists.

The search had ended at a part of the perimeter of the wood which bordered a row of small shops. It was a run-down area which he didn't know well, except that a number of Asian families and a few of Afro-Caribbean origins had displaced many former white inhabitants. Sandwiched between a newsagent and a hairdressers was a boarded-up shop with a weathered 'For Sale' notice affixed to its wall. Paul stood looking at the shop for some time before eventually crossing a road to take a closer look. Apart from the sealed-up entrance which fronted a pavement there was a door by one side of the shop which presumably led to a passageway between it and the adjoining hairdresser's. Paul waited until two Indian women swathed in heavy clothes had passed by, their faces pinched with cold, before trying the side-passage door. It was firmly bolted. He stood outside the derelict shop deep in thought while pedestrians passed by and a few cars came along the road. One car was a BMW and he looked at its number plate. It began with a 'J'.

He came to a decision, pulled out a mobile phone from his overcoat pocket and keyed the number on the estate agent's board. He was told that the price was negotiable; did he wish particulars to be sent him?

"I'm on a flying visit down here to do a bit of business," he replied. "Would it be possible for someone from your office to come right now just to show me round. I may not be down here again for some time."

After a pause he was informed, "Our Mr Cutler will be with you in about fifteen minutes if you don't mind waiting."

"So long as he makes it fifteen minutes and no more, all right. But I am on a tight schedule ... My name? It's Jones. Mr Jones."

He put the mobile phone away and wandered up and down the road to pass time and to create some body warmth. Within the allotted quarter of an hour, a red Vauxhall Astra slowed down and parked on a yellow line outside the shop. A young man alighted from the driver's seat.

"Mr Jones?"

"Yes. And you are Mr Cutler."

"The same, sir." A bunch of keys was produced and, after a wrestle with a lock, the shop door swung open. "Dammit," said the young man. "I should have brought a torch. No electrics. Place has been vacant for six months," he explained.

As he entered the shop, Paul was greeted by a strong odour which was difficult to analyse but contained elements of musty hay, bad meat and a sharp, faintly spicy smell.

"Sorry about the pong," said Cutler.

"What did the shop sell?"

"Pets, pet food, that sort of thing. The owner was an old lady who died. This is an executor sale. Usually executors are anxious to get rid of property, but these have hung on for the asking price. Too long. Now they're willing to negotiate, there aren't many people interested." As Paul peered through the gloom past a counter to a stairway at the back from which some light filtered down, Cutler continued, "Character of the neighbourhood has changed rapidly this year. Many of the newcomers are our brethren from the sub-continent where they eat dogs rather than keep them as pets, if you take my meaning, sir."

"I do indeed."

"The shop stayed open for a bit but did no business, and as the goodwill was virtually nil it got closed." Cutler moved forward. "Would you like to follow me, sir. Watch where you're stepping." He gave a laugh. "My boss would shoot me if you had an accident and there was an insurance claim. Might I enquire, sir, what you would require the premises for?"

Paul had intended to say, 'I represent Driveaway which is better known in the North than down here, but we are expanding. It's basically a driving school.' However, Cutler's last remark caused a last-minute change of plan.

"Funny you should mention insurance, because that's my line. Insurance and other financial services. Personal loans, and so on." If pressed for further details he could bluff his way through finances better than a pretence of wishing to run a driving school for motorists.

"Should do quite well in this area." Cutler said, opening a door at the rear of the shop. Light came through a window which looked as though it had last been wiped by a greasy rag. Dead flies littered the sill below. The room was furnished with a deal table, two cane chairs, and faded chintz curtains which hung from a drooping wire. Next to the window was a long grey blanket which Cutler pulled aside to reveal another door. He jangled the bunch of keys. "This leads to a small yard outside," he explained. "There's a brick-built loo, which I understand is flush operated and connected to main drainage. Would you like to have a look?"

"I would."

"Well, that's some progress," said Cutler cheerfully. "The last couple of viewers had already seen enough to know the place didn't suit."

Paul looked inside the toilet and pushed the flush handle. Cutler held his breath and then a faint gurgle and a trickle of rusty water splashed into the pan. Relieved at this evidence of some, if not full, working order he said, "It's one of those where you have to acquire the knack, if you take my meaning, sir."

"Maybe, but if there is some repair work needed it shouldn't cause a good plumber much trouble."

"Dead right," Cutler replied feelingly. "Anything else you'd like to see downstairs, sir?"

Paul walked over to the side of the small yard and gazed down a narrow passage to the bolted door beyond which was pavement and road. He went down the passage, gripped a handle and shook the door which responded with a loud rattle as though aggrieved at such rough treatment. "Seems a bit loose," he said, examining the bolt closely.

"I'm sure that could be fixed. if you are interested in buying."

"Of course. Now I'd like a quick look upstairs." Paul glanced at his watch. "As I explained on the phone, I'm on a tight schedule."

The two upstairs rooms, one leading from the other, were bare of furnishing except for an old iron bedstead on which a striped red and white mattress lay. As Paul sat on its side, Cutler again held his breath until his viewer stood up unharmed. There were always unknown hazards waiting in ambush to spring out and injure a viewer, and with lawyers chasing business with 'no win, no fee' deals people were apt to go to court on any pretext. "Mind the stairs," he said as they prepared to descend. "They're pretty steep and the light isn't all that good. I'll leave the bedroom door open until you're safely down."

Once more in the street he thrust some papers at Paul. "These are the particulars of the property and one or two others in the same price range." With a tentative note in his voice he added, "Can I ask, sir, whether you think it might suit?"

"It could do. I shall have to think about it, of course."

"Here's my card. My home number is on the back. Feel free to call me any time of the day or night... Might I have your address and phone number?"

"Certainly. I haven't got my card with me but if you have a pen I'll write it down."

Placing a piece of paper provided by the willing Cutler on the bonnet of the red Astra, Paul wrote, '33, Rosedale Gardens, Stockton-on-Tees' and added a phone number. Handing the paper to Cutler he said, "I can never remember my post code. The number isn't a home number, it's my mobile. This is strictly confidential. My wife and I don't see eye to eye on my job. It takes me all over the country and away from home for weeks at a time. So no letters, please, and contact only through the mobile."

"I understand. A wink is a good as a nod, if you take my meaning, sir."

Paul glanced at the young man's card. "It'll be nice to do business with you, er, James."

"Call me Jim please, sir."

"You are a Jim too. Now there's a coincidence. I'm a Jim. Jim Jones."

"Small world," said Cutler with hearty irrelevance.

"Certainly is, Jim. I'm fairly sure you'll be hearing from me. But remember. No letters. Wait for me to get in touch. Things are very tricky at home" – that at least is true, he thought – "very tricky, and I'm sure an ill-advised call or letter could knock any plan to start up a business down here on the head."

"I take your meaning, squire. You can rely on me."

They shook hands and Cutler sped away in his car. A smile creased Paul's features for the first time since the previous morning. His step was almost jaunty as he crossed the road and entered the wood once more. Pleased with the ease of getting young Cutler to accept the fictitious address, all he had to remember was too keep the mobile switched off whenever Shandy or Kimberley were around.

*   *   *

Wednesday was Sylvester's day off and while Paul, Shandy and Kimberley were having a breakfast at which only the clink of cutlery broke long uneasy silences, Sylvester was in bed, allowed – since he had started working – to have a lie in.

He lived in a road where ten years before there had been only British residents. After the arrival of two Greek-Cypriot families and then a Jamaican doctor, it was no longer regarded by the Brits as so exclusive and there were mutterings about a drop in house values. Next, another Greek-Cypriot family took up residence and then Sylvester's family arrived. His father was a pharmacist who had been to school in Jamaica with the doctor and they were close friends. Both had previously lived in Brixton but had felt uneasy about its atmosphere; about the no-go areas where drug pushers operated and the tinder-box potential whenever a black was wrongly arrested. Although there was no overt racism in the road where Sylvester lived – no National Front thugs, no windows smashed – the newcomers were pointedly ignored by neighbours who might have coined the very English phrase of 'we keep ourselves to ourselves'. Academically, Sylvester had not been a bright pupil at school and was regularly among the bottom three in his form, but he was a willing manual worker and had never played the sick-card to gain a day off. By contrast his younger sister, Coral, had a lively mind and was near the top of her form at a nearby convent school. Sylvester was proud of her abilities but would sometimes ruminate sadly, 'Where was I when the brains were dished out?'

But his thoughts when he awoke were not of the cold-shouldering neighbourhood, or of his sister's skill in finding the right word for every occasion while he was grappling in his mind with a pocket dictionary. He had come awake with the realisation that something was heart-sinkingly wrong. Moments later, he had remembered the rape scene and the panties which were beneath the mattress where he was lying. He would have to get rid of them but not before ... she had been pretty and white ... Jason Marchant should not have done what he did, definitely not, but in a way who could blame him? He hadn't used crude language like the other man... Yes, he must get rid of the pathetic remnant of a rape ... but not before he had one more good look at it.

He got out of bed and felt under the mattress – a moment of panic – it had disappeared during the night. Frantically his fingers scrabbled blindly around until he remembered he had hidden them under the other side of the bed. He retrieved a crumpled piece of white cotton and as his eyes focused on it he recalled how it had been wrenched off, over her thighs and down her legs, dislodging a shoe in the process. The memory became so vivid he hardly saw what he was holding. He became aware of stiffening flesh under his pyjama trousers.

He returned quickly into the bed and snuggled down, draping the panties across his face and pulling a counterpane over his head. Soon the counterpane seemed to take on a rhythmic life of its own; the vibration increased and ended with muffled grunts, and then a long sigh from under the bedclothes. He came up for air and after stuffing the little garment under a pillow, he relaxed. He would most definitely get rid of the item today. He'd drop it in a litter bin when no one was looking. At temporary peace with himself he drifted back into sleep.

The sound of his mother's voice banished a pleasant dream about a promised holiday in Jamaica next year, and the girl he was swimming with vanished for ever. "Time you were up and running, young fella. Know what time it is? Nearly ten. Now you get along to the bathroom while I make your bed."

"OK, Mom."

Since he had started work on early shift at the supermarket his mother had undertaken the chore of making his bed each day. He was almost out of bed, and rubbing sleep from his eyes when he remembered ... Oh, my God, panties under the pillow!

"Come along. What's keeping you, son. I got other work to do."

"Mom." A long pause.

"What now?"

"I been thinking."

"Lord be praised! He's been thinking!"

Another pause while Sylvester desperately attempted to fill a mental vacuum.

"Come on, son. Stop messing me around. Get yourself going."

"I been thinking, Mom."

"You have? Well, you could have fooled me. But they do say there's a first time for everything."

"No need to be like that, Mom. Sarcastic."

"Unless you claiming to be sick there is every need. I got other things to do beside standing here listening to fool talk about thinking. Now you get along to that bathroom pronto or I'll never do your bed again."

Some angel of mercy must have put the words into his mouth, like the evanescent dream, his mental vacuum disappeared.

"That's what I was thinking but you didn't give me the chance to say it."

His mother, now standing, arms akimbo, the personification of someone not to be trifled with, a woman who could make dextrous use of a rolling pin and not simply for making pastry, said: "I'm listening. I'm waiting for your pearl of wisdom which has taken so long to be born. Tell me, what you been thinking?"

"It's not fair on you having to make my bed every day, even on my day off."

"I'm not complaining."

"I know. But it makes me feel bad."

"Huh!"

"No honestly, Mom. Please let me make my own bed on my days off. I do appreciate all you do for me, and I know in some ways I been a disappointment to you and Daddy, but please Mom, let me make my own bed."

"First, I don't ever again want to hear you say you've been a disappointment to us, and second I think you got it right about making your own bed on your day off, and so" – she smiled – "I'll leave you to it."

When he was sure that his mother was downstairs, Sylvester retrieved the panties and looked for a hiding place until he was out of the bathroom. He wasn't going to risk leaving them under his pillow in case she changed her mind and returned to make his bed. After a few seconds of indecision he went to a wardrobe and stuffed the crumpled piece of cotton in a coat pocket.

On coming back from the bathroom he saw that it had been a wise move to change the hiding place. His bed was neatly made. Grinning to himself he made his way to the kitchen to be greeted with, "You're a lucky boy to get something to eat, you being so late."

"Thanks, Mom." Sylvester seated himself at a table in front of a bowl of cornflakes.

As he reached for a jug of milk his mother went on, "I did make your bed today, but" – she wagged a finger – "it's the last time on your days off."

"I saw. Thanks, Mom."

The finger-wagging continued. "Make sure you do it proper. I shall check on you. Don't forget: as you make your bed so you must lie on it." The restless finger curled back into the palm of her hand. "What you doing today?"

"I'm going down to the club. Some of the guys will be there. We'll kick a ball around."

He was referring to a recreation ground where youths of the locality congregated for various sporting activities. It had a club-house and was administered under strict conditions by a non-denominational church. No alcohol or smoking was allowed on the premises.

"I hope there aren't no Yardie kids there."

Sylvester paused from spooning cornflakes into his mouth. In a weary voice he gave the assurance required whenever he said he was going to the club.

"Mom, this place is so *respectable*. No drugs, no nothing except the clean fresh air."

"OK, OK, but watch it. The devil comes in many guises."

Sylvester sighed and continued with his breakfast. He loved his mother but wished she wouldn't treat him like an easily tempted ten-year-old. He was eighteen and knew right from wrong. Or did he? Was it right to have had a thrill fantasising that he was doing what Jason Marchant had done, he wondered. On balance, probably not. This problem solved, his resolution to dispose of the incriminating garment was strengthened. He would rid himself of any guilty thoughts that very day.

As he passed his mother, now polishing the hall floor he said, "Thanks, Mom. Love you."

"Love you too," she called after him as he ran upstairs, "though sometimes you don't deserve it," she added under her breath.

His good intention came to nothing. It would almost have been a profanity to dump the panties in the club's litter-bin, and then he forgot about them until he was almost home and went to pull a handkerchief out of a trouser pocket to blow his nose and found that instead he was holding an intimate piece of female underwear. Blood rushed to his face at the horrifying thought that he might have made such a misjudgement in his mother's presence.

He resolved that, once indoors, he would go straight to his room to hide the dangerous thing before his mother or smart-sharp little sister spotted it. His body temperature soared as if a thermostat were switched on to maximum as he imagined Coral, who sometimes irritatingly called him 'Silly Sylly', singing out, 'Mom, Sylly's got a lady's knick-knacks!'

Tomorrow, without fail, he would dispose of it.

Julian, a purple silk scarf threaded through a gold toggle around his neck, wearing a Turnbull and Asser shirt and a dark grey suit from his father's tailors, wandered into the outer office where Georgia sat by the telephone switchboard eating her lunchtime snack of tuna and lettuce sandwiches. She greeted him with, "Hello, darling. Come to slum with the workers?"

Julian made a show of peering about, even looking under a table, before saying in a puzzled voice, "Workers? I can only see one wage-waster filling herself with some ghastly concoction which looks like disposal from an offal factory."

Georgia laughed. As with Kennedy she enjoyed friendly sparring with Julian, and like Kennedy he was no threat, although Kennedy might have come on a bit strong if he hadn't been so taken by Martine. Georgia, who'd had some bad experiences with heterosexuals, saw no danger in light flirtation with Julian. "That's not a very nice thing to say, darling, don't you love me any more?"

"Oh, but I do. Madly. But I didn't come to bandy meaning-less words. I wondered if you knew when Shandy expected to be in. I've got a tricky question about the issue of an heir presump-tive."

A play on the words 'tissue' and 'air' flashed into Georgia's mind, was dismissed as being too feeble, and she said, "She should be in any time now. I know she went to see the Old Man this morning and she said she'd be in early afternoon. I've had to rearrange some appointments for her. She'll be busy so you can forget about your airs and graces."

Julian reached out and snatched at her last half-sandwich, took a bite from it, and gave his opinion. "Um, not bad," he said. "One should never judge by appearances, don't you think?"

"What the hell do you think you're doing," she asked indig-nantly. "You've got some front for a Johnny-Come-Lately."

"Speaking of which," he replied calmly, "as I understand it, first there was the Old man, then Shandy came along, and then you, and then Martine. Is that correct?"

Georgia's eyes narrowed; she suspected a trap. "What are you getting at?"

"I was thinking that technically you are senior to Martine, so why has Shandy left Martine in charge while she's not here?"

"Don't you try to drive a wedge between me and Martine…"

"Perish the thought."

"And don't try to wind me up. That's the trouble with you. You can be bitchier than any woman."

Julian put up his hands and recoiled as though physically attacked. "I'd no idea … I'm terribly sorry."

"You'd better be." She handed him the bite-marked half-sandwich. "Here. You started it, you'd better finish it."

"I'll take it as a token of your forgiveness for my unpardon-able gaffe."

She screwed up cellophane wrapping and threw it into a wastepaper basket. "Now, I've got things to do even if you haven't. So, on your way, Julian, darling."

He moved towards the door, turned and said, "Actually I came to ask the date of your birthday."

"Don't tell me you're an astrology freak."

"No. Well, sort of. I'd say you were a Leo."

"Wrong. I'm a Scorpio. I've got a sting in my tail, so watch it, boy."

"You have a birthday about now then?"

"Next week. All pressies gratefully received."

"And Shandy, what is her sign?"

"May the twenty-fourth makes her a Gemini."

"And the Old Man?"

"May the seventh. Taurus." Again her eyes narrowed with suspicion. "What do you want to know for?"

"Sheer idle curiosity. I reckon he must be in his late fifties. The Old Man, I mean."

"Maybe. Is that all or can I get on with my work?"

"Sorry if I've been a bore," he replied, sliding through the doorway. He felt pleased with himself having extracted the information he wanted to put him on the path of tracing, solely for his own interest, Samson's antecedents. Before he joined the firm he had overheard a conversation between his father and a friend in which his father had said, "I've got a feeling Samson might have been born on the wrong side of the blanket. Not that it matters a hoot. I'm damn grateful to the fellow for keeping the media off my back."

Nine

Shandy rapped on the door and went into her daughter's bedroom. It was in its usual disordered state with wardrobe doors open, clothes scattered on the floor, a miscellany of compact discs and cosmetic aids on the dressing table, one drawer in a chest of drawers sticking out to reveal a jumble of underwear, and with framed photos of pop stars crowding against family photographs on the top of the chest. School books were piled on a chair in the corner. Kimberley, still in a shortie nightshirt, sat on the side of an unmade bed facing the window. She was gently rocking back and forth to the music of a muted tape.

"Aren't you coming down to breakfast, darling?" Shandy asked.

Without turning her head Kimberley replied, "I'm not hungry."

"But you hardly ate anything yesterday."

"I'm not hungry, Mum."

"What's the matter, Kim?" As soon as the question was asked Shandy knew it was a foolish enquiry.

Kimberley turned her head; her face was pale and strained and her eyes red. "Nothing's the matter. I'm just not hungry. If I want anything I'll raid the fridge. OK?"

"I'll look in before I leave for work," said Shandy and closed the door noiselessly as though leaving a sleeping invalid.

As she walked into the kitchen, Paul asked, "Is she coming down?"

"No. She says she's not hungry. But if she doesn't want anything, we can't force her."

He paused from eating. "That's right. No point in trying to make her eat something she doesn't want... Pass the toast please."

She could hardly believe what she'd heard. Was this the man who yesterday was vowing to kill any rapist he could catch? Was this the father whose bursts of outrage at the violation of his daughter came close to the borders of insanity? In one way she was glad to be spared a show of outrage; and yet this would have been more understandable, even preferable, to his detachment. Covering her confusion she said, "I shan't be around, of course, but you'll be here if she needs anything. You aren't going out, are you? It's a miserable day and rain is forecast."

"I might go for a stroll, but Kimmy will be all right. She can look after herself."

Their daughter had been raped only two days previously and yet he was showing an indifference to her plight amounting to wilful disregard. Shandy was so bewildered by the inexplicable change of attitude that for a few moments she sat speechlessly watching him eating toast and marmalade as he read a morning newspaper.

They had been married for nearly twenty years and she had become attuned to his patterns of behaviour, nuances which indicated a mood change, and she had a good idea of what to expect in given circumstances, but now she was baffled. From professional experience she knew that many major marital stresses and difficulties were caused by sexual or financial problems between the partners. Paul was frustrated by her lack of libido and resented that he was no longer the primary bread-winner; but neither of these considerations applied.

In what she hoped was a casual tone of voice she asked, "Any idea where you might go for a stroll?"

Looking up from the newspaper he replied, "I thought of going to Brixton. Do you know if the market is on today?"

"Brixton!"

"If I have no luck there, and I doubt if I shall, I'll come back and see if anything is stirring in the wood."

"What do you expect to find in the wood?"

Without a trace of humour in his deadpan eyes or lips he replied, "Oh, I don't know. A teddy bear's picnic maybe."

His coldly delivered flip answer gave the explanation for his radical change of attitude. He must have crossed the line separating mental stability from insanity; an obsession with vengeance had overpowered his reason. The thought of what might happen if he should track down a rapist was too awful to contemplate. She rose from the table.

"I hope you know what you're putting Kim and me through," she said, before leaving the kitchen.

As she went up the stairs to the bathroom she thought: When the going gets tough, the tough get going. It was a matter of coping. 'Good old Shandy, you'll cope,' her sisters used to say as they added more straws to her camel-back. Yes. I can cope. I will cope. A good epitaph for me would be 'She coped well with life, now she can rest in peace.'

Brushing her teeth with more than customary vigour she steeled herself for coping with the day ahead. Setting aside domestic and emotional problems, there was the journey into town which nearly always involved traffic delays, gridlocks and hazardous cutting-in tactics from other frustrated drivers, an appointment with her solicitor about complications which had arisen over the sale of her mobile home in the south of France, dealing with her own and Samson's incomplete cases with only the back-up of a partly trained staff.

In time Julian might prove very good on genealogical enquiries, but at present he was short of tact when it came to dealing with clients. A superior, condescending arrogance was no way to handle a *nouveau riche* anxious to establish a pedigree. Old Maunder, whom Samson had taken on out of sympathy for an ordeal suffered at the hands of a criminal, was useful enough as a process server and for long watchful vigils outside houses where evidence was needed of the comings and goings of the occupants; but when he had no specific work to do, he would hang around the office offering to make unwanted cups of tea and generally interrupting their work with his excessive need to be helpful. Kennedy, who had been Samson's protégé, showed a lot of promise but was liable to get himself into scrapes from which he had to be carefully extracted like an abscess-prone tooth with twisted roots. Martine, now in temporary charge, had the persistence, thick skin, technical know-how and intuitive powers to make a first-class private detective but was still comparatively new. Georgia alone could be totally relied on.

As if it wasn't bad enough to be completely in charge of Samson Associates with the consultant awaiting a surgical operation, she had missed half a day at the office yesterday and today wanted to call at the local police station for a chat with Sergeant Broadbent which would delay her arrival at the office.

She had to oversee a varied workload, which in many respects was quite different from when she had started with Samson. There were now fewer divorce cases requiring evidence of adultery (including connivance at or condonation of adultery), many more enquiries into the private lives of high-flyers by prospective employers or head-hunters, in addition to advice on security, the service of writs, tricky negotiations where verbal promises made had been broken, a flow of missing-person cases from clients who believed the police files on their quest had been put aside to gather dust, or the Salvation Army's efforts to trace someone who didn't wish to be found had been unsuccessful. There were also occasional criminal investigations when a client had been dissatisfied by an absence of result or even of arrest by the police. The scope of all this work was now Shandy's overall responsibility. She was where the buck stopped and she had to cope with any eventuality, authorised or unauthorised.

After applying some light lipstick and a little blusher to lend colour to her pallid cheeks, she was ready to grab an overcoat and leave the house as soon as she had said farewell to

Kimberley. The goodbye involved more coping. The moment she entered the bedroom Kimberley burst into tears and Shandy quickly hugged her daughter and uttered such soothing words as 'There, there', 'It'll be all right, darling,' and 'I promise you can leave school at the end of term.'

As she hurried down the stairs she saw Paul waiting, wearing overcoat and scarf. "Thought I might cadge a life from you," he said. "Brixton is on your way."

It wasn't the right moment to get into an argument about the demon driving him. She gritted her teeth and said, "I'm late already."

"That's not my fault, is it?"

"No, Paul, it isn't our fault that I've been delayed comforting our daughter."

"Are you implying that I'm not willing to comfort her? It isn't easy when both she and you are keeping me at arm's length. But you'll both be grateful to me when I've brought these bastards to justice. Now, can I come with you as far as Brixton? It'll delay you further by approximately ten seconds while you drop me off. You can carry straight on up the A23. It couldn't be simpler."

She wanted to scream: 'You bloody fool, I shall have to back-track to our local nick if I take you to Brixton first,' but managed not to with a mighty effort of will-power. If she told him where she was going and why, he'd want to come with her. He would certainly question the police's dedication to finding the rapists, and that would make Bob Broadbent clam up.

"All right. You can come."

"Thanks a million, gracious lady. I'm so honoured by your permission to accompany you, in your very own car, a short but clearly inconvenient distance."

She ignored his sarcasm and put on her topcoat. The journey to Brixton passed without a word spoken. The traffic flow had congealed and the funereal pace of their car was in keeping with the tomb-like silence between them.

*   *   *

Before going into the police station, she had used her mobile phone to call Georgia to say she would be late again; the traffic had come to a dead stop.

She had hoped and prayed that Sergeant Broadbent would be on duty and to her relief he was standing near the entrance talking to a uniformed constable.

"Well, blow me down, if it isn't young Shandy," he said, a smile lighting craggy features, in which a large Roman nose was the most prominent, like a sudden burst of sunshine on an outcrop of rocks.

After conventional greetings had been exchanged she asked, "Could I have a private word, Bob?"

"Sure." To the constable who had melted into the background he said, "Will you take over for a few minutes, Reg. I'll be in interview room two if I'm needed."

"Tea?" he asked as they sat down at a small, bare table.

"No, thanks, I'm late as it is … I expect you know what's happened to Kimberley?"

"I do, and I'm very sorry for you and her." After the briefest of pauses he added as a polite and necessary afterthought, "And for your husband, Paul, of course."

"I wanted to know if there's been any progress. Samson's having an op and he wants to be kept informed."

"What sort of op?"

"Prostate. A routine job, but you know what men are like when there are threats to their intimate bits and pieces. He's Kim's godfather and is naturally concerned."

"I heard on the grapevine that he's retiring and I gave him a call. I gather you will be taking over?"

"I already have, although the staff haven't seen much of me the last couple of days. Has there been any progress, Bob?"

"Not a lot. Nothing from Forensics yet but I gather there are stains on the topcoat she was wearing which should be good for a DNA result. As for the BMW, it was reported stolen. The laugh is that is was stolen from the biggest crook in Norwood who'd just bought it for his youngest son. I wouldn't be in the thief's shoes if this guy gets to him first. Road rage won't be in it!"

"Who's that, Bob?"

"We call him 'Flash Jack' on account of the clothes and jewellery he wears. Real name, Jacques Duprez, originally from Martinique, so it's said. Don't know how he ended up here."

"What's his line? Drugs?"

Sergeant Broadbent shook his head vigorously. "No. Very high-class prostitution – MPs and top lawyers among their clients – and gambling. He's a sort of icon, if that's the right word, in the black community. Fancies himself as a sort of Robin Hood. Impeccable family life. Four kids, all males. Keeps clear of the drug scene but is absolutely ruthless when his own territory is challenged. We have two unsolved murders on file and the finger points at him, but that's all. It just points."

"Sounds quite a character. Getting back to the car, and talking of fingers, there should be prints on the steering wheel, and other clues, when it's found."

"Maybe, but I wouldn't count on it, Shandy. When they've done a bit of joy-riding they'll torch the car, and that's about all I can tell you up to date. Was there anything else?"

She hesitated before saying, "There is one other thing. I'd sooner you kept it to yourself unless you feel duty-bound to tell an inspector. I'm worried about Paul. He's taken it very badly. Talks of killing them, and you know what he can be like."

The fissures on Broadbent's forehead deepened as he frowned. "He'd better not try anything silly. His offence is still on file."

"I was afraid it might be."

"And having previous won't help if he does anything daft." He reached out and touched her arm with his hand in a compassionate gesture. "It's a tough time for you."

"You're right, but I can cope."

They both stood up. "I'm sure you can," he said. "Good luck and remember me to Mr Samson. It's been all change here since his day in the manor. I shall be leaving at the end of the year."

"I hope you have a long and happy retirement, Bob."

He gave a sad smile. "Don't know I want a long one. Since Ethel died things haven't been the same. Maybe I'll get a job as a nightwatchman."

He went with her to the front entrance. As they said goodbye she gave him a quick kiss on the cheek and once more his rough-hewn features were smilingly illuminated.

For the first time that day Shandy had a slice of luck. When she rejoined the A23 the traffic log-jam had disappeared and the run to Westminster Bridge was comparatively aggravation-free. Samson had recently given her the use of his slot in an underground car-park close to his apartment and she arrived at the office only half an hour overdue. By working though the lunchtime break, fortified only by cups of coffee and sandwiches purchased by Maunder, she was able to see an end in sight by five thirty in the afternoon.

She called Kimberley, and was pleasantly surprised at the change in her demeanour since the morning.

"I'm fine, thanks," she said. "Sandra's just left, and I'm going to make a meal for me and Dad. We're going to have tomato and basil soup, lamb cutlets, *petit pois*, tommies and chips, and finish with cheese and biscuits. Does it make you feel hungry? Shall we wait for you? When do you think you'll get here?"

Shandy thought better of her plan to go home. "No, don't wait for me. I've still got a bit to do here, and then I rather wanted to visit John and see how he's settling in at hospital. But if you need me at home I'll come straight away; your dinner sounds very tempting."

"There's no reason for you to come on my account, Mum. I'm all right. Honest. I'm sure Uncle John's need is greater than mine."

"If you're sure it'll be all right…"

"Positive."

Puzzled, and yet grateful for the inexplicable mood change, Shandy asked when Paul had come home.

"He got in about twenty minutes ago soaked to the skin and complaining about the lousy English weather. He's having a hot bath right now. Don't worry about him, Mum."

Her husband's sustenance was the least of Shandy's worries about him. He could starve or eat until his stomach burst; but she didn't say so. Instead she asked, "Do you know what he's been doing today?"

"No, and I don't want to. I'm trying hard to put all that behind me. That's what Sandra says I should do."

Shandy, who had long ago learned that advice from a peer-group friend was far more acceptable than parental counselling, said, "Good for Sandra. Well, Kim dear, I'll carry on here for a while."

"Bye then, oh, and give my love to Uncle John. Tell him I'm thinking of him."

It was after six thirty when Shandy wearily pushed aside papers on her desk and was ready to leave.

On her way out of the office she spotted Georgia seated by the switchboard leafing through a women's magazine.

"Still here, Georgia?"

"I'm not in any hurry. I thought I'd stay on in case you needed me for something."

"That's very kind of you. But what made you think I might need something?"

Looking boldly at her boss, Georgia replied, "I'm no good at mincing words, and it's obvious to me that you've not been at all yourself the last couple of days. Is something wrong at home?"

"As a matter of fact, there is. But I can cope."

"Of course you can. Everyone here knows what a great coper you are, but even the best coper in the world has to let it all hang out sometime." The boldness of her approach vanished and shyly, in a softer voice, Georgia continued, "That's why I stayed on in case you needed something: trouble is, most people take copers for granted. I don't, and I want you to know I'm here to share..."

She never finished the sentence. Tears had welled up in Shandy's eyes. She was unable to prevent sobs being wrenched from deep in her body or the teardrops running down her cheeks.

Georgia leapt to her feet, went to her and hugged her before leading her to a chair close to her own. Waiting until the sobs had subsided and cheeks had been dabbed with a tissue, she said, "Tell me about it. Is it something to do with Kim?"

"How did you guess?" Shandy asked in a slightly choking voice.

"It was just that. A guess." Georgia gave a tiny laugh. "Or maybe it's the famous women's intuition we hear about."

"Something terrible happened to her early on Tuesday morning."

"She was raped?" It was more a statement than an enquiry.

Shandy's eyes became wide with curiosity. "How the hell did you know that?"

"I didn't know. But I'm not stupid. I remembered something when you mentioned Tuesday. It flashed into my mind."

"Go on."

"I was having a bit of cross-talk with Kenco at the retirement party that day. He was something silly about being taken by force, and you jumped on him. Then you apologised. Said you'd had a bad morning and told us to start clearing up. I'd never seen you lose your cool like that before."

"I'm sorry I spoiled the fun."

"I was glad you did. It's a sensitive subject for me, too, but that was before Kenco's time. He didn't know any better."

Trusting implicitly in Georgia's discretion, Shandy spent the next half-hour unburdening herself of all her fears and worries. For once she wasn't coping; she had handed over to Georgia, who was proving her own potential as a coper.

The two women left the office together; Georgia to go to a flat in Highbury, Shandy to visit Samson in a private hospital situated on the border of north-east London.

Ten

An Indian male nurse called Nazir took Samson to his room on the first floor. It was functional with a sphygmomanometer and other medical aids near the bedhead, and comfortable with thick pile carpet, armchairs and television set, mounted high on a wall opposite the bed. There was also a bathroom *en suite*. The room overlooked a rose garden beyond which were more hospital buildings.

After switching on the television by remote control he flicked through the channels, settling for Sky Sports 2. A boxing match was in progress and, as a one-time junior heavyweight amateur boxing champion of the south-east, the sport interested him.

He had not been watching long when there was a knock on the door.

"Come in," he shouted. The door opened. "Shandy!" he exclaimed joyfully, "it's a treat to see you. Come and sit down. Bring a chair up."

She dragged a chair over to the bed. "Poor you," she said. "I bet you hate it."

"With a deadly loathing. But how are you?"

"I'm fine. How about you?"

"I'm already in need of a long convalescence. It's like Piccadilly in the rush hour here."

Taking a small gift-wrapped parcel from a holdall she said, "I got this for you. I was going to give it separately from the chess set after the party but when you told me you were having to go to hospital I thought I'd hang on to it until then." She handed him the parcel.

"A pressie. For me? Can I open it?"

"Of course."

He ripped off the paper covering from a book bound in red morocco leather with its title gold-blocked on the spine. "*The Royal Game*, Stefan Zweig," he read aloud. "How clever of you. It's a book I've wanted for years."

"I've leafed through it. The plot sounds miserable, but I expect you know it."

He nodded his head. "It's about a man who was obsessed with being a chess perfectionist which, among other things, resulted in a nervous breakdown. It was Zweig's last book before his suicide."

She appeared shocked. "I had no idea of that. Don't read the damn thing."

He laughed. "I probably won't while I'm in here. It's impossible to concentrate on anything for more than five minutes at a time. Anyway, how is Kim?"

A frown came to Shandy's forehead bringing with it tiny lines which in later life would deepen, and in ripe old age become furrows. "Bearing up, I think. She had mood changes. I'm never sure whether I'll find her cold and self-possessed or crying her heart out. It's a worry, and I have to say Paul isn't a great help."

"Still obsessive?"

"There's been a change. Now he seems not to care, and that worries me. I'm afraid he's up to something, but I can't guess what." She hesitated. "He has a very violent side to his character..." She lowered her eyes. "There's something I should have told you but never got round to it. Five years ago he went berserk in a pub. It was one of those pubs where kids are allowed in a playroom. Kim and a boy who was a bit younger than her squabbled. Kim hit the boy who squealed like a stuck pig. The boy's dad rushed in and cuffed Kim on the ear. Paul saw it and went mad. Not content with beating the man up he went on a rampage after the landlord had tried to restrain him. Worse than that: when the police arrived he had a go at them too. He was taken away in handcuffs. He wasn't allowed bail and when his case came to court he was fined eight hundred pounds for the damage and sentenced to three months. Because he'd been in custody for that amount of time he was set free." She looked up to me Samson's gaze. "Luckily all this happened when he was between jobs. I know I should have told you at the time..." Her voice faded away.

"If it's of any comfort to you," he said, "I knew about it, but didn't feel it was my place to raise the subject. I knew that when you were ready to tell me, you would."

"You did? How did you know?"

"I read about it in a newspaper."

"Does Georgia know? She was with us at the time."

"She never mentioned it, and neither did I... Was this the only time you saw him being violent?"

"Before we were married, there was an incident. Again it was in a pub. A big lout tried to get fresh with me. Paul went for him like a tiger. The lout's mates separated them and told them to settle things outside. They looked gleeful, sure that Paul would be pasted. He wasn't. A few minutes later he was back in the pub. He had a slight graze by his right eye and when I asked if he was all right he said, 'I'm fine, but you should see the other guy.'"

"The fracas didn't put you off him?"

Shandy shook her head emphatically. "The reverse. I thought he'd be a good protector, and," she smiled, "it isn't altogether displeasing to have two men fighting over you."

Samson had remained silent during both accounts. Now he spoke slowly as if measuring each word. "And so you think that if he finds anyone who he believes, rightly or wrongly, committed the crime against Kim, he would kill that person?"

"I do. Don't you?"

"I'm afraid to say it's a strong possibility. If I wasn't trapped here, I'd have a word with him. Try to make him see sense."

Doubtfully she replied, "That might help a bit but I don't think it'd be any use. I think he's gone beyond reason and we're in a dead calm before a deadly storm." She stood up. "I ought to be going. To see what's happening at home. Wish me luck."

"I do. You'll come and see me again?"

"Don't count on it too much. I'd hate to disappoint you. But I shall try to see you every day."

"That'll be a hell of a journey for you at weekends."

"You are worth it, John dear." She bent over to him, taking care to avoid the drip-bag, and kissed him on the cheek. "Is there anything you'd like me to bring next time?"

"There is. A bottle of whisky. A litre bottle."

"Is that all?"

"Is that all! It'll be a life-saver."

"A single malt?"

"That would do nicely."

Lying in bed, and thinking of the episodes of Paul's violence, Samson remembered the tiny striations across Shandy's brow as she related the details of each incident. He had never known her to frown before, but presumably there had been occasions when she had been perplexed, angry or embarrassed, and he simply hadn't noticed. In fact, now he thought about the matter, he had always seen her as a presence rather than as a person. It was a lack of visual awareness when one is so familiar with a person that they become a sort of disembodied entity and it requires a dramatic event to restore them to full being. It was different for those 'in love' who would notice every minute alteration of the beloved's features. Samson knew he wasn't falling in love with Shandy even if he had, for the first time, noticed lines on her forehead; and he hadn't any desire to be in love with her. Their rock-solid relationship was based on mutual respect and caring, and it would stay that way.

Almost every evening since Paul's compulsory redundancy Shandy had experienced vague apprehensions as she neared home, not because she feared any violence (he had never abused her physically) but sometimes his resentment at being unemployed while she earned money made him bad tempered. He would find fault with everything she did, or he would be coldly non-communicative throughout the remainder of the evening.

Tonight she was more apprehensive than usual. Apart from the uncertainty of not knowing what his mood would be, she was anxious about Kimberley, and she would be arriving home much later than normal. As her car turned into the road, she saw that he had switched on the outside lights. This was a good sign. When there were no lights it meant either that he had forgotten, which seldom occurred, or that his resentment had become loaded with self-pity, or she could expect to be welcomed with undisguised hostility.

They were sitting side by side on a settee; Paul had a glass of whisky beside him. Kimberley jumped to her feet.

"Come and sit down, Mum. You must have had a busy day. I'll get you something to eat."

Paul turned his head, smiled and said, "Hello, dear," before continuing to watch a game show on television.

Some tension eased out of Shandy as taut muscles relaxed. "Thanks for the offer, Kim, but I can get my own." She needed to be alone to assess the unexpected sight of father and daughter sitting quietly together as they viewed what Paul, in a carping mood, would refer to as 'electronic wallpaper'.

"I'll give you a hand," Kimberley volunteered, and followed Shandy out of the room.

As she prepared a pasta dish, Shandy asked, "Things all right? Between you and Dad, I mean."

"Like I said on the phone, he came in from the rain and went up and had a bath straight away. He came down and switched on the outside lights while I started cooking. I called out when it was ready and we sat down in here. It was like the old times, before he lost his job. He chatted away about past holidays and asked where I'd like to go next year."

"No mention of you-know-what?" Shandy asked.

"Not a word. It was right off the agenda, thank God. Do you think he's OK again?"

"I hope so. I do hope so."

"But you aren't sure?"

"Not one hundred per cent. Did you ask what he'd been doing today?"

Kimberley shook her head. "I thought about it but chickened out." Sounding slightly apologetic she added, "I was afraid I'd hear something I don't want to hear. Like I said, I want to put all that behind me."

"I understand and don't blame you," Shandy replied sympathetically. "In your place I would have done the same." She paused for thought before continuing. "There are times when it's best to let sleeping dogs lie. Anyway, changes in his behaviour aren't your problem; they are his and, because I'm married to him, partly mine."

When Shandy's meal had been finished, Kimberley went upstairs to her room. Later, after watching a newscast, Shandy excused herself as needing an early night. Paul said, "If the late-night film is any good I'll watch it."

Not once had he mentioned either Kimberley's rape or where he had been during the day.

Paul was tired. If circumstances had been normal, he would have gone to bed at the same time as Shandy; but circumstances were not normal. There was the abnormality of being in a warm double bed with a very attractive wife who would claim the time of the month, her own tiredness, or any other lame excuse possible to avoid what in better times were known as 'conjugal duties', who would employ any and every ploy known to womanhood to prevent intercourse; and there was the abnormality of his daughter having recently been raped.

He had no wish to watch a late-night movie, he wanted to be alone to think, undistracted by wife or daughter. Nevertheless, he sat down in his favourite armchair opposite the television set, placed a recharged glass of whisky on a small piecrust beside him, switched on the television by remote control, and turned the sound down, to gaze almost sightlessly at electronic wallpaper. Although he had given up smoking some months before – his breath smelling of tobacco had been another put-off in Shandy's quiver of anti-sex arrows – he had never completely lost a craving for nicotine and today had bought a packet of twenty cigarettes. There was no doubt in his mind that smoking eased stress and he felt under considerable stress as an unemployed man with a frigid wife and a raped daughter. He took out the cigarette packet, from which five were already missing although none had yet been smoked in the house, and rose from the armchair to hunt for an ashtray. When he had given up smoking, all ashtrays had been removed from sight, but where had Shandy hidden them? Good thinking time was wasted while he searched fruitlessly. In the end, he got a saucer to grind out stubs and flick in ash.

Once more he settled down to gaze at silent images pursuing each other on a smoke-silver screen. It had been a satisfactory day. In Brixton he had gone to the market in Atlantic Road. Vendors stood by stalls mainly selling fruit and vegetables. Some whites mingled among the ethnic mix of purchasers. Mugging and pick-pocketing were reputedly rife in this area and Paul had made sure his wallet was securely zipped up in an inside pocket of his jacket. No mugger would get the better of Paul Bullivant.

He remained on sharp-eyed alert throughout a stroll up and down the market which lay in a section of the street close to an Underground station, and like a spy reconnoitring dangerous enemy territory, when passing a black man, he would glance quickly towards his left hand. Few wore anything on their hands and those men who did were old, and wore woollen mittens which covered the palms of their hands leaving fingers free.

When he had surveyed the whole of the market area he strode purposefully towards a selected target, a fruit stall at which guavas, pawpaws, melons and other fruits were on sale. An Afro-Caribbean vendor had two children beside him, and it was the children who had attracted Paul's attention. They would make a useful conversational talking-point. The boy was playing with a Yo-Yo, watched by his younger brother or playmate, who patiently waited for his turn with the Yo-Yo.

After a careful examination of the fruit on display, Paul bought some oranges and a bunch of bananas. While waiting for change from a ten-pound note, he struck up a conversation with the seller. "Nice kids," he remarked. "Are they yours?"

"Sure are."

"I've got a boy, probably about the same age as your elder one. How old is he?"

"Harry, tell the gentleman how old you is."

Without pausing from displaying his skills with the Yo-Yo the boy looked up at Paul and said, "I'm eleven,"

"Same age as my boy. On half-term are you?"

"Sure am."

The boy then demonstrated his prowess by executing the manoeuvre known as 'walking the dog'.

"Very good," Paul praised, "that deserves something." He took a pound coin from the change handed to him and to the father said, "Is it all right with you if I give him this?"

"OK by me. Kind of you."

"What about me?" the smaller boy asked, and received an admonishment from his father.

"Jamie, you got no business troubling the gentleman."

"He isn't troubling me." Paul selected two smaller denomination coins and handed them over.

"He shouldn't have asked," said the father.

"If you don't ask you often don't get," Paul replied. "My boy's always asking for something. The latest is a replica revolver, something that really looks the business, not a plastic toy. I've looked everywhere, but you just can't get one in any of the shops. You don't know where I can buy one, do you?"

The fruit-seller gave him a long, calculating appraisal before replying, "You want a fake shooter that looks like the real thing?"

"That's right."

"I may know someone who could help. No promises."

"Of course not."

"It'll cost."

"About how much?"

"Can't tell you exactly. Say, about fifty."

Paul whistled between his teeth. "That's a lot for a fake."

"Maybe. But it don't take much to turn a real good fake into a weapon. You get my meaning?"

Paul appeared to consider the matter. "My boy certainly wants one. I don't know…"

The vendor lowered his voice and after a sly glance to right and left said, "Maybe Daddy could play with it too. Make it a party toy. Scare friends. Good for laughs."

At this point Paul realised the man hadn't been deceived by talk of his non-existent son. He was stepping into dangerous territory. He hesitated momentarily before deciding to go ahead. In for a penny; in for a pound; go for broke.

"That's an idea," he said. "I could have some harmless fun with it. I'd want to have a look at the goods first."

"Naturally."

"When could that be?"

"I'll be here tomorrow, Friday, and then not again till next Tuesday."

"I'll be here same time tomorrow," said Paul.

"Like I said. No promises. No guarantees."

"Understood."

Another customer had arrived and was testing a melon for ripeness.

"See you then, man." The vendor went to the new customer.

From the fruit stall Paul had gone to a telephone booth in the post office further down Atlantic Road to make a call to the CID handling Kimberley's case. After some delay, he was told that enquiries were still being made, witnesses were being sought from some who had attended Sharon's party to ascertain whether anyone had noticed the H-registration BMW. To date a blank had been drawn. There might be forensic evidence available should a suspect be arrested.

"And that's about all we can say at present, Mr Bullivant. I note your daughter has described the car as dark or darkish. I wonder if she can be a little more specific. Dark blue, dark green, dark grey, black?"

"I don't think so. I've already asked her that. But I can try again."

"Just a detail, sir, but much of our work consists of putting small details together in the hope of a clearer picture emerging. But rest assured, we are doing our best."

"I'm sure you are. I've always supported our police force. Finest in the world. I hope all the talk about 'institutionalised racism' doesn't make your job even more difficult."

"Thank you for your call, Mr Bullivant." The line went dead.

As he left the telephone booth he saw a police car which had parked nearby. It drove away at some speed but not before Paul had thought he recognised the driver as an officer he had seen before somewhere and it passed his mind that during the conversation with the CID his call might have been traced and a patrol car sent to verify him as a bona fide caller. Or am I seeing shadows where there are none? he wondered. In any event, the police did seem to be working on the case.

Advertisements, during a break in the movie, were now soundlessly chasing each other across the screen. Paul stubbed out a cigarette and poured himself a final pre-bedtime drink.

A last cigarette was lighted as he settled down once more in the armchair. Yes, it had been a satisfactory day. From Brixton he had gone to the wood and this had been followed by a meeting with estate agent Jim Cutler. A faint smile momentarily lightened Paul's face as he remembered saying, 'I'm a Jim too'. He had already worked out his next move with Cutler which, to be effective, would depend on catching the man who had lost most of the index finger of his left hand. He knew it was a needle in a haystack situation, a long shot of astronomical distance, but he clung to the belief that the perpetrator of a crime will, sooner or later, return to the scene of the crime. Shandy could call him obsessive. Let her. But he knew he had plenty of common sense. She might regard his behaviour as over the top; but he knew it was the rational reaction of a loving father determined to bring his daughter's violators to justice. That is, the justice of the British law courts after he, Paul, had taught whomever he caught a salutary lesson.

Another smile flitted across his face as he recalled how, at breakfast, in reply to Shandy's, 'What do you expect to find in the wood?' he had replied, poker-faced, 'A teddy bear's picnic maybe.' She had been so taken aback by the dismissive reply that she had nearly spilled the coffee from the cup in her hand. You keep me at a distance in bed, he had thought, now it's your turn to know what it's like to be kept at a distance.

His marriage might be unsatisfactory, but thank God Kimberley's brief annoyance with him appeared to be over. During the evening spent together before Shandy's return she had been more like the old Kimmy whom he loved so dearly. She kissed him lightly on the cheek before retiring upstairs to her room and had said, "Thanks, Dad, for not mentioning it."

At one point he had almost asked about the car's colour, but now was glad he hadn't. He determined to earn further favour by avoiding the subject which, in turn, would add to Shandy's confusion. As these and other thoughts crossed his mind he closed his eyes. Soon he was asleep. He woke with a start at ten past three, switched off the television, all the lights inside and outside the house, and yawned his way to a bed where his wife was sound asleep.

He undressed quietly and climbed into bed. Without any change in the rhythm of her breathing she shifted her position to face him and her arm stretched out and flopped on his chest. In the early years of marriage, it had been how she liked to fall asleep. In those days he would wait until he was certain she was deep in slumber before releasing himself from the pinioning arm. The memories of happier days unsettled him. He waited a long time before gently removing the arm which prevented him from sleep.

The memory of love which had all but withered away brought sadness which spoiled slightly what had otherwise been a very satisfactory day.

Throughout the roller-coaster ride of their marriage certain constants had remained straight and level, and one of these was that Paul always made the early-morning cups of tea and brought them to Shandy who would still be in bed. This procedure never varied, however much they may have bickered and argued during the previous evening. It was no different today, Friday, although Paul hadn't retired to bed until after three in the morning.

As he stood in the kitchen waiting for the kettle to boil he recalled with amusement how Shandy must have been confused by his apparent change from vengeful father to one who couldn't care less about what had happened to his daughter. It was a fitting punishment for treating him as an obsessive. Paul was the type of man who believed in retribution for those who upset the norms of social or domestic behaviour, particularly if an incident affected him. Punishment could be mild or heavy: in Shandy's case it was very mild; if he caught the rapists, or one of them, it would be extremely heavy. An unwanted thought then entered his mind. What if Shandy attributed his changed attitude to something which had nothing to do with Kimberley? What if she, recalling an affair he had once had, thought he had found another woman?

Before redundancy from the construction company he had been an employee of some importance. He had his own room at company headquarters as deputy head of the estimates and tenders division, and had been responsible for hiring and firing staff in that division. He had realised the company was in difficulty when he had been instructed to dismiss many employees. But it had been a shock when, after the last man had left his room on the verge of tears, Paul was summoned by a director and himself told to pack up and leave that same day. He had travelled home by taxi, having been brusquely told to leave the keys of his company car at the reception desk.

The kettle boiled and he poured hot water on two tea-bags. He continued thinking of the days when he had been someone of significance, a time when he had been the main provider at home and he had regarded Shandy's job with Samson Associates as a hobby. His affair had been with Peggy, a chirpy, cheeky blonde in the office services division who had burst into his room when a Christmas party was in full swing, eyes aglow beneath sparkles of silver dust in her hair and said, "Come on, Mr Bullivant, join in the fun. All work and no play makes Jack – or should I say Paul? – a dull boy."

He had let her drag him down to a noisy, smoke-filled basement where alcohol was freely available. "I know how much you contributed to this bash," Peggy said leading him by the hand to a makeshift bar. "You are entitled, if anyone is. I mean," she added with a quick admiring look, "entitled to drink the place dry. I don't mean entitled to anything else, or do I?" Too much drink had loosened inhibitions and later that evening they both went back to his room where they became torridly unfaithful to their respective spouses. The affair had continued until early summer when a jealous rival for Peggy's affections had sent a poison-pen letter to Shandy. She had challenged him at a time when her own sexual coolness was rankling with him and they had blazed into a mega-size quarrel. Eventually he had apologised and she had forgiven him. As for Peggy, she left the company shortly after the showdown between Paul and Shandy.

He fished out the tea-bags and added milk to each cup. Perhaps it was as well he had remembered Peggy; he would change his tack once more and forego the amusement of confusing her. He would try to be as he had been before the rape; in short, give the impression of being neither obsessive nor too laid back.

The opportunity to put into practice this alteration of attitude came when, having finished her cup of tea, she said, "We really must get a Teasmade. It would save you having to traipse up and down the stairs for second cups."

"I don't mind. I've nothing much else to do."

He had intended to ask her for another lift to Brixton but he didn't want her to become suspicious that he had found another woman. It was a nuisance, but he would have to go by public transport to see the fruit-seller.

"Any plans for today?" she asked with studied casualness.

"I thought I might look at my CV again," he said. "Tart it up a bit, and check through the appointments in yesterday's *Telegraph*."

At least he still gets up early enough for me to have a few minutes longer in bed, she thought. He's playing games, I'm sure that's behind the chopping and changing. He's trying to throw me off the scent of his obsession … or that's what I thought, but maybe there's something else as well. I don't believe the stuff about revising his CV; that's eyewash. Getting another job has taken second place to finding out who raped Kim. Prime suspect is a black man with a missing finger, and God help him if Paul ever meets him.

From the bathroom above, the hiss of a spraying shower came the sound of Paul whistling. Whistling while he showered was associated in her mind with the days early in marriage when there had been what she called 'love-making' and he called 'sex' during the night. It was an expression of satisfaction and at one time had amused, even gratified, her, but he'd had little to whistle about in recent months. So, why was he whistling now? It was inconceivable that he'd suddenly found another woman, or was it? Surely not at a time like this when their family life had been so violently disrupted. Could it be that the Peggy woman had come back into his life? Had he, ever since the affair, kept her on 'hold' in some way and now, half-crazy over Kim's rape, had turned to her for comfort?

It was a hypothesis unworthy of consideration; yet there must have been some explanation for his mood-swings. Assuming that he was still hell-bent on dealing out justice to the rapists – which, knowing him, would be severe – and that the game he was playing was designed to throw her off the scent, he would be in serious trouble if his mission was successful. Their marriage was going through a rocky patch but she was still his wife, conscience-bound so far as possible to stand by her wedding vows. What was needed was for a surveillance to be kept on him, and who better to observe his movements at a discreet distance than a private detective?

From this though came the realisation that no one was better placed than she to mount such an operation, a ploy that would kill two birds with a single well-aimed stone. If he were shadowed by someone with a mobile phone, the alarm could be raised if he caught a rapist, and intervention made before he inflicted grave injuries on the man, and it would also be clear whether he was having secret trysts with a woman.

The whistling from the bathroom stopped but Shandy's thoughts raced ahead. She disliked the idea of asking someone from another firm to undertake the job of watching her husband's movements, but who in her office could be entrusted with such a delicate task? At the firm's pre-Christmas dinners when partners of staff were always invited, Paul had met Georgia, Martine and Kennedy, and so these were eliminated. Julian and Maunder remained. Julian was a non-starter on account of inexperience. Old Tom Maunder was the perfect answer to the problem. He was accomplished at merging unnoticed into any background, accustomed to keeping watch for hours on end, and unquestionably loyal to Samson whom he regarded with dog-like devotion. But if Tom Maunder was to be used for tailing Paul, she ought to obtain Samson's agreement to the plan. He was the firm's consultant, he should be consulted on such a sensitive matter; moreover, if he agreed (and she had little doubt that he would) she would put the idea to Maunder and say that Mr Samson thought he was just the man for the job, a statement which if not strictly accurate would give Maunder a fillip.

Kimberley joined them for breakfast. She was nervous and worried because nothing had yet been done about her leaving school. The second half of the term had begun on Monday and it was now Friday. The headmaster might not be available over the weekend. With a reproachful glance at Shandy she said, "You promised, Mum."

"I did. I'll give him a call today. I meant to do it yesterday but I got so busy that—"

Paul interrupted. "I can do it, if you like. It might come better from her father. Man to man, and all that. And I won't take any nonsense from him."

After another quick look at her mother who gave the slightest of nods, Kimberley said, "Thanks, Dad. It's just that I want to know where I stand."

"Of course you do, Kimmy dear."

Shortly afterwards, Shandy left for the office, glad that a sort of harmony had been restored to the family.

Eleven

Sylvester had gone to bed the previous evening with a headache and a high temperature. His muscles and joints ached and he couldn't get warm even though his mother turned the central heating up to maximum, and a painful cough kept him awake most of the night. When he staggered down for breakfast his little sister, an honest child, said, "You look awful, Sylly."

"I feel awful."

"It's back to bed for you, my boy." His mother spoke in a voice which he instantly recognised as brooking no argument. Nevertheless, he tried.

"But Mom, today is pay-day."

"Pay can wait. You'll have all the more when you get it."

"I might lose my job."

"Don't try to fool me, boy. Nobody gets sacked these days for being sick once in a while. That's right, Daddy?"

Josiah Manley was a small, quiet, patient man, who seldom spoke unless addressed and was happiest when busy dispensing prescriptions at the pharmacy which employed him. A methodical worker who had never made a mistake, on more than one occasion he had queried a doctor's prescription and thereby saved a customer from receiving a faulty anodyne. He had mastered the art of non-commitment, partial or total, and so when his wife repeated he question he replied, "You may well be right, Mother."

"I am right. Back to bed, Sylvester. I'll call the store and tell them you won't be in until Monday at the earliest."

"What will you say is the matter with me, Mom?"

"I shall say you've got the flu. That's what it is, eh, Daddy?"

"I'm not qualified to give a medical opinion, Mother."

"Of course you are. You deal with medicines all day long. It's the flu and I know it. Now you get some antibiotics from the shop today and bring them home."

"I can't do that."

"No such word in the English language as 'can't'. Why not?"

With a long-suffering expression ruffling his kindly features Josiah Manley patiently explained, "I can't dispense anything without a proper prescription, and if it is a strain of influenza then it is a viral infection and antibiotics are of no benefit unless there is a secondary infection in which case..."

"Spare me the book-learning, man," his wife interrupted irritably. "What's best for the flu?"

"Aspirin is a basic remedy. There are a number of brand-name products for treating influenza, which can be purchased without prescription over the counter. And, as you say, bed rest."

"There you are, Sylvester. Take notice of what your daddy says. Bed rest. Now, off you go; I'll bring you a hot-water bottle. Go on, boy, get going when you're told."

And so Sylvester returned to his room but before getting into bed he removed the panties, which he now cursed himself for having taken in the first place, from under the mattress. He would have to find another hiding place as his mother, in her zeal to care for him, might insist on stripping the bed to put on fresh sheets. He opened a wardrobe door. A pair of old trainers lay at the base of the wardrobe out of sight. Taking one out he stuffed the panties inside it, replaced the trainer, and closed the wardrobe door.

Possession of the panties was now a waking nightmare. A terrible jinx. Almighty God, maker of all things, judge of all men, was showing his divine anger at Sylvester's theft of a white girl's undergarment.

He kneeled by the side of his bed and prayed to the Lord Jesus to intercede on his behalf to forgive his sin and lift the intolerable burden of wickedness from his conscience.

He had barely finished his prayer and scrambled into bed when the door opened and his mother walked in carrying a hot-water bottle. "Coral is right," she said. "You don't look so good, but your momma will get you right."

But he knew he wouldn't feel right until he had rid himself of a piece of flimsy white cotton.

It hadn't taken Samson long to discover that in a private hospital it was impossible to play a game of chess without a series of interruptions breaking his concentration. The day after admission to the hospital there was a knock on his door and Mr Timson, his consultant, entered the room.

"How's my patient today?"

"Fine, thanks."

"Good. Monday is my day for operations here and all being well we'll do you then. Dr Morton the anaesthetist will check you over in the afternoon. She's a lovely lady. You're a lucky chap to have her." Timson moved over to the window. "It's a wonderful day outside. One of those November days when poor weather is in remission and Mother Nature shows off the last of the summer's late finery before baring her body for the winter." He paused, taken aback by his own rhetoric, before adding, "Not up to Shakespeare perhaps, but then I doubt if the Bard would have made much of a urologist." He gave an infectious chuckle, which brought a grin to Samson's face before leaving with the promise, "I'll look in on you over the weekend." After he had gone Samson wondered how a man whose job involved the exploration of some of the less pleasing functions of the human body could generate such *bonhomie*.

Remains of his last meal of the day had been cleared away before Shandy arrived. From a bag she produced a wrapped bottle.

"Ta-ra! Your whisky, sir."

He stripped off the paper and gave an exclamation of approval. "Glenmorangie!"

"How's it going?"

"The op is on Monday."

"It'll be good to get it over."

"It will, even with the setbacks."

"What setbacks?"

He gave a mirthless laugh. "My, er, manhood may be affected."

"Sod that," she said, "who cares, if you don't."

"No one, I guess."

"I certainly don't. Comes a time in most people's lives when sex is an overrated pastime, and can be positively damaging to a relationship. Ask me about Paul!"

"I've sometimes wondered about that. I had an idea…"

"Wonder no more."

"How is he?"

She frowned. "Odd, isn't it? You can live with someone for twenty years and find you don't know them, understand them, any more. He's become secretive, that's the only way I can describe it. I catch him looking at me in a way I don't recognise, and when our eyes meet, he looks away. I'm convinced he's plotting something…" Her frown deepened, increasing the incipient lines on her forehead. "I don't see how he can possibly find the men who did it, but if he does, there will be someone's murder… Do you think I'm being melodramatic?"

"No, I don't. And I agree with you, the chance of him finding the guys is in the region of a million to one. I've been thinking about it. According to Kim, one was black, one was white and from up north, and there were possibly another two. Why should a black, presumably from South London, be with a white, pre-sumably from Yorkshire, or Lancashire? Drugs are the obvious connection. Could be a sort of shuttle service. Manchester gets short of the stuff and comes to London, or vice versa."

Shandy pondered his idea. "You may be right, but it doesn't stop me being afraid for him. We may not be in love any more, but he is my husband and the father of our daughter."

"How is she coping?"

"Up and down. Brave one minute and a frightened child the next. I just hope it doesn't put her off men altogether." She squeezed his hand. "There are decent ones around."

"I wish I could do something. Have a word with him."

"Well, you can't, and he'd only become more defensive, more secretive. But there is something I'd like to sound you on."

"Go ahead."

"As you say, it's a million to one shot he'll find them, but to make doubly sure I'd like to have him watched for a while." She removed her hand. "What do you think? Am I being paranoid?"

"You're sensible, Shandy. Both feet on the ground, and you know the answer to that better than I. But who would watch him? Not someone from an agency?"

"No way. I was wondering about Tom Maunder. What do you think?"

He made no reply.

"Well?" she asked.

"If you want to know. Not much."

"Why not?"

"It would be a full-time job which would mean taking Tom off any other case he might be needed for, and for an indefinite amount of time."

"I should have known you'd take that line," she said, more in self-reproach than as a criticism of his view.

"I know you're very worried about Paul, and probably with good cause, but the problem won't be solved by setting one member of staff to shadow another member's husband. That would create even more problems, particularly if others in the firm found out. They could think it might be their turn to be shadowed next. The only way you could have Tom employed in watching Paul would be to tell all the staff why you are taking such a measure, and we both know that just isn't on."

"You're right," she sighed.

"Eventually he'll see the futility of his animosity, Kimberley will hopefully come to terms with her ordeal, and life will revert to normality."

107

Her head was lowered, her eyes downcast, and her shoulders slumped. She had nothing to say.

To fill the silence, he continued, "I know this has come at a bad time when I'm out of action and you've had to take over running the firm. I know you've got a hell of a lot on your plate, but I've every confidence in you. You'll win, Shandy, you'll win."

She looked up at him and quickly away again but not before he'd seen tears in her eyes. "Thanks for the vote of confidence," she said. "I shan't let you down. You, the firm or myself."

After he put the handset down, Paul wished he had taped the conversation. He had prepared himself to talk tough, for where Kimmy was concerned he would stand no nonsense. The reaction to his call did more than take the wind out of his sails; it was a hurricane, which dismasted his vessel of determination and left him drifting wordless. The headmaster had said, "I've been expecting you to ring me, Mr Bullivant. Of course Kimberley won't be back at school this term and there is no statutory requirement that she should continue schooling; although, I have to say, she shows great promise and would almost certainly win a place at university."

He could recall fragments of what followed which, added together, and put into order, began with a reference to the local newspaper, *The Advertiser*, which "contains no reference to the ordeal suffered by a schoolgirl... Copy for Friday's edition of the weekly must be in by Tuesday evening at the latest..." Thoughts of revenge had occupied Paul's mind to the exclusion of Press coverage, and he had deliberately kept Shandy from discussing any incidental outcome of the rape in pique at having been called obsessive... "It is always difficult to balance legitimate public interest against private considerations," the headmaster had said. "She is a brave girl and I'm sure that in time she'll be right as rain."

There was more. Disjointed half-sentences which floated in and out of his mind during the day, but as soon as he had put the handset down he went upstairs to where Kimberley had returned after breakfast. Her bedroom was her sanctuary, the only place where she could come to terms with her trauma.

"Come in," she called in response to his tap on the door. She was lying on her back on the bed, still wearing a dressing gown over a short white nightshirt which had on its front the imprint of Mickey Mouse and the words, 'Mice 'n' Easy'.

She shifted to allow him space to sit down beside her. "I've just been on the phone to Mr Symons," he said.

She immediately sat upright and came close to him, as if needing protection from something the headmaster might have said.

"What did he say, Dad? You did ask him if I had to go back to school?"

He laughed. "Ask? I told him you weren't."

"You did? And what did he say?"

"Well, he didn't like it much, said you had a lot of promise and he was hoping you'd be going to a university, but in the end he caved in."

"And I don't have to go back?"

"No. You don't have to go back. Ever."

"Oh, Dad! You are brilliant!"

She threw her arms round his neck and planted a kiss firmly on the side of his face. Then she flopped back to resume her prone position. "I want to put it all behind me. Get on with my life," she said.

"I'm positive that's the right attitude, sweetheart. Mine is slightly different. I'd like to see the thugs punished, but if the punishment was to be legal – a term of imprisonment – there would have to be a case heard in open court and neither you nor I, and possibly your mother either, would want that, would we?"

"No fear!"

"But you wouldn't mind if they could be punished for what they did without going to court or any publicity, would you?"

As he spoke he looked directly into her eyes and he saw her answer there a split second before she said viciously, "I'd love it, love it, if the men that did it to me were castrated. That'd teach them a lesson!"

The savagery of her words set the seal of approval on his intentions.

Twelve

Friday was a day for action and he had planned it in four parts. The first part had been the call to the headmaster of Kimberley's school, which had been successfully accomplished. Her total endorsement of his desire to inflict punishment was a bonus. The next part was the easiest. It was simply a visit to the bank to draw out money from his current account.

He had received a lump sum as compensation for being made redundant and although it was more of a silver-alloy handshake than a golden one, it was sufficient with his savings to allow him to contribute a fair amount to the expenses of running a home, the remainder being found by Shandy from her salary as a partner in Samson Associates.

A branch of his bank was within fifteen minutes' walking distance of where he lived. He set off under a sky that was a moth-eaten grey blanket through which irregular patches of backing blue cloth could be seen. At the bank he drew out one thousand pounds in cash, mostly in fifty-pound notes. He hoped this sum would cover the day's expenses.

When he was made redundant he had been obliged to surrender a company car, and as Shandy had used their car to drive to the office, his only means of transport to Brixton were bus or taxi. He chose the former and during the journey he thought of the day ahead. By evening everything should be in place for a showdown with the man he most wanted to find, the driver of an old BMW. Three men, possibly four, had been in the car but only two had participated in the rape. One, a white, was probably back home in the North; but even if he wasn't, Paul felt far less animosity towards him than to the black. His twisted reasoning was primitive and tribal; sexual intercourse forced on a white woman was deplorable and unacceptable, but somehow more tolerable than a black male raping a white woman, an act which not only defiled the woman but was an insult to the entire white race. His searing rage at what a black man had done to his beloved daughter had by now driven the memory of his own illicit desires for her deep into the recesses of his subconscious mind. To him, Kimberley's white robe of virginity had become a bloodstained rag. He vowed that, if it took a lifetime, he would find the black responsible for her degradation. He was prepared to wait, whatever the weather, for the criminal to return to the scene of his crime and, if he didn't come back after, say, a fortnight, then he would widen the area of search.

He felt a surge of elation at the prospect ahead; he had lost his job but he had found a purpose.

He felt like someone who had infiltrated enemy territory as he threaded his way between market stalls. The feeling was a throwback to childhood days when he had played daring games of Cowboys and Indians with other boys, days when a recreation ground had become a wide prairie and a backyard a tented encampment; only now the prairie was a street littered by bits of refuse and the tents were shops, many having familiar household names.

The fruit-seller greeted him with, "What'd you like today, sir? I got fruits from all over the world! Grapes from Algeria, loose dates from Egypt, strawberries flown in from California, tomatoes from the Canary Islands, oranges from South Africa, mangos, pawpaws and melons from the West Indies, fresh vegetables grown here in England... What can I get for you?"

Paul realised that purchase of unwanted fruit was the price to be paid for the information he needed. He spent almost eighteen pounds on perishable produce which he could not take home unless he could think of an explanation which would satisfy Shandy's curiosity. At last the seller nodded towards a stall-holder with dreadlocked hair on the opposite side of the street.

"You might get something from him, sir, but if you do or if you don't, it's no business of mine. I don't want to know."

"Right." With this single word and without thanks Paul, now laden with two large plastic bags containing fruit and vegetables, crossed the street. He was extremely careful not to bump into anyone, even though many shoppers were white, as the bags would prevent free use of his hands in any argument. He avoided any eye contact with other pedestrians, like a spy on his way to a secret rendezvous.

The dreadlocked man, whose stall seemed to contain a miscellany of second-hand engineering artefacts, gave Paul and his bags a contemptuous look.

"You want somethin'?" he asked in a rasping voice. Taken aback by the hostility in the question, Paul hesitated. The stall-holder asserted himself further: "You hung-up, man?"

Paul didn't require a translator to understand he was being taunted, but in enemy terrain, with fists clenching bags, he was in no position to make an issue of the man's rudeness.

"C'mon, stretch out and straighten up. You want somethin'?"

Smothering a strong impulse either for fight or flight, Paul said icily, "Your friend over there said you might be able to sell me a replica handgun."

The stall-holder looked across at the fruit-seller and replied, "Ain't no friend o'mine."

Paul had endured enough. "OK, have it your way. I've lost nothing; you've got a lost deal." He looked at the wares on display – used car dynamos and magnetos, monkey wrenches, wire, cables, old TV sets, trays containing cog-wheels, nuts and bolts, and many other items – and said, "It would probably be crap anyway, like the rest here." He turned away to make his exit. He was angry enough to drop his shopping and stand his ground, but he was conscious that his back was now exposed to the enemy.

He heard the stall holder laugh and say in a wheedling tone, "C'mon, man, don't be like that. I'm only kidding. I got what you need. Come back here."

It went against the grain to respond to what amounted to a command, but for the sake of his plan Paul needed a replica gun. He turned.

"Let's see it then."

"See it? Here? You may be crazy, I'm not. You want a looksee, you follow me around the corner."

He whistled and made a gesture to indicate a short absence to the adjoining stall-holder, and walked away. Paul, filled with doubts about the wisdom of going anywhere with such a companion, followed. His apprehensions were unfounded. The other man went only as far as the nearest boarded-up shop and waited for Paul to join him in its doorway.

Then, turning his back on the busy street scene he invited Paul to stand closer to him with, "C'mon, man. I ain't goin' to try an' fuck you."

Overcoming his revulsion, Paul once more did as he was told, trying not to inhale a smell of body odour mingled with a stale sickly perfume. A package wrapped in oilskin was produced from an inside coat pocket, the oilskin carefully unfolded to reveal a neat black automatic handgun. "You know what sort this is?"

"No."

"I tell you. It's a perfect workin' Smith and Wesson nine-millimetre with double-action hammer. Safe to carry even with the safety off. This here, where your thumb-print would be, is the magazine-release catch—"

Paul interrupted. "Is this a replica?"

"Is it hell! It's the real thing, man. An' don't give me no shit about wanting it for you kid. You want it for you. OK?"

"How much?" Paul asked tersely.

"Two hundred."

"The guy I spoke to yesterday said fifty."

"He did? Buy one from him then." Paul made no comment. "You don't want? That's OK by me, but I ain't standin' here any longer. Take it or leave it. I'll throw in six rounds if you want. No extra charge. Have we got a deal?"

Paul nodded his head and while he reached for his wallet to count out the money, the vendor, after loading the gun, wiped it clear of his fingerprints with a spotted white and red kerchief. He replaced the gun in the oilskin and an exchange of money and gun took place.

After ramming the package into one of the plastic bags, Paul hurried away, another phase of the day's plan completed, only one left to discharge; but it could be difficult, and if he failed the whole carefully constructed edifice could be blown apart like a house hit full-on by a cruise missile.

He called the estate agent's office where Cutler was employed. Paul was put through to him straight away. He came to the point at once.

"Jim Jones here, Jim. It's essential that I see you a.s.a.p. Any chance if I come round right away?"

After receiving an affirmative he took a taxi and within twenty minutes was shaking Cutler by the hand.

"Has the shop been sold yet, Jim?"

"Not yet, Mr Jones."

"Good, because I am very interested indeed."

As he spoke Paul looked around the room, searching for a point of mutual contact. Early in his career, when he had been selling insurance policies, he had learned the importance of finding common ground with his prospective client. This might be a picture hanging on the wall of a room in the other person's house. Paul would profess admiration for the quality of the art. There were no pictures in Cutler's office but there was a clean ashtray on the desk which separated the two men. Having expressed interest in the lack of sale of the shop Paul broke off to say, "Do you smoke, Jim?"

"Not with clients, unless they do."

"Fair enough." Paul produced a packet of cigarettes. "You won't mind if I smoke then?"

"Of course not. Go ahead."

Before Cutler could reach into his pocket Paul had said, "Here. Have one of mine."

Paul lit both their cigarettes, and said, "Did you know that this is the only drug which soothes when one needs soothing and stimulates when stimulation is required?"

"Is that so?"

"And yet smokers are treated like pariahs. It's all right to drink but not to smoke. But whoever heard of a smoker going out and killing someone because of the effects of tobacco? Drink has killed thousands of innocents."

"That's true."

Discussion of the virtues of cigarette-smoking and the irrational prejudices of the anti-smoking lobby continued until Paul was certain a bridgehead had been secured and the time to begin an assault had arrived.

After flicking ash into the ashtray, he began: "I must take you completely into my confidence. I hope my trust won't be misplaced. I think you already know that my wife and I don't get along well, to put it mildly; well, I am partly responsible for that. I have a woman friend, someone who is very dear to me. Like me she is unhappily married. Her husband is a brute who beats her up. She is terrified of him. With the aid of a small mortgage, I could pay the purchase price of the shop you showed me. A mortgage wouldn't even be necessary as she has some money of her own, but it wouldn't be fair to expect her to fund part of the purchase without first seeing the property. Are you with me?"

Cutler's attention to the story had visibly increased the moment Paul had mentioned a lady friend. A gleam came to his eyes and Paul lowered his voice, he leaned forward over his desk so as not to miss a word. "I'm with you," he replied, eager to hear more. Not only was he curious as to where Paul's confession was leading but he sensed a sale of a property which had hitherto been as unsaleable as a dead dog. To pull off the sale, and at the asking price, would be a plumed feather in his cap.

"The problem is that, like me, her home is in Stockton. She is too frightened to come down here to view it in case her husband finds out. Her only chance of seeing it would be when she is certain he would be away for at least one night. Now it

occasionally happens that his business detains him overnight –
he is in the import-export line – and when he can't get home he
rings her up, usually fairly late in the evening. She has her own
car and is willing to drive through the night, which depending on
traffic conditions would take four to five hours, have a look at
the property, and travel back arriving home before her husband.
The only snag is that if she arrived in the middle of the night,
your office would be closed and no key available."

At this point Paul stubbed out his cigarette, sat back and
awaited Cutler's reaction. It was unexpected.

"That isn't the only snag. The electricity is off and so your
friend would have to view by torchlight. Most unsatisfactory."

"I don't know that is a disadvantage, Jim. Let's not mince
words. At present the place is distinctly grotty. Electric light
would emphasise this. It would probably look better in torchlight, particularly if the torch battery was on the blink."

He laughed to show no offence was intended and after a
moment Cutler joined in the laughter. "You're right there," he
said. "So, have you any suggestions, Mr Jones?"

"Do you have a spare set of keys?"

"Yes."

"So if I had one set, you would be able to show someone else
around if necessary?"

Cutler fidgeted and looked embarrassed. "If it was down to
me, I'd be happy to oblige, if you take my meaning. This is a
small branch of a big chain of estate agents. Apart from the
manager and me, we have a full-time assistant in the office and
a part-timer who, when she's here, shares this room with me. I
don't have the authority to release any keys without referring the
matter first to the manager."

"Would he be a problem?"

"He's a bit of an old stick-in-the-mud, if you know what I
mean. Does everything by the book. Very religious. Goes to
church two or three times every Sunday. Not the sort who'd be
sympathetic to what you've just told me. Don't get me wrong,
Mr Jones; I myself have a lot of sympathy."

"Can't something be worked out?"

Cutler looked doubtful. "Maybe he'd be agreeable if you put down a holding deposit, but the trouble with that is if your friend doesn't come down for some time we can't hold on indefinitely; and anyway before he agreed my manager would want to be assured of *bona fides*, if you take my meaning."

"It looks as though we've reached a dead end, unless…"

Cutler perked up. "Unless what?"

"Unless we had another set of keys made for my use on the understanding that I returned these to you immediately on demand. I have six hundred in cash on me towards a holding deposit which I would let you have as hostage to my honesty and whether or not my friend likes the place, two hundred of that would be yours. I would promise to keep regularly in touch with you in case another buyer comes along who is willing to purchase at the full amount as I would be. Within reason, I'm willing to sign anything you want signed to give a sort of validity to what is otherwise an informal agreement between us although, in my opinion, it is better left as a verbal understanding. In emergency you can get in touch with me on my mobile, but only use it in discretion." He paused and took out his wallet and began counting out twelve fifty-pound banknotes. "If you feel this is not enough, I should certainly want something in writing and that, of course, would mean we could hardly mention the two hundred I'd like to give you for your co-operation."

Cutler seemed transfixed by the small pile of notes on his desk.

"Have we got a deal?" Paul asked.

Cutler picked up the money. "I hope I'm doing the right thing."

"No more than I do for myself," Paul replied with false intensity. "I'm not only gambling on you, Jim, not to let me down, but I'm taking a huge gamble with a lovely lady's and my future. Should things work out for us, you would be an honoured guest at our wedding."

Paul stood up and extended his hand. Cutler did likewise and, as they shook hands Cutler said, "I'll let you have the spare keys now and have another lot made from the master set. After all, you won't want to come back down here all the way from Stockton just to collect some keys, and I don't suppose you want me to post them to you in case your wife... Enough said?"

"Good thinking, Jim," Paul replied, and he meant it.

On leaving Cutler, he went to a nearby pub. It had been a pleasant morning and he felt like a celebratory drink and a meal.

After lunch he went to the wood where he intended to patrol the path and be close to where Kimberley had been raped on the Tuesday. It was now Friday and he was becoming familiar with one or two regular users of the way through the wood. The inhabitants of the immediate area were predominantly white and he hadn't as yet seen a single black face except for one or two middle-aged women. It was when he received a curious look from a tall, grey-haired man who habitually took his dog for a walk through the wood that he realised suspicions could be aroused by his presence; after all, there had recently been a report of a flasher in the neighbourhood. He decided to keep away from the path as much as possible and to concentrate his presence near to the clearing where the crime had taken place. A fallen tree provided a seat, and he had a newspaper crossword to pass the time. His cigarette consumption increased and a number of butts lay close to the fallen tree.

It had been a fine morning but by late afternoon the sky, glimpsed through branches on which a few brown leaves retained a tenuous hold, had become a uniform grey overcast. A chill had entered the air and he decided that tomorrow he'd bring a bottle of scotch with him. Not once did it occur to him that by normal standards his behaviour would seem bizarre, and not once did he consider he was wasting his time. As winter took its early grip on the changing season, the hours of daylight grew fewer and today dusk, its gloom accentuated by the shade of trees, appeared to fall even earlier than expected. At five o'clock he decided to go home.

He called out loudly, "I'm back, Kimmy."

There was no response. Usually there was a reply of some sort. An 'OK, Dad' or 'I'm in the kitchen'. Absence of any acknowledgement sent a dart of anxiety into his being and he hurried upstairs. A knock on her door and entry into the bedroom were simultaneous. She was sitting red-eyed on the side of the bed and her friend, Sandra, was beside her with a comforting arm round her shoulders.

"Sorry," he said, backing out and closing the door quietly.

Downstairs, he switched on the television. Just as it didn't occur to him that for anyone to make an act of vengeance virtually the whole purpose of his life was abnormal, nor did he think that Shandy, tired after carrying a burden of extra work due to Samson's retirement, might appreciate something having been done towards the preparation of an evening meal – even just peeling a few potatoes. In a sense, he had regressed to a state of early childhood. He seemed to occupy a central position while, outside, the world spun around the all-important self. And in his own centre, lacking the daylight of reason, the black flower of obsession prospered within him.

He was still in front of the television, with a packet of cigarettes and a gin and tonic to hand when Shandy arrived home. These days there were no little greetings or courtesies on meeting after having been apart; she said, "Where's Kim?", he replied, "Upstairs," and she disappeared. Some twenty minutes later she and Sandra came down. He heard the front door shut and Shandy came into the sitting room.

She sat down and said, "I'd like a sherry."

If getting meals ready was a woman's job, fetching drinks was the man's. Without demur Paul left the room. When he returned with a schooner of dry sherry, he noticed the television had been switched off. Shandy wanted his full attention.

She said, "Kim is terribly worried that boys, decent boys that is, are going to avoid her. That little bitch Sharon reckons it was Kim's fault her parents found out about the party, and she's been spreading it around that Kim only got what she'd been asking for."

"Worried that boys will avoid her?" This was a new, unexpected dimension to the tragedy and superficially of no importance.

"Trevor hasn't been in touch since it happened, and he knows about it."

Unaware of the conspiracy between his wife and daughter to keep him in the dark about boyfriends, he knew only of Trevor, a nineteen-year-old who wore thick-lensed spectacles and idolised Kimberley with an adoration which made her untouchable, almost sacred. He would take Kimberley to the cinema or the theatre and, if required, escort her to a party. It was a pity he had been otherwise engaged on the night of Sharon's party. He was polite, well spoken and he called Paul 'sir'. Apart from Kimberley, his devotion was to his job with a small firm who specialised in 'the development of multi-functional electronic guidance systems for the visually impaired'. He had explained to Paul, with the embellishment of technical jargon, his part in a research project, and Paul had decided that Trevor was a suitable companion for his Kimmy.

When Shandy had finished bemoaning Trevor's non-communication, Paul said, "I think he's just respected her privacy, as one does in times of sorrow, or bereavement... When are we eating, by the way?"

Shandy tensed in her chair and her eyes widened slightly. "Eating! I don't know when you're eating, but I'm having mine when I've finished this sherry, unless I decide I'd like another."

He had been sitting, half facing her, and half towards the blank television screen. Now he turned to face her fully. "What's that supposed to mean? You're having yours?"

"Didn't Kim let you know? I phoned while you were out this afternoon. I asked her to get your meal as I didn't know when I'd be home. She must have forgotten. I've got myself a kebab."

"Well, thanks very much! That's great!"

"You are capable of knocking up something for yourself, aren't you? You've had all day."

He sensed the disdain of the worker for the layabout in her voice and it was enough to ignite the anger. If she wanted a row she could have one. He wasn't going to put up with her supercilious airs simply because she had a job and he had none. Anyway, how was she to know that he hadn't spent all day job-hunting?

"I find it strange," he said, "that you can sit there, sipping sherry, and worrying because Kimmy's boyfriend hasn't been in touch when you are ideally placed to find the men who screwed her. I thought Samson Associates was supposed to be a detective agency. I guess I should have know better after the bull-terrier fiasco. You couldn't even find a bloody dog!"

He was referring to a case, two or three years earlier, where a Crufts champion had almost certainly been stolen by a rival breeder. The dog had never been found and circumstantial evidence of the rival breeder's guilt wasn't strong enough to bring a prosecution.

"Couldn't even find a bloody dog!" he repeated with a derisive laugh.

"Are you trying to wind me up, Paul?"

"Wind you up? Why should I want to wind you up? It's just that the thought occurred to me that since your job involves finding missing persons, and the two who raped Kimmy are in that category, and you are now the big chief, you might have put someone on to finding who did it. Or maybe you have, but kept it from me. Have you used any of the resources at your disposal to get these criminals?"

Shandy maintained self-control by speaking slowly. "A terrible crime has been committed against our daughter and, as you know, crime is in the first place for the police to deal with. It is the policy of S.A. not to interfere unless asked by the police for our assistance, or they've reached a dead end and our client wants us to take over the case with a view to bringing a civil action. There is a grey area between these two but we aren't in that area yet."

"And at the rate you're going, you never will be. So far as I can tell, the police have done bugger all, your precious agency is scared of upsetting the police, and I'm the only one who's concerned about bringing these bastards to justice. Or, failing that –" he added menacingly "– bringing justice to them."

Stung by his dismissal of her firm, Shandy said, "I'm not going to get paranoid or obsessive about it. You mentioned our resources, yes, we do have resources and if the police get nowhere with their enquiries I shan't hesitate to use them."

"Resources? What resources?" he scoffed.

"I wouldn't dream of telling you."

A sneer was wired from his face. "Why not? Are you saying you don't trust me?" His voice grew louder so that he was almost shouting, "And speaking of trust, I'm beginning to wonder about you and John Samson. You seem much more concerned about his welfare than mine."

Shandy stood up. "I don't have to take this," she said.

He was a man who took pride in keeping lean and fit; his reflexes were sharp; over-indulgence in alcohol and cigarettes had yet to take a toll. Before she could reach the door he had leapt out of his armchair and barred her exit.

"Let me through, Paul."

"Why wouldn't you tell me what your resources are? You don't trust me, do you? Why the hell should I trust you?"

"Please let me through."

"Not until I have an answer."

"John is an old and dear friend who I've known longer than I've known you. There never has been, and never will be, anything remotely like an affair between us. I have never been unfaithful to you which is more than you can say—"

"Oh, yes. Bring that up," he interrupted bitterly.

"You started this argument. Now, please let me past."

"Where do you think you're going?"

Anger, rigidly suppressed, began rising to the surface. She clenched her fists and when she spoke it was icily deliberate in contrast to his intemperate voice. "I am not your servant. I do not have to account to you for where I go."

"No, you're not my servant," he shouted, "you are my so-called wife, and some wife you've turned out to be! All you think of is your career. Some wife! Some mother!"

He knew this last shaft had hurt because she flinched, but she wasn't to be shouted into submission. "Somebody has to keep this house going," she retorted. "I won't call it a home."

"I suppose I'm to blame because I can't get a job. Do you think I've not been trying? You've seen my mail each day. 'Thank you for your enquiry but we regret we have no position available.'"

123

As he was speaking the door behind him opened and Kimberley appeared. She was close to tears. "Why are you shouting, Dad? I can't stand it."

He was instantly contrite. "I'm sorry, sweetheart, I lost my cool. We had a difference of opinion on the best way to tackle this thing. Your mum wants to do it by the book. In other words, let the police do what they can first of all. I'm not so sure. I want to do it the unorthodox way – to take the matter into my own hands and act without delay. Your mum's way is the most sensible; but I find it hard to accept."

"Oh…" Kimberley put her hand to her mouth; it was the stage gesture of someone who had suddenly remembered an important message too late for it to be of use. "I said I'd…" She turned to her mother, "Mum, I completely forgot. I was talking with Sandra and it went right out of my mind. You asked me to get Dad's dinner."

Before Shandy could speak Paul jumped in with, "Not to worry. I've got an idea. Why don't you two go out for a meal. Have it on me." He felt for his wallet. "I'm perfectly happy with the kebab… No, I insist… No arguments, please."

Shandy found her voice. "Forget the kebab. I'll get something."

Paul was adamant. "No way. You've had a busy day. There's that new Indian restaurant – what's it called, Spice House or something? You both like Indian food, and you know I'm not mad about it. I'd like you both to have a nice curry. You'd like that, Kimmy?"

"Well, yes." She hesitated. "You could come too."

Seeing the opportunity to repair some of the damage done by their argument, and keen to support Kimberley in whatever positive she suggested, Shandy added her weight. "Good idea. The three of us haven't been out together lately. And we don't have to have a curry; we could have a Chinese or whatever you like."

By siding with their daughter Paul was aware she was turning the tables on him, putting him on the back foot. She didn't really want to be trapped into making halting and aimless conversation in a restaurant, knowing that the one subject of utmost concern to all three was taboo. Probably after a busy day she didn't wish to go out at all.

"It's kind of you both, but I've got things I want to do here."

He gave Shandy a challenging look, defying her to ask what he had to do, and when she lowered her eyes, a sign that his challenge wasn't to be taken up, he continued, "Besides, I rather fancy a kebab. Haven't had one for ages."

He ate the kebab while they were changing their clothes. Within half an hour they had left, and he was free to think and plan. Although he still clung to the belief that a criminal will eventually return to the scene of his crime, he realised it was becoming impractical to haunt the wood for long periods each day. Not only would he be noticed and possibly reported to the police as an undesirable, a flasher or worse, but the weather would deteriorate. Already the chill of winter was in the air. He would have to extend the area of search for a black man whose left hand was minus an index finger, and to undertake this effectively he needed transport; a small car, a banger would serve the purpose.

After pouring himself another whisky he settled down with pen and paper to work out exactly how much he could afford to spend on a car.

Before the catastrophe of being made redundant he had taken pride in providing everything for the small family unit, including Kimberley's education at a private school, all household and holiday expenses, and so on. Everything Shandy earned at Samson Associates was hers to keep and she had bought the mobile home in the south of France, which was now being sold, and an apartment in Puerto Pollensa, Majorca. Recently, however, she had been spending more on everyday necessities – not that she mentioned this – but he noticed that what he was accustomed to giving her for provisions was no longer enough. Although she didn't approve of his whisky-drinking, she would buy scotch; but then she was herself drinking far more wine than previously. It was certain she wouldn't add cigarettes to her shopping list. A mischievous thought flitted in and out of his mind. He could say, 'Why won't you buy cigs for me? You'll then have justification for refusing sex...'

He reckoned that after the expenses incurred that day he still had more than nine thousand pounds in liquid assets. At the present time this was more than enough to buy a decent car, but all he needed was a small, easily parked car in which to travel short distances. How would he explain to Shandy why a car was necessary? Easy. He'd say it would be helpful in job hunting. It would enable him to visit more centres where jobs were advertised. He was going to lower his sights and take on more or less anything that offered a worthwhile wage. He was now thinking in terms of 'wages' rather than 'salaries'.

He went to a cupboard where newspapers were stacked for collection and recycling, and he found the latest issue of the *Streatham Free Press*. Under the column headed 'Cars for Sale' he saw: 'Fiat Uno. Good condition. 7 yrs old. MOT and taxed. Snip at £1,500'. A telephone number followed.

He dialled the number, and a deep, unmistakably Afro voice answered. Paul asked about the car's mileage, the number of previous owners, its engine capacity, colour, and finally arranged to visit an address between Streatham and Brixton in the morning. He had intended to ask whether a near offer would be acceptable, but a mist of anathema descended at the thought of haggling with a black man.

The truism that a new purpose in life often brings new enthusiasm held good for him. He felt something akin to excitement as he went to fetch an A to Z of London. Poring over the street atlas he decided that the area of operational search would be limited to approximately a two-mile radius to the north, west and east of Streatham. This coverage would take in Brixton, Norbury, Tulse Hill and Herne Hill, all of which had a fairly high population of black inhabitants. That his search was like looking for a specific sand-dune in the Sahara desert and could last a lifetime without any result didn't deter him. He had total self-belief and confidence that the man he sought would be his to punish before – if the fellow was in a fit state – he handed him over to the police for formal arrest. He was now a total slave to an obsession, and like all such slaves regarded himself as master of his destiny.

He thought about buying a dog to accompany him on his visits to the wood. Dog-walking was an acceptable reason for a continuing presence, but the idea was shelved when he thought of all the drawbacks of having responsibility for a canine friend, not least being Shandy's certain objections to it being in the house.

The sound of her car arriving home broke his train of thought. A key turned in the front door and he was glad to hear the sound of animated talk; it indicated that the outing had gone well and therefore that Shandy should be receptive to his purchase of a car. Not that she could veto it; but he didn't want a day of satisfying achievement to be soured. After Kimberley had gone to bed, he was about to mention the car when Shandy pre-empted him with, "Crossing fingers I think Kim is over the worst. It was a good idea of yours for us to go out for a meal. I was beginning to worry about her staying indoors all day, but she's broken the ice. It's the first time since that awful morning, and she took it well."

He said, "Good," in a voice which lacked expression or emotion. It was the sort of flat remark he might have made if she had commented that her own car was running well after a recent service.

"Good? It's more than good, it's terrific."

Naturally he wanted her to recover fully from her ordeal and be his bright Kimmy once more, but the longer she remained in a twilight of shock the more intense became his desire for retribution. Having found a powerful objective, apart from obtaining a fresh job, he didn't want it vitiated by her returning to normality too soon.

"Yes, you're right. It is terrific," he said.

"Of course it'll take time. She'll have her downs."

"That's true."

"But she's on the mend. Christmas is coming up and then the New Year. It'll be time for a new beginning."

"Yes, a new beginning."

"What's the matter. Paul?"

"Nothing's the matter."

"Yes, it is. I know you. Has something happened while we were out?"

"No, nothing at all, except I've been thinking of getting a car."

"A car? What for?"

"So that I can get to employment agencies quicker. It takes ages by public transport."

"Maybe it does, but what do you expect to find elsewhere that you won't find locally? It's obvious you aren't going to find anything suitable to meet your qualifications and experience in employment exchanges. You aren't a brickie, plumber or electrician. In the construction industry you were in management."

"Only junior management."

She shrugged her shoulders. "Well, get a car if that's what you want. I hope you'll keep it parked in the road. There isn't room for two cars in what passes for a drive here."

"OK."

A silence spread between them, and it wasn't the silence which indicated a peaceful contentment existing between two perfectly attuned people. It was uneasy: the quiet of a truce between warring factions. It created a tension which demanded to be snapped like overstretched elastic.

In the end, Shandy spoke. "I've had a long day. I'll turn in."

"I'll be up later."

Without a further word she left the room. He heard her high heels clatter on the parquet floor of the hall before she reached the tread of the stair carpet. It was only when he heard the click of the bathroom door closing that he rose from his chair and went to the drinks cabinet to pour another whisky. On returning to the chair he saw the ashtray with four cigarette butts squashed in it. She must have noticed it, and smelled the smoky atmosphere but had said nothing.

Why should she? He was still the man of the house with all this position implied, wasn't he?

She was asleep, or feigning sleep, when he went to bed.

Shandy had felt euphoric when she returned home with Kimberley after their meal. Her daughter was facing the outside world; an important step on the road to full recovery. The shadow of a sneaking sense of guilt which had dogged Shandy since the rape was fading away; it was the guilt of a too conscientious person who feels that she has put her own interests before those of others dependent on her. Had she been neglecting her daughter and husband on account of her work at Samson Associates? She had, she thought, been so involved· in taking over from Samson and becoming head of the firm that inevitably she had been staying late at the office and coming home too tired to cook a meal. Instead she had brought back something from a takeaway; a Chinese, or Indian meal or even fish and chips. At other times a ready-to-eat meal had been taken from the deep freezer, defrosted in a microwave, and served within half an hour. That such neglect had no connection with her teenage. daughter going to a party at a friend's house was immaterial to her.

Although Paul would not have believed it, she also felt a sort of guilt for her sexual coolness, which had been partly caused by the speed with which he would gain satisfaction and then turn over and go to sleep, leaving her stranded on a plateau of orgasmic frustration.

As she drove home with Kimberley beside her speaking of the possibility of taking a degree through a correspondence course, she decided that tonight she would respond to Paul's needs in bed. It proved to be a fragile decision, unable to withstand the chill of his unemotional reaction to her good news about Kimberley's apparent emergence from a state of housebound isolation. He was more concerned with buying a car on the pretext, which she didn't believe, that it would help him in a search for employment. Instinct or an intuitive faculty told her that the need for a car was connected with his obsession to find the rapists which, in spite of his pretended change of attitude, had penetrated his psyche like some evil maggot. This understanding lifted the nagging burden of sexual guilt from her. Her next move, when the time was right, would be to state a strong desire for separate beds and if, as a result, he found another Peggy, so be it.

She was asleep, her back to his side of the bed, when after a final whisky and one last cigarette he finally made his way, a little unsteady, upstairs.

Thirteen

Under pressure from his wife and for the sake of a quiet life, Josiah Manley telephoned his old friend from Jamaican days, apologised for calling him on a Saturday, and asked if he would come to check on his son's health. The boy was feverish, had a high temperature, and although it seemed like a case of influenza for which his pharmacy had many remedies, it was better to be safe than sorry.

Dr McCloud, one of whose ancestors had been a bold sea-rover before succumbing to that charms of a dusky Carib maid, gravely told Josiah not to apologise as it would give him pleasure to be of some service to a good friend from the old days back home. After a further exchange of compliments, Dr McCloud said he'd be on his way within the hour; and Josiah related the news to his wife before going out to a large green-house in a small garden where he cultivated orchids. If there was to be a crisis, he reflected, it always occurred over the weekend, but he brightened slightly at the thought of his wife, now in the kitchen, preparing his favourite meal of codfish and ackee.

The doctor arrived well within his allotted time and after a thorough examination of Sylvester said that yes, indeed Sylvester had the flu, and he wrote a prescription for what he and Josiah both knew was a populist panacea but would quell the anxieties of a worried mother. He also wrote a sick note for the manager of the supermarket where Sylvester worked, and after a cup of coffee made from arabica beans grown on the Blue Mountains, he departed.

Josiah heard his wife upraising their son with, "You ungrateful boy, what do you mean, you don't want a week off work? Course you do, and you will!" On his way back to the greenhouse Josiah smiled to himself. Sylvester might not be great on book learning but he was a chip off the old block when it came to work. Just as Josiah longed to get back to his pharmacy on Monday, so Sylvester wanted a quick return to his place of employment. Both males were activated by a desire to escape from the nagging dominance of Mrs Christabel Manley but, Josiah reflected, as he entered the welcoming warmth of the greenhouse, it was worse for Sylvester who had to put up with the incessant teasing of his younger sibling. Coral, pretty as well as clever, would one day be a harmful little armful for many a boyfriend. But at present that day seemed as remote as the dreaded day when Josiah would be obliged to retire from the Streatham branch of a national chain of chemist's shops where he was a valued and trusted employee.

It was not an epidemic, but that weekend many Londoners were sick or falling sick with feverish colds and influenza. On arrival at the offices of Samson Associates on Saturday (a full working day for the firm) Shandy found a message on the answerphone from Brian 'Kenco' Kennedy, who was in bed with what he described as 'the lurgy'. He hoped to be in on Monday, if it cleared up by then. Martine arrived snuffling and blowing her nose, red-eyed, and complaining of a bad night's sleep. Julian asked if he might leave early; he could catch up on genealogical research over the weekend, surfing the Internet on his own computer. All serious research was done on the computer; the days were over of visiting country churchyards to decipher inscriptions on moss-covered graves or going in person to the Public Records Office. With the dedication of a true online believer, Julian explained that he had copies of software such as

Broderbund's *Family Tree Maker*, and Cyndi's list of genealogical sites, in addition to having access to the Family History Library in Salt Lake City. He cited four web sites which provided genealogical information before Shandy threw her arms in surrender and cried, "Enough! Enough!"

On his way out of the office the ever-dependable Georgia called out, "Skiving again, Julian?"

"Oh, get asterisked, darling," he replied.

"I will, darling, but not by you. Or are you making me an offer?"

He poked out his tongue at her before making a rapid exit.

Old Tom Maunder checked in and was promptly sent out again to keep watch on a rakish sprig of the nobility who was depleting the family fortune by gambling and by lavish expenditure on a mistress who had enticed him to join a drug-smuggling ring in an attempt to recoup losses.

However, staff shortages were the least of Shandy's tribulations. She had three investigative reports to write up and a number of interviews for a secretary to work on a permanent basis for Samson Associates. A series of temporaries had proved an unsatisfactory solution to secretarial problems. Georgia, Kennedy and Shandy herself could all use a word processor; but for a reason Shandy had never fully understand Samson, who could type with two fingers on an old Olivetti portable, had set himself against having a permanent secretary. Shandy suspected it was lack of space in the office that was partly the reason for his stubborn resistance to change. His own room, now hers, was large and impressive; all other rooms were considerably smaller and involved sharing. Permanent staff dislike sharing with temps even more than sharing with each other; even Martine and Kennedy didn't wish to be in one another's company all day and sometimes all night too.

Whenever Shandy had suggested a move to a larger office she had met with an implacable wall of concrete resistance on the grounds that their present office was in a prime location at a reasonable rent and to move could only send the team down market. The outer office where Georgia worked could accommodate a secretary. The problem now facing Shandy on a dreary November day was finding the right person at the right salary.

By seven thirty that evening she had interviewed nine prospective secretaries, written up two of her own reports, dealt with a number of telephone enquiries, two dissatisfied clients who wanted reductions on their bills of cost (Samson's fees were notoriously high), been through a muddle of papers on Kennedy's desk to see if anything required attention, had an hour-long interview with a man whose wife had flagrantly cuckolded him and who wanted to entrap her *in flagrante delicto*, and another interview with an elderly woman whose grandson and sole heir had gone missing while back-packing in the Far East and who wanted him found and brought home whatever the cost as she had terminal cancer and wished to see him once more before she died.

In between these chores she had telephoned Kimberley to ask her to get an evening meal for herself and Paul. She had asked how he had been that day and was told he had been emptying their garage, an integral part of the house, of accumulated junk which had been transferred to the loft.

"He's been out and bought himself a little blue car," Kimberley explained, "and says he's going to keep it in the garage. I told him he wouldn't be able to get it out if you were parked in the drive."

"What did he say to that?"

"He said you'd have to move yours then. He said he didn't fancy parking in the road outside."

To this annoying information Shandy replied, "I'll see you later, dear," and hung up, seething with anger at Paul's cavalier statement. And now, on her way home through traffic congested by pre-Christmas Saturday evening shoppers, she wondered what sort of reception she would get, and whether the lights outside their house would be switched on.

A man, shot through the back of his head at close range, was identified by his fingerprints as Jason Marchant, a small-time crook thought to be involved in drug trafficking. His body had been found in an alleyway close to Acre Lane in Brixton shortly after daybreak on the Saturday when Shandy had been obliged to come home late.

On the previous day, a burned out BMW had been found on a lay-by south of Leeds. The owner of the car had not been traced through DVLA records as number plates had been removed before the vehicle had been torched, and as yet no connection had been made between the dead man and the burned out car. It would not be long, however, before the engine number would reveal its owner to be 'Flash Jack' Duprez and the link made between him and Jason Marchant, but there was no sustainable evidence that Duprez had ordered the murder of the man responsible for stealing the car he had bought recently for his son's use.

It had been careless boasting by the youth who had been detailed to keep watch while his two older companions raped Kimberley that had sealed Marchant's fate. An associate of Duprez's had heard the boast of a BMW having been nicked for the entertainment of a pal from the North for a spot of joy-riding, which had led the three to Streatham and the discovery of a party there. The youth had stopped short of mentioning the subsequent rape as it gave him little street cred to have played the subservient role of keeping watch while the two older men enjoyed themselves. Moreover, his scarf had been left at the scene of the crime and it had disappeared when he had returned a few hours later to retrieve it. There was no percentage in mentioning this part of the night.

Shandy waited impatiently at the junction of the A23 and Acre Lane for traffic lights to change from red. She was not to know that she was so close to the place where the corpse had earlier been found of the man who had raped her daughter.

The lights changed to green and a block of vehicles moved slowly forward. A quarter of an hour later she reached the road where she lived and was glad to see the outside lights of her home had been switched on. Paul had obviously had second thoughts about leaving his new car in the garage because a blue Fiat Uno was parked in the road directly outside the house.

Soon after they had married and bought the house she couldn't wait to get home, but now, after switching off the engine, she sat still for a few moments before climbing wearily out of the car. There was no longer any thrill in homecoming, only uneasy apprehensions.

In the Manley household Sunday was not a day of rest, it was the day dedicated to praising the Lord and all His works. A bible reading and prayers before breakfast preceded worship at a Baptist Church where little Coral's shrill soprano and her mother's vibrant contralto, stoked by the burning coals of Josiah Manley's basso profundo, and Sylvester's fervent tenor, put the family in the premier league of hot gospellors.

Grace before lunch was a peaen of gratitude to the good Lord for the food about to be served – any suggestion that Josiah's earning might have contributed to the cost of the meal would have been akin to blasphemy. In the afternoon the male Manleys were allowed a certain degree of freedom to pursue their interests, provided these were not tainted by undue worldliness, before a second round of worship at church.

However, this Sunday, on account of his influenza, Sylvester was excused the visits to church and took no part in family prayers. And yet it was not so much a day of rest as a day of bed-rest, marred by a disproportionate sense of guilt over cotton panties stuffed inside a shoe in his wardrobe. He was a superstitious youth and he believed, as his mother had taught, that the Lord brings eternal damnation in hell-fire to those who fall into evil ways. His high temperature and sweating body was, he had no doubt, a foretaste of the punishment he would receive after death unless he rid himself of his awful secret.

While the rest of the family was at church he knelt by his bed and prayed. He asked for divine guidance on the matter of disposal of the article he had foolishly taken and begged forgiveness for his sin. It was then that a miracle occurred. Although there was no voice in his head, the Lord answered his prayer with a blindingly clear revelation. He must, as soon as possible, return the panties to the exact place he had taken them from. Once he had done this his guilt would be purged and any sin connected with the intimate article of clothing would be forgiven.

On climbing back into bed he went into a deep and peaceful sleep from which he eventually awoke feeling refreshed. His temperature had fallen to near normal and his mother, when she brought him some nourishing soup, on noticing the difference attributed his amazing recovery to the power of prayer on his behalf led by no less a person than the preacher himself at the evening service.

Sylvester went along with her theory on the efficiency of mass prayer but he privately knew it was his prayer, and his alone, which had influenced the good Lord.

When clearing the garage of junk and lumber, Paul had come across an old suitcase which contained, among other things, photograph albums and papers which had belonged to his father, and various other family memorabilia and trivia including a box which held no fewer than seven cut-throat razors and two leather strops. All the razors were still lethally sharp and he selected one before putting the rest back in the box. It would need only a quick swipe with such a tool to sever a scrotum from its penile mooring. A rapist would deserve no less punishment.

His problem was where to keep the razor and the newly acquired handgun until he caught the men who deflowered his lovely daughter. Unlike Shandy, who knew the truth, he imagined his daughter had been a virgin. Where, he wondered, was a safe place to hide the two weapons? He was unaware that in a different part of town a man with a missing finger was facing a similar quandary with Kimberley's panties.

In the end he wrapped up the gun and razor in a piece of oily cloth which he secreted under the front passenger seat of his car. A previous owner had fitted an alarm which should, he hoped, be enough to deter any thief from trying to steal the car.

For an hour or two on Sunday afternoon, November lost its grip on the drab weather and Shandy drove in sunshine to the hospital where Samson awaited his operation.

He asked almost at once, "How's my god-daughter?"

"Still very much up one minute and down the next. When I left she was on an up. Her boyfriend, Trevor, called in to see her. She'd thought he'd gone off her, but he was just giving her a bit of time to get over the ordeal."

"And how is Paul?"

"I'm convinced he's game-playing, but I'm not sure what the game is. His behaviour has become much more normal but I suspect he's covering something. It's a pretence. To be honest, John, I'm scared for him. He's bought a car and says that transport will make it easier to find a suitable job, but it could equally be used to search a wider area for the men who raped Kim. I just hope he isn't stupid enough to get mixed up with the Yardies or in some gangland vendetta."

"Have you been on to CID?"

"Not since Friday but they've promised to let me know if anything comes up. Although it's been all change with the personnel, your name still means something..."

"Nice to know."

"...and Bob Broadbent is still around. He's promised to keep an eye on the case and to let me know of any developments."

Shandy stayed with her old boss for just over an hour before going back to Streatham. As she rounded the corner of her road, she saw that Paul's car was no longer parked there. Indoors, she found Kimberley and Trevor seated side by side in the sitting room watching television. They were so self-consciously apart she guessed they had been closer before they'd heard her arrival. She hoped her hunch was right; it would be another small sign pointing in the direction of recovery.

"Any idea where Dad's gone?" she asked casually.

"Haven't a clue," Kimberley replied. "He just said he was taking the dog for a walk meaning, I suppose, he was going out for a run in his new toy. How is Uncle John?"

"OK. He'll be glad to get tomorrow over. He sent you his love."

Trevor spoke for the first time. "There you are, Kim. I told you that you were much loved."

"I don't know about that. It's my confidence I've lost as much as anything."

Shandy disappeared quietly leaving them to discuss methods of building up confidence.

When Paul returned it was with a huge bunch of chrysanthemums purchased at a supermarket in Tulse Hill. Supermarkets were a magnet to so many people that it seemed worthwhile visiting a few in his area of search. He hadn't as yet seen a single black man with an insufficiency of fingers but wasn't in the least deterred. In time the police files would be closed on an unsolved case; his file would never be closed while the rapists remained at large.

"What lovely colours," Shandy exclaimed when he handed her the bouquet of flowers and she gave him a kiss on the lips.

Her kiss surprised, but did not excite him.

"Everything's all right, isn't it?" she asked.

He knew at once that what she meant was, 'You've given up trying to find those men, haven't you?' and the unspoken question made him realise with a degree of bitterness that in kissing him she had been acting a part. He instantly replied, "Yes, everything's fine now."

Fourteen

It was seven fifteen on Monday evening when Samson, clad in a white gown, and already half-dosed by pre-med injections of a sedative and a painkiller into his rump, was wheeled into the operating theatre. Almost at once after an oxygen mask was put over his face, he slipped into oblivion. Two hours later he awoke in the recovery room with his left arm connected to a saline drip and with an irrigator on his wrist. Back again in his room he was soon asleep. At eight o'clock the following morning Mr Timson came to see him and reported that the operation had gone well. His prostate had shrunk and was very hard; the tumour attached to it had blocked the passage through which urine should pass. "We must now get you back to peeing properly," he said, "and get the appropriate muscles working again."

Six days later, and virtually clear of incontinence, he was fit to be discharged. Shandy drove him back to his flat. Against his wishes she had hired an agency nurse-cum-housekeeper to look after him and cook his meals for a week or so. "Mrs Collas won't like that," he complained referring to his regular cleaning woman, "and I shall get flak from them both."

"You'll survive," Shandy retorted crisply.

He had come to terms with cancer which had been temporarily controlled but not cured; he now faced a

141

confrontation with the facts of retirement. Had it been too premature?

"I hope I shan't be sidelined," he said as they neared his flat.

"What do you mean?"

"Consultant is a nice title to have but it's pretty meaningless. Like a company or club president; one is nothing more than a figurehead."

"It was your choice, John. You weren't pushed." Realising she sounded a shade too brusque Shandy went on in a softer voice, "Don't worry. I shan't be so silly as to undervalue your opinion on tricky cases or staffing problems."

"I'd planned to indulge myself with holiday cruises; revisit in luxury some of the places I'd seen living fairly rough below decks. And countries I'd never had the chance to visit. I know I'm a late starter in the culture stakes but I wanted to learn more about ancient Greece and the Roman civilisation. In late years I find I have an appetite for history. When not travelling I though of getting material for a history of Time."

"History of Time? When did Time start?"

"Probably trillions of years before the Big Bang. The sheer immensity of Time acted like a detonator. The Russians are working on a theory that the unimaginable vastness of Time can actually cause movement."

They were now travelling along Piccadilly and within walking distance of his flat. "Luxury cruises and writing a history doesn't appeal to you any more?" she asked.

"Not as much as the stresses and excitements of what I've been doing for the last twenty plus years." He gave a heavy sigh. "But we shall see."

Defying his mother's wishes for once, Sylvester pronounced himself ready to resume work two days after his miraculous recovery. In spite of her dire warnings about a relapse, and that he needn't expect her to look after him if he took ill again, he returned to his job in the stockroom at a store in Norbury.

In ordinary circumstances, covered by a sick note issued by the worthy Dr McCloud, Sylvester might have taken advantage of two more days at home. He didn't feel up to moving crates of bottles or emptying sacks of potatoes but, in his mind, the panties had become part of a fearsome jinx. An atavistic instinct told him that they would be the cause of some unspeakable evil befalling him. He knew that he must rid himself of them by taking them back to the clearing in the wood where they has been purloined.

It was a day in which the transition from night to day was a seamless grey and he was glad that nobody was around as he entered the wood. Leaving the path he walked stealthily into the clearing looking furtively around to check if by an extraordinary mischance someone else was there. Satisfied that he was alone he took the panties, now slightly grubby and off-white, from his pocket and hung them on the bush where he had found them. As he left the clearing, his lips creased in a smile and his stride became jaunty.

From time to time during the next few days he returned to the clearing hoping to find that the panties had somehow become dislodged by wind and rain and were now on the ground completely out of sight. He could, of course, have put them there and covered them with fallen leaves but even to touch them again could be unlucky. As a first-generation Jamaican born in England, he knew about duppies and how malign these spirits could be when guarding a jinxed object and he had no intention of offending them.

Brian Kennedy and Georgia were always first to arrive at the office. However, two days before Samson was discharged from hospital, Julian was already waiting on the pavement outside. He would never have admitted it, but he wanted to impress Georgia with his self-considered brilliance as a genealogical researcher.

She greeted him with, "Well, look what the wind's blown in."

"Ha! Ha! How witty! How clever! How original!"

"Don't be like that, darling. Come in and make me a coffee."

A few minutes later, with her seated by the switchboard, and him on a chair next to her, he remarked as casually as he could,

"I've found out something very interesting about the Old Man's antecedents."

"I'm not sure I want to know," she replied guardedly.

Julian wasn't to be stopped from staggering her with his acumen and all-round mastery of his chosen line. Aware that her concentration and attention would be limited he kept the technical know-how to a minimum and came rapidly to the dramatic point. "You know, of course, who Saint-Saens was?"

"San what?"

"Charles Camille Saint-Saens born in Paris 1835. He was of humble origins—"

"Like me. A right commoner, you mean?"

"I don't mean anything of the sort, and please don't interrupt," he said tetchily. "As a result of my research I went to Haddon Manor in Hampshire and from family records discovered that in 1863 a member of the Saint-Saens family stayed there for a couple of months and seduced a serving girl called Betsy. No surname available. However, after a boy child was born, the family who had sacked her relented and took her back into their employ. She now had a surname – he paused for effect – Samson!"

Georgia shook her head. "Sorry, I don't get it. She was called Samson, so what?"

"Said quickly, don't Saint-Saens and Samson sound alike?"

"So do Bogart and Bogarde but that doesn't mean Humphrey was related to Dirk."

"You are being deliberately perverse, Georgia. I don't see why I should cast my pearls in front of people like you."

"Get you!"

"I can see I'm wasting my time," he said, adding waspishly, "I expect your knowledge of famous opera is on a par with your knowledge of famous composers—"

"You're right. Told you I was a commoner. I don't know nuffin'."

"Then let me throw a little light on the Dark Continent you call a brain. Saint-Saens' most famous opera is called *Samson and Delilah*."

In the pause while Georgia was working out a snappy put-down, Shandy walked in. She'd had an exceptionally good run into town and was earlier than usual. When she had gone to her room Georgia spoke, and it wasn't a put-down or sarcasm at his expense. She said, "If I were you, Julian, I'd keep the info you've given me to yourself. I shan't tell anyone. Whatever you do, don't tell the Old Man, not if you want to carry on working here. You'd be *persona non grata* and that, darling, is Latin for 'No one wants you round here so get lost'."

He stood up. "I suppose it was silly of me, but I wanted to share what I'd discovered with someone, and I chose you."

He looked so crestfallen that she was touched. She turned up from her chair, said, "You're a sweetie sometimes," threw her arms round his neck and planted a kiss fair and square on his lips, and she didn't let go for about five seconds.

When free from her embrace, looking flustered, he exclaimed, "Really!"

"Such a waste of a nice-looking guy," she murmured, sitting down in front of the switchboard.

"I'm getting out of here."

Her laughter followed his departure.

Not long after her arrival, Shandy's phone went and Georgia said, "Detective Inspector Tapsell from the CID for you."

"Put him through."

She listened intently as the inspector brought her up to date on Kimberley's case. The burned out BMW had been identified as having been stolen. It had belonged to a Mr Jacques Duprez who had been interviewed. He had purchased the car for his son, and the car was certainly the one used by the rapists. It was probable that one of these men had since been murdered but as yet the proof lacked sufficient hard evidence.

"We believe three men were involved," the inspector continued. "If we are right in thinking one of them has been killed in reprisal – or punishment, if you like – for stealing the car, although I stress we can't prove this, then two men are left. One presumably has disappeared up north and we have no leads at all who the other might be. This doesn't mean we are shelving the case, but I thought you and your husband should know the score."

"Thanks. I appreciate that. This man who was killed – did he have a finger missing?"

"I can categorically say no to that."

Shandy thanked the inspector once more before finishing the call. She wasn't sorry for the man who had died in what was undoubtedly a piece of gangland vengeance, but she was disappointed that he had a full set of fingers. If she could have told Paul that the man he had been hunting had been found dead it would put an end to his obsession.

He listened in silence to her account of the conversation with Tapsell and when she had finished he simply said, "One down, two to go."

Kimberley's reaction seemed stronger. "Serves him right," she said, "I hope he rots in hell." However, it was spoken not with venom, but rather as though she was saying what she imagined was expected of her.

Their attitudes although both expressed with a degree of firmness sounded curiously detached which Shandy guessed was misleading so far as Paul was concerned. He was still intent on bringing all to justice, or his idea of justice to all. As for Kimberley, her moods continued to fluctuate but had become less extreme.

Why do I worry about them, Shandy wondered, I've got enough to worry about in running a business, for a business she was finding out was the nature of the agency. It was then she realised how much she was missing Samson's solid presence in the office.

For Paul, what had been an obsessive purpose was becoming a way of life. Walking down streets and going in and out of supermarkets and other stores would have been an aimless exercise but for the missing finger validating his actions; moreover, it kept him from being stuck indoors. Trevor, Sandra, and one or two other friends were visiting Kimberley, and with each visit her CD player seemed to become louder. He no longer felt able to demand that the volume be turned down. Also, she was beginning to go out more herself and, with nothing to look at outside except an everlasting pall of grey, the lights and sounds of busy streets were a kind of stimulant.

November merged into December and the first snow of winter fluttered down from a cloudy expanse. Bing Crosby singing that he was dreaming of a white Christmas seemed to be playing in almost every store and if it wasn't this unrelenting proclamation that the so-called festive season had arrived there were choirs of angels being urged to sing praises and exalt the Lord God of Hosts. Looking at the left hand of every black man within visual range had become a conditioned response. On one occasion at a petrol station he had peered too closely at a man whose hand was wrapped around the nozzle of a pump. "Somethin' botherin' you, pal?" the man had demanded aggressively and Paul had been obliged to reply, "No, nothing," and hurry away. He seldom visited the clearing in the wood.

Originally he had planned to take his victim, at gunpoint if necessary, to the empty shop premises. Here, after tying the man up he would grill him about rape until he extracted a confession, and if the man didn't confess, Paul would find ways of showing him it would be in his best interests to do so. In his car he kept the equipment for this operation – handgun, razor, torch and a length of cord with a slipknot noose ready to slip over the victim's wrists after he had been ordered to put them behind his back. The principal snag to this plan was the increasing pressure being put on him by Jim Cutler to come to a decision on the purchase of the property which, of course, Paul had not the slightest intention of buying. All he wanted was a place where he could hold a captive without fear of being found.

In Cutler's most recent call to Paul on his mobile he had issued an ultimatum. "Unless you are prepared to pay a full ten per cent deposit and sign an agreement to purchase subject to formal contract, Mr Jones, I regret to say I must ask that the keys you hold be returned without further delay. I'll give you one more week to come to a decision."

"I shall want all the money I've paid you back. All six hundred pounds."

"You shall have it back the moment the keys are in my possession."

The line went dead.

Paul would have much preferred to have his quarry holed up in a private house rather than a public place but, if the worst came to the worst, he could always take the man to the scene of the crime and interrogate him there, but this would be a riskier procedure; a passer-by might hear something and stop to investigate.

And then, about a month after Samson's retirement party and with six days of the ultimatum still in hand, he decided to go back to the wood one last time. It was cold and damp, and he intended staying for only a few minutes. On entering the clearing almost the first thing he saw was something that resembled a wet handkerchief hanging on a bush. It hadn't been there on his previous visit and he went over to investigate.

Using finger and thumb he plucked it from the bush and held it away as though it was contaminated. It slowly unfolded and he saw he was holding a pair of female briefs. Realisation that these were possibly, even probably, Kimberley's panties crashed into his mind with such force that the impact seemed to reverberate through his body and leave him breathless. So he had been right all along! Criminals *did* return to the scene of their crime!

Realisation was followed by a sense of frustration. If only he had continued his watch instead of going here, there and everywhere, he could have caught the rapist. Such a gilt-edged opportunity was unlikely to occur again. He stuffed the sad, damp garment into his overcoat pocket and hurried home. Kimberley should be able to identify it. But when he reached his house he found it empty. A note on the kitchen table said, 'Dad, have gone to the pictures with Sandra. Back about six. Luv, Kimmy'.

Disappointed by her absence he took the panties from his pocket and spread them beside the note on the table. There was no tag on the waistband to indicate a place of purchase.

Otherwise they seemed a fairly usual pair of cotton briefs with a fillet of lace directly above a gusset made of some silky material. He glanced at his watch and then at the gloom outside. It was too late to continue his search in Norbury and anyway, what was the use? He had missed the boat and it was a boat which would never return to that port of call. He went to the drinks cabinet and poured himself a stiff whisky.

When Kimberley returned with Sandra he was slumped in an armchair, his eyes fixed on electronic wallpaper which he couldn't be bothered to switch off. The two girls had disappeared upstairs by the time he had stirred himself. A minute or two later he gave a knock on Kimberley's door and walked in. Sandra was seated in front of the dressing table and Kimberley was brushing her long and lustrous auburn hair.

Kimberley turned round. "Dad," she exclaimed, "I didn't know you were home."

"I got in ages ago." He held out the panties. "Look what I've found."

She put down the brush. "What do you mean? Found?"

"In the clearing," he replied. "They were in the clearing."

Her eyebrows arched in bewilderment. "Clearing? What clearing? What are you talking about?"

"The clearing where..." He was about to say, 'where you were raped', but conscious of Sandra's presence, and aware that the subject of rape was taboo, he broke off in mid-sentence. "Are these yours?" he asked bluntly, holding up the garment.

She went forward to examine. "I don't know. Where did you get them?"

"I've told you. In the clearing."

Understanding dawned on her face as a rosy flush of anger. "Christ Almighty! Don't you ever give up? I'm trying hard to forget and you come barging into my room while I've got a guest, brandishing a pair of knickers!"

His mouth sagged open. His darling Kimmy had never spoken like this to him before. Two options were available. He could either be the heavy-handed father and rebuke her for insolence in speaking like that, or he could leave the room with as much dignity as he could summon. He chose the second. "I'm sorry to have intruded," he said stiffly and left.

However, instead of being demoralised by her outburst, his desire for vengeance was rekindled. Let them think he was obsessive, let them think he was mad, but his search would continue. There was still a chance that one of the rapists – perhaps the one with a missing finger – was somewhere in the district.

He steeled himself for Shandy's return from work. Now odd man out in the household of three, he expected her reaction to be much the same as Kimberley's and was pleasantly surprised that her main reproof was that he had moved the evidence which should have remained *in situ* until the police were notified. One look at the item was enough for her to confirm that it had almost certainly been Kimberley's, as it was identical to a pair of pants she had washed more than once which was no longer in her chest of drawers. She said that she'd hand them into CID on her way to the office in the morning, and if CID wanted to know how he'd come by them she'd have to tell them that he, Paul, visited the spot from time to time and was desperately keen that the rapists be caught. He guessed she would refer to his behaviour as obsessive, but he refrained from making an issue of the matter. Later in the evening Kimberley gave a half-apology for her flare-up; he said it was his fault and *rapprochement* of a sort between them was restored.

Next day, and with only five left before the expiry of the ultimatum, the weather had changed; a belt of high pressure had moved eastwards bringing a clear blue sky and a heavy frost. His spirits rose as he drove towards Norbury, which probably had a lower black population than Brixton or Herne Hill, or even Streatham, but was within the radius of his search. He parked his car in the car-park of a medium-sized SupaSava Store where he intended buying a lunchtime snack.

He was on his way to the check-out with a wedge of Stilton, lettuce, tomatoes and a packet of water biscuits when, passing through an aisle which had tinned foods, he saw a young black man in a blue overall stamped with the store's logo putting cans of baked beans on a nearly empty shelf. His gaze was transfixed by the man's left hand. Its index finger was nothing more than a stump. As Paul paused, amazed by his good fortune, the man placed the last of the cans on the shelf, picked up an empty brown cardboard carton, and turned so that Paul saw him full-face. Paul was so close that the man almost bumped into him, said, "Pardon me, sir," and went on his way. Paul followed him at a discreet distance until he entered a door marked 'Private – Staff Only'.

In a state of elated shock, Paul paid for his purchases and hurried to the car-park. After making sure that anyone using the staff entrance at the rear of the building would nevertheless have to go to the front and the main road to get anywhere away from the premises, he drove out intending to maintain a vigil even in this meant staying on a yellow line. Eventually, after cruising up and down in the car, he was able to park by the kerb on the main road in one of the few spots permitted. From here he could see the front entrance to the supermarket as well as the car-park exit.

He began a foot patrol up and down the street, always keeping the store in sight. It was unlikely that the black youth owned a car; nonetheless Paul tried to scrutinise the driver of every car leaving the supermarket. It was his intention to keep watch until dusk; even if he didn't see the man again he knew his place of work. He ate his lunch in the car with the engine switched on to provide some heat in its cold interior.

It was exactly ten past three in the afternoon when his quarry emerged on foot from the car-park exit carrying a spray of red carnations wrapped in a cone of paper. He crossed the road and went to a bus stop. Within a few minutes he boarded a bus bound for Streatham. Paul followed in his car and during the journey adapted his SupaSava plastic bag for use as a holdall for the accessories needed for the capture and detention of his quarry.

After the young man had alighted from the bus, he was slowly followed until he turned into a road flanked on each side by semi-detached, architecturally identical houses. Paul quickly parked his car by the roadside, grabbed the holdall, locked the car door and on foot followed his target who was now some seventy yards ahead.

When the man took a short road which led to the wood, Paul's heartbeat increased with a surge of adrenalin. A benign fate was giving him another opportunity. The criminal was returning for a second time to the scene of his crime. Paul extracted the gun from the holdall and rammed it into his overcoat pocket.

The man entered the wood unaware that he was being pursued by someone bent on exacting retributive justice on what he deemed to be his day of justification while, for his victim, it would be the day of reckoning.

Fifteen

At the SupaSava store where Sylvester worked the staff were allowed discounts on a number of items. Among these were flowers purchased from a stall near the entrance. Madhu, who had been moved from a check-out counter, was in charge of this stall, and it gave Sylvester an opportunity to chat with her if he bought some flowers or a pot plant. Now and again he brought home flowers for his mother who had resumed making his bed and the carnations were a thank-you for this favour.

It had been a sunny day and he decided on this way home to check whether the panties had yet dropped from the twig and were now completely out of sight. As he neared the wood he could hear birds singing; perhaps they had been fooled by the fine day into thinking spring had arrived; yet, as he got close to the clearing he noticed something that had struck him once or twice before. No birds sang there, as if they knew some evil had happened and were avoiding the place. The thought that possibly at night ghosts met here sent a shiver down his spine and he resolved that, once the panties had disappeared from view, he would never visit the site again. Like the birds, he would avoid it.

He left the footpath and entered the clearing. He looked, and looked again. No sign of the panties. They must have fallen to the ground. With a light heart, as if divine absolution had been granted to a sinner, he went over to the bush to look down on the carpet of leaves below. He kicked at the leaves to see if somehow the panties had become covered by a late fall and while he was kicking a voice behind him said, "Are you looking for something?"

Sylvester spun round to see a man holding a gun, which was pointed at him. Although the man was a stranger, Sylvester was sure he had seen him somewhere. The sudden appearance surprised him, but he wasn't afraid. Maybe it was because in his other hand the man held a bag with the store's name and logo on it, the same symbol that appeared on the paper which wrapped his carnations.

"Have you lost something?" the man asked. He came a step closer and repeated the question, not loudly – but there was an edge of menace in his voice. "Have you lost something?"

"No."

"So you're not looking for a young woman's briefs? Her knickers?"

A terrible dread seized Sylvester; it was so immediate and so strong he almost fainted. He opened his mouth to speak but no words came; his mind had gone blank. A click as the man took the safety catch off the gun sent a wave of terror through Sylvester. "Answer my question or I swear I'll use this."

Sylvester dropped the bunch of carnations and raised his hands above his head. He managed to say, "Are you a cop?" That he might be cornered by a policeman was the only explanation, but how did the man know he was looking for the girl's knickers?

"No, I'm not a cop. Put your hands down, pick up the flowers and turn around."

Sylvester obeyed the instruction.

"Turn right around. I want your back to me."

Gripped by the awful uncertainty that he was about to be executed, Sylvester began trembling violently. He did as he was told and then speech came to his dry mouth. "Please don't shoot me, mister. I can explain everything."

"I'm glad to hear it. You've got a lot of explaining to do. But not here, and not yet." A pause followed a silence broken only by a slight rustling sound. The man spoke again. "Turn to your left."

Sylvester swivelled to his right.

"To the left, you fool!"

Sylvester continued his motion until he was facing the way demanded. As he did so he saw the SupaSava bag had been emptied and was now on the ground and one of the man's overcoat pockets was bulging. He heard the man move over the fallen leaves and towards him and a moment later felt something hard press against his spine.

"Hold those flowers in front of you with both hands... If you try anything, I'll shoot and bust your spine. If you survive, you'll be paralysed for the rest of your rotten life. Get moving."

Unsure where to go, Sylvester stumbled forward. He was pushed past some bushes along a track made by Paul during previous visits. At one point he stopped, uncertain where next to go.

A voice behind him said, "To the left, if you know your left from your right, and don't stop again or I'll let you have it. Think what it would be like to be paralysed from the waist down. Maybe from the waist up too. You wouldn't be able to rape any more white girls."

Sylvester was appalled. "I ain't raped anybody!"

"Shut up! You speak when you're spoken to. Not otherwise. You understand?"

"Yes, sir."

They reached the perimeter of the wood. "Hold it," said the man and he moved a short step forward to look down the road. Traffic seemed fairly heavy. A number of cars were coming from one direction, and most of the vehicles were carrying at least one child.

"Bloody kids coming out of school," said the man. "Step back, and keep those flowers down."

"Where you taking me, sir?"

"Shut up! Another peep from you and it'll be curtains."

A shudder ran through Sylvester's frame. He was at the mercy of a man who was obviously mad. He had no idea how long they waited for the road traffic to abate; it seemed an age, but at last the road was clear, both visibly and audibly. On the other side there were no pedestrians.

The man said, "Move! Fast!"

Holding the flowers with both hands like a broad sword, Sylvester charged across the road. He came to a stop close to a doorway.

"Turn right! Stay still!"

He heard the sound of a key inserted into a lock. A door swung open.

"Inside!"

Sylvester stepped forward into a room which smelled like the zoo at Kingston. The door slammed shut.

"Keep going. Up those stairs."

Sylvester's brain had been clogged by a miasma of fear, but now some light penetrated it. Knickers and rape. The man must think he was responsible for what had happened to the white girl that terrible morning in the wood. Having worked this out, he felt better. The guy wasn't mad, simply misguided. Once he was allowed to speak he would explain everything. He could even name one of the rapists. It went against the grain to snitch on anyone, but it was a case of every man for himself. If the guy went after Jason, that was Jason's problem.

They reached what seemed to have once been a bedroom, judging by a striped red and white mattress on an old iron-frame bed.

Poked forward by the gun held against his back Sylvester was forced against the bed.

"Drop the flowers."

Sylvester let go of the bunch of carnations which fell to the floor where they were kicked under the bed. One broken bloom remained, blood red against a brown floorboard.

"Lie down on your stomach."

"Please, sir. Let me explain. I wasn't..."

"Shut up! You can explain later. Now, lie down."

Once he was face down on the damp, musty-smelling mattress, Sylvester was ordered to put his hands behind his back. Again he obeyed. He had little reasonable alternative, for the man, if not mad, was close to being unhinged.

A slipknot was pulled tight over his wrists and further knots made before he was instructed to lie on his back. He wriggled over. Another piece of cord was used to secure his ankles to the bed-ends so that his legs were splayed open. Lying on his back with his legs wide he felt very vulnerable. As the man raised his gun and pointed it towards the region of the genitalia he began to struggle with all his might.

"I'm tempted to shoot now," the man said calmly, "and leave you to die here, but I'll give you a chance first to explain why you raped my daughter."

"I didn't rape, sir, please sir, believe me, sir."

"But you were looking for her panties, you don't deny that?"

"I don't deny it, sir, but…"

"For your information, I found them. Did you put them back after stealing them as a trophy for the rape?"

"No trophy, sir. I swear it."

"I don't believe you. I'll tell you what happened. After you and your friend desecrated my daughter with your filthy sperm, you went. But you realised you'd left your scarf at the scene and you went back to get it. But my daughter had a torch and she shone it on you and, like the coward you are, you bolted. She was quick enough to see you had a finger missing. Now then, do you deny it was you she shone the torch on?"

"No, sir, I don't deny it, but I can explain."

"Go on then, and it had better be good."

The gun which had dropped slightly was raised to its original target. Sylvester who had previously been tongue-tied now gabbled with feverish speed.

"I go early to work, sir, at the SupaSava store in Norbury, and one morning last month I was going through the wood and I hadn't been to have a pee before I left home and I felt the need. So I went to a spot I'd used before and had a pee. I just finished when I heard steps running. I hid behind a bush. Next thing I knew was seeing a girl being chased by three men. She must have caught her foot in something because she fell over. The men dragged her off the path and near to where I was hiding—"

"Just a minute. Stop there. You saw what was happening and you did nothing to stop it?"

"I was scared, sir. That's the honest truth. There was three of them."

"Go on."

"It all happened very quick, sir. It was soon over—"

"And you did nothing. You are a bloody coward. What are you?"

"A bloody coward, sir."

"And why are you a coward?"

"Don't know, sir."

"You're a coward to tell me a pack of lies and not take responsibility for what you and others did to my daughter."

"No, sir, that's not true."

The gun was waved threateningly. "Are you calling me a liar?"

"No, sir. No way."

"You're sticking to this absurd story about 'having a pee' as you put it?"

"It's true. I'm a Christian, God-fearing boy, sir, and I swear by Almighty God that I spoke the truth."

The man's face had been coldly impassive but a flicker of doubt crossed it. Sylvester was slow to verbalise but quick enough to assess the reactions of others. Years of teasing by his little sister had taught him to judge from facial expression whether it was safe to aim a pretend swipe at her, and he could read his mother's face more easily than he could read a book. Encouraged by the brief show of doubt on the man's face he pressed on.

"I knew one of the men, sir, he was at my school. Older than me and a big bully. He's had one prison sentence that I know of. His name is Jason Marchant."

"Jason Marchant. Is he black?"

"Yes, sir."

"And the other man, or men. What about their names?"

"There was one on look-out, sir. The scarf was his. He may have been white or black, but the man with Jason was white."

"His name?"

"I never seen him before, but he sure didn't come from London. Not from the way he spoke."

The gun was lowered. "Might he have come from the North?"

"He might, sir. Probably did, sir."

"You deserve to be punished for not trying to protect my daughter, but before I decide on what punishment you merit I'm going to check on your story. It'd better be true or you can say goodbye to what passes as your manhood."

"It is true. I've already sworn by Almighty God."

"You'll be in almighty trouble if it's not. For your information the black who raped my daughter is already dead. When I say 'Black Man's Wheels', do you know what I mean?"

"No, sir."

"This fellow stole a BMW belonging to another black. A big mistake. He got himself killed."

"Sir?"

"So I'm going to check whether the dead man's name was Jason Marchant. Your future depends on confirmation."

The man gave a twisted grin which was far more menacing than any smile. Sylvester shivered but whether it was from fear or the cold damp of the tenement he didn't know. It was now almost dark and the man switched on a torch. "I don't want to fall downstairs and break my neck," he explained, " and you'd better pray to your Almighty God that nothing happens to me while I'm away, or else it'll be slow starvation for you."

A key turned in the lock of the door and Sylvester was left to brood on his last remark.

Shandy came home earlier than usual. Almost at once she said, "Where's Kim?"

Paul handed her a note. She read it aloud. "'Have gone to Trevor's for the evening. Be home about ten. Luv. K.'"

For a while they talked about their daughter and decided to wait until the New Year before reaching any firm decision on whether she should continue her education (their wish) or whether she should go out to work (her preference).

Then he suggested eating out at a French restaurant which had recently opened near Herne Hill. On the way there, with him driving her car, he said, "By the way, that fellow who got himself killed for pinching the BMW, what was his name?"

She thought. "Inspector Tapsell didn't give a name. I don't remember a name. The killer was someone called Duprez, I think. Why?"

"Just curious."

The subject was dropped, not to be picked up again. The restaurant food was good and the wine excellent. Con-versation between them flowed more easily than it had for some time. At the end of the meal he turned down her offer to pay. "It's sweet of you, but I still have a bit left," he said. And my pride, he thought.

On the way home Shandy received a call on her mobile. It was from Kimberley. Could she stay on until eleven? Mr Brown, Trevor's father, would run her home. A brief consultation, and an affirmative was given.

Indoors, he poured out two brandies and when these were finished he said, "How about an early night?"

"What about Kim?"

"She's got a key, and I can let her in if she hasn't got it with her."

Quite unexpectedly he saw she was looking at him in a way she hadn't for many months. He risked a grin and a wink.

"You look like a man with something on his mind," she said knowingly.

"I have."

"On your mind?"

"Somewhere."

"And where would that be?"

He winked again.

She laughed. "All right. You're on."

In the bedroom she was amazed by the ferocity of his love-making.

"Hey, what's got into you?" she protested with an uncertain smile.

He didn't reply but continued kissing her all over her body. When finally their limbs entwined their climaxes were almost simultaneous.

He rolled off her and, both exhausted by the passionate encounter they lay in each other's arms. She was first to speak. "That was something," she said.

"It was," he agreed.

"I could easily go to sleep now," she said at length.

"You do that. I'm not quite ready yet. Think I'll get up and wait for Kimmy."

"Are you sure?"

"Perfectly." After kissing her lips lightly he slid off the bed and began to dress. By the time he was ready to go downstairs she was breathing deeply and evenly in a contented sleep.

She came awake with a start at the sound of a door banging. The noise came from the direction of Kimberley's bedroom. She glanced at a bedside clock. It showed the time at just before ten, so why was Kim home when she'd phoned to ask if it was all right to come home later? Shandy decided to investigate.

She found her daughter leafing through a fashion magazine.

"You're back early, dear."

"Oh, hello Mum. They are such a *boring* family."

"Boring? Is Trevor a bore?"

"He's the most boring of the lot. Mrs Brown's a cow, Mr Brown's a bore, and so is Trev's sister."

"I'm sorry to hear that."

"Don't be. I was bored out of my skull and decided to come home."

"Is Dad downstairs?"

"Isn't he with you?"

"No."

"Well, he's not downstairs."

"Where can he be?" said Shandy more to herself than to her daughter.

"Search me. Gone out for a walk maybe."

"What? At this time of night?"

"He does go out a lot these days. He's been a bit peculiar ever since – you know what."

Shandy made no comment and Kimberley said, "Do you think I'd make it as a fashion model? I think I'd like that. I could take a college course."

"Perhaps, but let's talk about it in the morning, dear, when your father is here."

Shandy left the room. Instinct, intuition or a sixth sense told her that something was terribly wrong and she didn't know how to cope with the feeling.

Sixteen

Cold and fearful, Sylvester listened intently to hear whether his tormentor had left the premises or was playing a cruel cat-and-mouse game. He heard the outside door shutting; he was now alone and helpless in a strange place. He ached for the warmth and security of his home and vowed that if ever he returned there again he'd let little Coral bait him as much as she wished. He'd even encourage her.

He thought of his mother and wondered what she would do if she were trapped in similar circumstances. The answer was immediate: she would pray to the good Lord for deliverance from evil. Silently, but with lips moving, he recited the Lord's Prayer. What would his father do? Answer: the same as his mother but with a lesser display of emotional conviction.

He then formulated a prayer of his own, beseeching God to give him the strength to endure whatever terrors lay ahead. His prayer ended with the request that God give him guidance what to do. Once more the answer came instantly: Get yourself free, young man.

Underneath his short topcoat and attached to his trouser belt was a flick-knife, or switchblade as it was sometimes called. If he could reach it and press a button a sharp blade would spring out which maybe he could manipulate to cut the cord tying his wrists. To get hold of the knife he would first need to sit up and lean forward as far as possible.

His legs tied by the ankles to the bed-ends provided leverage, his stomach muscles were strong and firm, and at the third attempt he was sitting upright on the mattress. He had to free the tail of his topcoat before he could reach to fumble for the knife. By straining hard against the binding cord which cut into his flesh he could just get his fingertips to the knife handle, but the knife was on the right side of the belt, which meant his left hand was the nearer one to it – and his left hand had no forefinger. He cursed the day when he and a friend, both aged twelve, thought they would chop up sticks for firewood, thereby earning a little extra pocket money. While Sylvester held a piece of wood his friend brought down an axe on to it, but a knot in the wood sent the axe-blade off course and neatly sliced off Sylvester's finger. An attempt to sew it back had proved fruitless and the last he saw of it was when it was dropped in a litter bag to be taken to the rubbish dump.

But ruing the day, and cursing himself and his erstwhile friend for their juvenile stupidity, wouldn't set him free. After a short rest, he resumed the struggle. At last, and with painful burns scored into his wrists, he managed to stretch the cord enough to enable him to pull out the knife by using his thumb and two middle fingers. With his thumb he pressed the button and the blade shot out. It was now a matter of manoeuvring the knife to sever the cord. This was more difficult than he had anticipated, as the knife kept slipping and he had to take care not to cut himself. To lose another finger would be God's judgement for his ineptitude.

He had no idea of time lapse – it seemed many hours – but eventually the cord was sufficiently cut to allow him to break loose. He quickly cut the binding from his ankles and now free he slid off the bed and on to his knees beside it. With his eyes closed he thanked the Almighty for having listened to his plea and mercifully given him strength and encouragement.

He was still on his knees when he heard a noise from downstairs. His captor had returned. He leapt to his feet. There wasn't time to get to the casement window, open it and jump, and anyway the drop might be too far.

As he dithered uncertainly he heard footsteps slowly coming up the stairs, each tread a little bit louder than the last as if he, the captive, was intended to hear and to fear.

If that was his captor's intention it had the opposite effect. In spite of being called a coward by the man, Sylvester didn't lack courage. At school he had stood up to bullies and after one particularly bruising fight had been left alone. It was as a result of that fight that he had bought the flick-knife, not for aggressive purposes but as a defence. His mother, who knew of the fight, knew also of the knife but had never commented on it; his father had simply said, 'Well done, son'.

His knife was his friend and his friend was with him now in his hour of need.

After good sex, Paul always felt much more at peace with the world. Good sex blunted the edge of his naturally self-assertive, readily aggressive personality. For him, good sex was the best tranquilliser. But it had to be good sex, not average sex, routine sex, or 'OK-if-that's-what-you-want sex'. Good sex was like a memorably tasty meal, it left one with a feeling of replete satisfaction; it was even better than the sense of bursting pride from pulling off an excellent business deal. The best feel-good factor came from good sex. Good sex was the most effective panacea for every psychological sickness, and that evening with Shandy had provided very good sex indeed.

However, like the scenic impact of a breathtaking sunset spread-eagled across the western sky, the effect of good sex was of limited duration, but as he hurried back to the disused shop where his captive was held he was still in its incandescent afterglow.

A desire for vengeance had been dissipated; he now had little inclination to put his victim on the rack.

The fellow's story was credible and probably he had been nothing more than a hidden, unwilling spectator of a rape. He should, of course, have intervened to stop the evil assault – in similar circumstances he, Paul, would have fought off the assailants – but perhaps it was expecting too much of an ignorant young black to behave like an intelligent, responsible white man; and it would have been a three-against-one contest.

Within a quarter of an hour Paul had reached his destination. He was about to enter the premises when he was stopped by a thought which had forced its way into his one-track mind. It was the blindingly obvious fact that his victim would be the prime witness at any rape trial. He was in a position to make a positive identification of two, if not all three, of the men. He could identify the body of the car thief now presumably in a morgue awaiting a formal inquest. If he were to be punished now he might be unwilling to testify at a later date against the two men, still alive, if they were caught.

He opened the front door and, after switching on his torch, stepped inside. He climbed the stairs slowly, not to intimidate, but because he was deep in thought. The fellow would be set free, but only after it had been made clear to him that this act of extreme clemency was dependent upon him keeping his mouth shut about his captivity and his willingness to testify against the rapists at any court trial. If he failed to honour either of these obligations, he would be hunted down and would have to pay the ultimate price – a painful lingering death at Paul's hands.

Certain that this was the right course to take, Paul inserted the key in the lock of the upstairs bedroom. Everything then happened at once. Before the torch was knocked from his grip Paul glimpsed a flash of bright steel in its beam. His reaction was so swift that the knife did nothing more than rip his coat sleeve. In the split second before the torch clattered on to the bare floorboards, Paul had swung round and aimed a blow at his unseen attacker. A moment later the two men were locked in a deadly struggle for supremacy.

As his captor stepped through the doorway Sylvester sprang forward. With his left hand he aimed a blow at the torch and caught Paul on the wrist, causing him to drop the torch; with his right hand, which held the knife, he was about to lunge towards the man's heart, but in the last microsecond pulled the blow so that it harmlessly tore at an overcoat sleeve. It was not the time or place to analyse why he had changed direction; but it was caused by something inside him taking control to prevent an attempted murder.

The torch came to rest against the skirting board and its light threw a segment of the room into relief. In the struggle both men fell to the floor. As they rolled into the lighted area and came to a stop Sylvester managed to be on top. But Paul had a vice-like grip on the wrist of the knife-wielding hand. A searing pain ran up Sylvester's arm but it was nothing to the agony of the wrist lacerated by the prolonged effort to free himself. As Paul's grip tightened even more Sylvester couldn't prevent a scream escaping. The sudden unexpected noise caused Paul to try to shift from under the other man and to lift his head. At the same moment that his head came up, Sylvester, no longer able to hold the knife, pushed it away form his hand. It dropped, point downwards, directly into the side of Paul's neck piercing the carotid artery.

It was doubtful whether Paul would have survived even if paramedics had been available but what made death certain was his attempt to pull out the knife just as Sylvester tried to do likewise. Their uncoordinated joint effort slit the artery and blood gushed out in spurts driven by the pulsations of his heart. Before he died, his voice clogged with blood, Paul whispered, "No need for that. I wasn't going to harm you."

His heart stopped beating and the blood flow became a trickle. It had begun to dry up before Sylvester, deeply shocked by the catastrophic outcome of the fight, hauled himself off the dead body. In half-light thrown by the torch he saw a huge dark stain of blood on his coat. His fingers were sticky with blood. He let out a terrible cry which might have come for a mortally wounded animal, got to his feet and rushed from the room, leaving knife and torch behind. He stumbled down the stairs and into the street, and he began running as fast as he could mindless of direction.

*   *   *

"John."

"Shandy."

"I know it's far too late to be calling you."

"Not a bit. I'm hardly ever in bed before one a.m. and it's not yet midnight."

"Even so, it's far too late."

"It's never too late, or too early, for you to call me. Is something bothering you?"

"It's Paul. He's disappeared. This may sound crazy, coming from me, but I'm sure he's in some sort of trouble. I'm worried stiff. I just had to speak to someone. To speak to you. He's only been gone for an hour – an hour and a half at most – but we had a good evening together, one of the best for ages. I went to bed and dozed off. I woke up with Kim coming home and she told me he wasn't around. She's gone to bed and I've been lying awake. I know it's ridiculous, but it's not like Paul to go out late like this. I'm sure something is wrong, badly wrong, and I don't know what to do. I feel awful about ringing you up..."

"Don't. The traffic should be fairly light at this time of night. I'll be with you in half an hour or so."

"I don't want to—"

"Shandy, it's not what you want; I want to come over."

"But I might be being stupid. Paul might come back before you get here and then—"

"Then I'll go back, glad everything is all right."

"But—"

"No 'buts', please. I'm on my way. I'll see you anon – if not sooner. Bye."

When he arrived she opened the front door before he had a chance to ring the bell. "I don't want Kim to be woken up," she whispered. "Come in."

In a voice lowered to match hers, he said, "Paul not home yet?"

She shook her head. Once inside the sitting room, she related all that had occurred since she and Samson had been in touch, including a passing reference to their love-making which had immediately preceded his disappearance – "so there's no dissatisfaction on that score," she added – and concluded with, "I can't think where he might have gone."

"Could he have gone to where Kimberley was raped?"

"At this time of night?"

"You suspect he's been there more often than he's admitted."

"Not at this time of night."

"Is it far?"

"It's about three quarters of the way through a small wood which begins at the other end of this road."

He stood up. "Let's go then."

Startled by the suggestion she could only say, "What? Now?"

"You've got a torch?"

"Yes."

"It's the only place I can think he may be. So, let's go."

There was enough street lighting until they reached the wood where he switched on the torch. She took his arm, and despite her apprehensions, managed to joke, "If the neighbours see us, half might say, 'We always knew she was a bad lot.'"

"And what would the other half say?"

"They'd say 'Good for her!'"

"It's more likely they'd say 'Lucky him'."

She gave his arm a little squeeze and they walked in silence until she said, "It's here."

"Well, he isn't." he replied as they entered the clearing and he flashed a beam of light around.

"Nothing is here except that plastic bag." He went across and looked down at the bag. "It hasn't been here long. It hasn't been flattened by the elements, and it still has small air pockets." He stooped and picked up the bag. "There's something inside." He handed her the torch. "Here. Hold this. I'll see what it is."

He took out what appeared to be a slightly curved six-inch piece of black wood and with finger and thumb opened up a shining steel blade. "It's an old-fashioned cut-throat razor. Have you seen it before?"

"I've never seen one before."

"So it isn't Paul's?"

"No. He uses an ordinary razor. A safety razor."

"There's something else." From the bag he pulled out a screwed up paper bag. He opened it carefully and she shone the torch on a piece of biscuit and the remains of a slice of Stilton cheese.

He heard her indrawn breath. "Don't tell me you recognise this," he said.

"I don't, but it's Paul's favourite snack. Stilton, biscuits and a tomato or two. And he's very keen not to leave litter around. It's typical of him to put unused food in the bag it came in, and put that inside a larger bag to be disposed of later."

Samson snapped the razor shut. "We shouldn't leave this lying around," he said putting it back into the plastic bag. "SupaSava store." He turned to Shandy, "Do you know where that is?"

"There are quite a few south of the river. I think Norbury is the nearest."

He walked round the clearing, flashing the torch up and down and all around.

Shandy kept close to him. "I wouldn't care to be here on my own. It's a spooky place."

"I can't see anything else unusual," he remarked. "We'll go back and I'll come again when it's daylight."

"You must stay the night."

A polite argument followed which ended with him accepting her offer of a bed in the spare room.

"Assuming the bag was Paul's, and it didn't belong to someone with the same taste in occasional snacks, how do you account for the razor and the bag being left in the clearing?" she asked.

"I can't, but I'd guess Paul met someone there by arrange-ment or chance and they left together. Nor can I explain the razor – except possibly that he brought it along as some sort of pro-tection, which seems unlikely, or that there were other things in the bag which he took with him; though it beats me why he should leave the bag behind."

Speculation continued for another hour before both went to their separate beds.

Samson, fascinated by the dimension of Time which itself had many lesser dimensions, had sometime wondered why human beings appeared to be genetically programmed so that the amount of sleep needed at each age seemed, on average, to resemble a smooth downward curve on a graph. In other words, at the top of the graph a baby might need, say, eighteen hours sleep per day; but a man or woman of seventy-plus could get by on four or five. He himself, still some way from seventy, was therefore a blip in the graph and he needed only four.

He awoke early in the morning, got up, dressed and went on tip-toe downstairs. Shandy, also fully dressed, came out of the kitchen. "Coffee?" she enquired.

"Later. I'd like to get out now before many people are about. Paul didn't come back during the night?"

"No."

They walked together to the clearing. The first light of a cold, grey day was filtering through the treetops when they arrived. Samson, torch in hand, walked slowly round the perimeter of the clearing. He completed two circuits before returning to a point where he stopped and said, "It looks as though a rough path may start here. Let's see if I'm right, and where it leads."

He had gone about fifty metres when he paused, stopped and picked up something from the ground. It was the head of a red carnation which had been detached from its stem. Passing it to Shandy he said, "It's fresh. Can't have been here very long."

"I don't know. Carnations stay fresh quite a long while."

"Nevertheless, a very odd thing to find here. Someone has obviously been this way recently and lost either a buttonhole or a bloom from a bunch of carnations. Does the SupaSava chain sell flowers?"

She thought for a moment, and then, "I think they all do. The ones I've seen have a flower stall near the entrance, close to the tobacco kiosk."

It was Samson's turn to be thoughtful. "Interesting," he said. "It's a very long shot, but suppose Paul met someone in the clearing, or even at a SupaSava when he bought his lunch, and the person he met had a bunch of flowers, and both decided to come through this part of the wood although there is no clearly defined track. Where would they be going?"

"I've no idea."

"Neither have I, but we'll carry on until either the track peters out or we arrive at habitation."

Within five minutes they had reached the road where the disused pet shop was located. There was nobody in sight and after a solitary car had passed by they crossed the road. None of the other shops in the shabby parade was yet open. Samson read the estate agent's board, took out a notebook and wrote down a telephone number. "Estate agents are often useful sources of local knowledge," he explained.

She smiled. "I was aware of that."

He was instantly apologetic. "I'm sorry. I was seeing you as Paul's wife, not as the principal of Samson Associates, purveyors of private investigations to the gentry."

"You are forgiven."

He peered at a stain on the upright of a door frame which showed up reddish-brown against faded white paint. "What do you make of that?" he asked.

She looked closely. "It could be a smear of paint or…"

Her voice faded away as a terrible thought crossed her mind.

He finished the sentence for her. "Or something more sinister." Without much hope of a result he pushed at the door latch. To the surprise of both, the door swung open.

He didn't mince words. "We both know the mark could be a bloodstain. It could have been made by someone who left the premises in such a hurry that he forgot to lock the door… or possibly he didn't have the key. I'm going inside."

"I'm coming with you."

"As you wish," he replied in a voice which conveyed that her entry would be by her choice, not his.

They covered the downstairs area. Samson made the only comment. "It stinks," he said. "I'll look upstairs."

On opening the door of a bedroom, he saw Paul's body on the floor with blood dried from a gash in his neck and the blood-stained blade of a knife lying against his throat. Before he could

172

prevent her, Shandy was standing beside him, white-faced, with her eyelids pinned back by shock. She swayed on her feet and thinking she was about to faint he put his arm round her as a support.

"I'll be all right," she murmured.

"You go downstairs," he said. "I'll join you in a minute."

"I can cope," she replied.

"I would sooner you waited downstairs."

"What are you going to do?"

"Have a quick look around. See what there is here besides that." He indicated a broken carnation near the bed. "And then I shall phone the police."

"I want to stay."

"Why?"

"If the killer gets caught and is put on trial we don't want a smart defence lawyer questioning your uncorroborated evidence. Alleging, for instance, that you moved the body or in some way altered the room."

They both knew that a personable barrister with a glib tongue could sow the seeds of doubt in the minds of jurors and so, grudgingly and yet with admiration for cool assessment in a time of extreme stress, he said, "All right, but stay here by the door."

Spotting a bunch of carnations wrapped in paper under the bed, he bent down and gently pulled it out. "SupaSava," he read aloud before replacing the flowers. He turned to Shandy. "You didn't see me touch that?"

"You didn't. I would swear on oath that you touched nothing."

Standing upright once more he looked down at a piece of twisted cord which lay on top of the striped mattress and at a separate length of cord tied to railings at the bed-end. He made no comment but went across the room where a torch was lying on the floor. Taking a handkerchief from his pocket he carefully wrapped it round his right hand so that no fingerprints would be left after picking it up, then he carried it across to Shandy who, ashen-faced, stood in the doorway, her eyes following all his movements closely to avoid staring at the corpse.

173

"Do you recognise this?" he asked.

"It looks like the spare we kept at home but I couldn't be absolutely sure."

"The battery is nearly dead but there's a bit of life in it. I'd guess it's been on for some time."

He took the torch back to where it had been lying and placed it on the floor in exactly the same position as it had been before.

Then he went to Paul's body and knelt beside it, the handkerchief still around his hand which he ran across the pockets of the dead man's overcoat. He frowned as he pressed against something hard and then, moving very slowly and taking care not to disturb the pocket's outline more than necessary, he felt inside and pulled up the butt of a black automatic gun. Turning to Shandy whose gaze was riveted on his actions he said, "It looks like a Smith and Wesson nine-millimetre. It's safety catch is in the off position; it's ready for use. Did you know about this?"

Dumbfounded, she shook her head in an emphatic negative.

Again using infinite care he pushed the gun back into the pocket before standing up. "You haven't seen any of that," he said, this time as a statement, not a question. After a quick final survey of the room he went to her. "Let's go."

In the street outside the building he used his mobile phone to call a taxi to take her home before he rang up the police. "I'll wait for them here and join you as soon as I can."

"I'm not looking forward to breaking the bad news to Kim."

"Do nothing until I'm with you, and then let me handle it."

"Will you? Do the talking, I mean. I'll be there too but in the background until she needs me."

"Of course I'll do the talking." He paused. "I think you've been fantastic," he added.

The ghost of a smile passed her face. "Thanks. Coming from you that is quite a compliment."

Seventeen

Sylvester ran, and ran, and ran. He got a second, a third and a fourth wind. But he couldn't run away from the image in his mind of blood spurting from the dying man's neck and the look of uncomprehending hurt in his eyes as he uttered his last words.

Sheer panic fuelled his legs but when the adrenalin dried up and when his thigh and calf muscles could no longer take the strain, he slowed to a trot before coming to a stop, panting like an old steam engine. He had come to a halt by North Dulwich railway station.

From here he staggered a short distance to some school buildings close to which was a playing field with goalposts and a few benches for spectators. He slumped down on to a bench and temporarily banishing the dreadful memory from his mind tried to work out what he should do next. Home was the place where he needed to be, but he couldn't face his mother and say, 'Mom, I've just killed a man.'

At length he decided to go home and to leave again after he had changed his clothes, without disturbing his sleeping family. The next problem was to orientate himself. He knew Dulwich was east of Herne Hill which was east of Streatham, and so he needed to go west.

It was a clear, cold, frosty night. As he looked heavenwards at the stars, he prayed to the Lord for guidance. 'Seek and ye shall find' was the answer he received so he decided to go in the direction he was facing. He would keep the pattern of stars as a checkpoint to prevent himself going round in a circle. Having rested he felt able to begin the journey and he made a silent sacred pledge that if the Lord saw fit to take him home he would serve the Lord faithfully for the rest of his life.

An hour later he arrived at the semi-detached three-bedroom house, which had a narrow passage running down one side next to an integral garage. Sylvester's bedroom was over the garage but, as the garage's length extended beyond the length of his bedroom, there was a ledge on its roof which, if he mounted could provide access through a window to his room. It wouldn't be the first time he had used this method of entry, although on most previous occasions he had taken a step ladder from the garage to help him up. Tonight, however, he couldn't risk the sound of a squeaky garage door awakening his parents. He was obliged to use a rainwater butt for a foothold, and a short length of drainpipe for the final assault on the garage roof.

He was able to reach a latch to open a window, which he climbed through. For a few moments he stood still, listening intently for any noise that would indicate he had woken someone. Satisfied his entry had not aroused anybody, he closed the part-open bedroom door and switched on the light. He now moved quickly, divesting himself of his bloodstained coat and changing from his working clothes into the suit worn only for church on Sunday. From a cupboard he took a large leather bag which he packed with a change of clothing and, being no lover of winter, he included a thick woollen crew-neck sweater. He decided to keep on the black laced shoes which he wore to work, but he put in a pair of comfortable trainers. Having packed the bag almost to bursting point, he zipped it up and went to a drawer by the bed where he kept the key to a metal box containing cash saved and a Post Office deposit-account book. From the box, hidden behind a pile of magazines and paperbacks, he removed all of his worldly assets, £125 in cash and £550 on deposit at a meagre rate of interest.

Now ready to leave he switched off the light. It was difficult to descend from the garage roof hampered by the bag and the stained coat but he managed it and, on firm ground once more, he hurried away. It was as he gave a backward glance, a final look at the home he had known all his life, that he realised he hadn't reopened his bedroom door and, a second or two later, remembered that he had left his passport behind. This document of identification had been acquired the previous year when Josiah Manley had taken his family on holiday to Jamaica for a fortnight.

During passages of connective lucid thought since the death of his captor, Sylvester had selected Jamaica as the best place to flee to and hide. He had enjoyed his stay there and had met distant relatives who might be willing to provide shelter until he could plan a future. This escape route was impossible without a passport. He suddenly felt overwhelmingly tired. His steps faltered as he wondered where to go now. He began swaying from side to side like a drunk as a heavy cloud of fatigue pressed down on his eyelids. He desperately needed to lie down and rest, and at that point in the night even the gutter looked attractive; he could use a kerbstone as a pillow.

The wood was now only five minutes away but he would sooner die than ever go there again. It was a wicked place, haunted by evil spirits. And then – it may have been his rest in the school recreation ground at Dulwich which prompted the idea – he thought of the nearby recreation ground, where he and friends would meet for games of football. At a corner of the field was an old shed where worn-out equipment and other lumber was stored. The lock on its door had been broken some weeks before and hadn't been repaired. There was talk of demolishing the shed and taking its contents to a rubbish tip. It would be the ideal place for two or three hours' sleep, and he could also leave the heavily stained coat there concealed among other junk.

With a supreme effort he dragged his unwilling limbs there, opened the door and fell down to the floor. He was instantly asleep.

*　　　*　　　*

Recovered from his operation, Samson began to have misgivings about his retirement. He was a worker, and a life filled with leisure-time activities had never appealed to him except in those moments, usually when downcast, when he had flirted with notions of ocean cruises and a cottage near a harbour in a small fishing village. However, in his opinion self-doubt was an emotion to be avoided lest, like a mouse with a chunk of cheese, it nibbled away at one's confidence and a proper sense of self-esteem. And so, when he found himself precipitated back into the lifestyle he favoured most he was not displeased.

Even though he had not met DI Tapsell, he found that his reputation had survived as someone who in the past had been of help to the police. After reporting briefly on the circumstances which had brought him to the disused premises, and promising later to go to the police station to make a more detailed statement, he returned to Shandy's home, prepared to break the tragic news to Kimberley of her father's death.

He had no relish for such a task. Extreme care would need to be taken not to send her over the edge into a breakdown. He certainly would gloss over the bloody details of death and might even lie and say the cause of death was unknown and was probably a heart attack. It was a mystery why Paul should have been in a deserted premises, but the police had been notified and until there had been a coroner's inquest it was best not to speculate. The worst scenario would be if Kimberley wrongly attributed his death, from whatever cause, to herself and she became consumed with a sense of guilt.

As it happened, his fears on behalf of Kimberley proved to be groundless. When he arrived at her home he was amazed to find the daughter comforting the mother. Apparently when pressed by Kimberley for an explanation for Paul's absence Shandy's ability to cope had been tested beyond endurance and she had burst into tears and told Kimberley everything sparing her only the more grisly aspects of the death. Red-eyed, she gave Samson a watery smile before telling him of the events prior to his arrival.

"Kim has been wonderful," she said in conclusion.

"It's nothing more than you deserve, Mum. You've been wonderful to me."

"I really ought to get going soon," Shandy went on. "I'm late already. I was wondering if..."

"Wonder no more," Samson chipped in. "You won't be going to the office today. I'll take over."

"I'd be ever so grateful. Just for today."

"Think nothing of it. I'm going to the nick first to make a statement – incidentally you'll be asked for a statement too – and then I'll go back to town. I think you should take the rest of the week off. I shall be only too happy to be back at my old desk for a day or three. But I shall also try to discover why Paul went to an empty disused shop and who was with him."

Shandy and Kimberley exchanged a quick look and both began speaking at the same moment. They broke off, and Kimberley said, "You tell him what we think."

"Kim and I have been talking about it," Shandy began, "I know we haven't thought it through but it seems likely—"

"Very likely," Kimberley interrupted.

"Very likely that Paul cornered one of the men he was after and there was a fight which he lost."

She paused, waiting for Samson's reaction.

"The same thought crossed my mind," he said, "but we must be careful not to prejudge the issue."

"Why not?" Kimberley asked. "Why shouldn't we have opinions?"

He knew it was not the time to argue about the difference between a prejudgement and an opinion. The strain of the situation was showing on both faces awaiting his comment, and so he simply said, "You may well be right, but I must get going. I'll be in touch."

Minutes later he was on his way.

From the police station he went straight to the estate agent's where Jim Cutler worked. After introducing himself as a private investigator acting on behalf of the widow of a man found dead at the premises advertised for sale by Cutler's firm he began on a series of questions. He learned that the police had been in touch with Cutler and had asked him to call at the station later in the day. It seemed that Cutler had said he was ignorant of who the dead man might be and that anyway he had no business to be on the premises. However, under Samson's relentless questioning he began to crack and the truth emerged. By turns nervously assertive and resentfully compliant he told how he had been duped by a man who had given the name of Jones into thinking he was a *bona fide* client. The man had spun a story about wishing to set up an enterprise with a woman friend in an area far away from his wife and had needed the keys so that he could show his friend the place. It was, of course, most irregular to accede to such a request but the prospective client had been very plausible and the premises were difficult to sell. The property had been on the market many months.

"How much did he leave as a deposit?" Samson asked.

"Er, four hundred pounds."

"Is that all? That's less than one per cent of the asking price. I take it you have evidence of this. The widow will require that."

Cutler shifted in his seat. "It was an informal arrangement. There's nothing in writing."

"In other words you were paid more. How much more? Three thousand? Four thousand? I warn you, Mr Cutler, you are swimming in dangerous waters. The widow won't be pleased with your account, nor will the police be, or whoever runs this firm."

Cutler was visibly rattled. "All right. He gave me six hundred."

"And the rest."

"It was six hundred, I swear. Two hundred was for me for accommodating him." Cutler pulled open a drawer in his desk and took out an envelope which he slapped in front of Samson. "Here it is. Six hundred in fifties. You can count it."

"Hand it to the police," said Samson, sternly contemptuous. "I don't accept bribes."

"For Christ's sake! It isn't a bribe!"

"In that case," said Samson, "I'll take it and give it to the widow, and I'll give you a receipt for the money."

"The police don't have to know, do they? I mean, what's passed between you and me is confidential, isn't it?"

Before answering the questions Samson counted out six hundred pounds, put the money in his wallet, tore a page out of a notebook which he always carried, and scribbled out a receipt.

"Here you are. I think you should tell the police everything you've told me. Come clean. Apologise for misleading them in the first place. Say you didn't want to be involved but on reconsideration decided to tell the truth. They won't be angry. It'll tie up one loose end, so far as they're concerned. They'll almost certainly want you to identify the body to make absolutely sure that the dead man is your Mr Jones."

Cutler was dismayed. "Must I? Tell them, I mean."

"If you don't, I shall. It would be better coming from you, don't you think?"

"I suppose so. I hope none of this gets back to my boss, if you know what I mean."

Samson stood up. "That's your problem. Now I have other things to do. Goodbye, Mr Cutler."

He was glad that the crew of S.S. Samson Associates seemed pleased to have their Old Man back at the helm; he had always prided himself on running a happy ship. Not that Shandy had been unpopular; it was the unpredictable absences during her short tenure which led to uncertainties that, if not checked, would develop into dissatisfaction. No employee who needs to consult number one before giving advice to a client likes to find there is no number one, only a far less experienced number two.

When Samson went out either on casework or for a private reason he invariably first made sure that, barring the unforeseen, his staff were capable of managing a workload without supervision, and that at least one person, usually Georgia, knew when to expect him to return. To date, on account of her own domestic difficulties Shandy had not been able to fulfil these requirements adequately.

Georgia and Julian were in the outer office as he was about to leave on the day following Paul's death. "I shall be out for about three hours," he said to Georgia, "If anyone wants me personally, take their number and say I'll call them back. Everything all right?"

"Fine, thanks. Mr Samson."

"And you, Julian? No urgent problems?"

"I'm fine too."

"How's the ancestral line of Sir Malcolm Graham going?"

"Very well."

"And Jasper Peddle?"

"I've come across a murky bar sinister there."

"Illegitimacy runs in all the best families."

"In Victorian times the Peddles were great patrons of opera. Do you like opera, Mr Samson?"

"I like some arias very much but I'm not an opera buff although there is one I should like to see – now what's it called? – ah, I remember, *Samson and Delilah* by some French composer."

With that, and eyes a-twinkle, Samson made his exit leaving a stunned silence behind him.

Julian spoke. "Did you tell him?"

"No way. Honest."

"Are you sure you didn't say something?"

"You calling me a liar, darling?"

"No, of course not. It must be a coincidence."

"Don't count on that. The Old Man is very smart. Anyway, it doesn't matter. Now run along or my lust will get the better of me and I'll give you a smacker you'll never forget."

"That really would be a fate worse than death," Julian retorted before scampering back to his room.

It had not been possible to deduce from the paper wrapping on the carnations from which SupaSava store the flowers had been purchased. Samson intended to visit all stores in the chain within an eight-mile radius of the woodland in the hope that he might find a salesperson who could give him a clue to the identity of the buyer of the carnations who, in Samson's opinion, was almost certainly not Paul. The store at Norbury was the nearest to the wood and as he drove there Samson tried to estimate the date and time of purchase. As it was now Thursday, 7th December, and Paul's body had been discovered on the morning of Wednesday, it was fairly safe to assume the flowers had been bought on Tuesday. The actual time of the sale was impossible to guess but, on the basis that a perishable commodity is likely to be acquired later rather than earlier, particularly if it is a gift for a girlfriend or for the decoration of home, Samson thought Tuesday afternoon was the most likely time. He realised that his mission had little chance of success, but it was an avenue of inquiry which had to be explored.

An Indian girl wearing the name badge 'Madhu' was serving a customer when he entered the store at Norbury. As soon as she was free he stepped forward to admire some bunches of carnations. "Do you sell many of these?" he asked.

"They are popular, yes."

"The red ones look nice."

"They are nice, yes."

"I'd like a dozen, please." While Madhu selected and wrapped the flowers Samson engaged her in trivialities searching for an opening which would enable him to ask questions vital to his enquiries, but the door of opportunity remained closed, and so he had no alternative but to lean against it with his considerable weight.

He paid for the flowers and said, "I wonder if you could help me. I need to know if you can remember selling a dozen red carnations on Tuesday, probably during the afternoon?" As soon as he had spoken he knew that she would not be co-operative.

"Why do you want to know?" she asked suspiciously. "Do you represent management?"

"No, I don't." He produced his card and gave it to her. As she read it, he went on, "I've been instructed by a woman whose husband has been found dead and I'm looking for someone who may have witnessed the death and can therefore help in enquiries which I and the police must make."

Her quick indrawn breath and a nervous tic by her left eye told him that his journey had not been wasted.

"Excuse me," she said, moving away.

"Certainly, but I should like to see your supervisor or the manager of this store. Could you take me to either?"

She hesitated, plainly disconcerted by the request.

"It is a popular line, as I have already said. There were four or five sales of carnations that afternoon. Other flowers too. Roses are very popular. I can't remember them all."

"I don't expect you to," he replied smoothly. "But there is one you do remember. Perhaps it wasn't so much a sale as a gift. That is no concern of mine. I've told you I'm not from management. I'm not trying to entrap you. But if you won't tell me, I shall have to go to management."

She gave an anguished look as another customer picked up a bunch of freesias. "I can't talk here," she said with a note of desperation in her voice.

"Do you get a break?"

"I'm due for one in half an hour, but it's a short one and I can't leave the building."

"I notice there's a coffee shop here. Can you meet me there in half an hour?"

The man who had picked up the freesias was impatient. "Are you serving, miss?"

"Yes," she said to him and turning her head said yes to Samson.

He queued for a cup of coffee and went to sit at a yellow formica-topped table where he could watch shoppers coming and going. Christmas decorations were strung across the ceiling beneath which at almost every table were either pensioners passing the time until Time took their mortality, or trolley-laden housewives exchanging gossip while their small children, the future generation in the eternally repetitive cycle of life, buzzed noisily around. Before he became bored with the sameness of a constantly changing scene, Madhu arrived. She hadn't joined the queue; she didn't want anything to drink. She came to the point straight away.

"I may know this person you wish to see as a witness," she said, "but before we go any further I need to know that he is not in trouble."

"I hope he isn't, but I can't make any promises, and that is what the police will say if and when they come here."

"This is very difficult for me."

"I understand that. The best I can do is to treat anything you might tell as confidential for as long as I can."

"I would like to know more. What have carnations purchased here got to do with anyone who may have witnessed a death?"

"Possibly nothing. I am as much in the dark as you. But if you have a name or an identity, and you let me have it, I can find out whether the person named was a witness."

Speaking with her eyes lowered she said, "It is very difficult for me. The man works here and very recently we have become friendly. He wanted flowers to take home to his mother and I let him have some. It was no big deal. Employees are allowed to buy certain things at reduced prices anyway. What worries me is" – she raised her eyes to meet his – "he hasn't been back to work since we said goodbye at about three on Tuesday afternoon."

"Has he rung in to say he is off sick?"

"No. He was away with flu, but that cleared up. There has been no communication from him. I asked the supervisor when I came in this morning."

"Nothing from his family?"

She shook her head. "Not so far as I know."

"Do you know his home address?"

"Not the exact address, but I can get it."

"Can you get it for me while I wait?"

"I hope I am doing the right thing."

"You are. If he has done nothing wrong he has nothing to fear, and if he is in trouble it won't help to run away; and it is help he may need more than anything."

Once more she avoided looking directly at him and gazed down on the table, but this time he sensed it was more from embarrassment than from concern over allowing flowers to go cheaply or without charge.

"I mentioned that recently we had become friendly," she said. "I must explain there is nothing more than that. Nor could there be. I am already…"

Her hesitation lasted so long that Samson broke the hiatus with, "You are already spoken for?"

"Yes, exactly. Sometimes he seems a little bit lost. Vulnerable. I have heard also that the man in charge of the stores is harsh with him and gives him the worst jobs. I feel sorry for him. You understand?"

"Perfectly. But tell me, does he strike you as a man who would under great provocation become violent?"

"Violent? Not at all. That is not to say he could not stick up for himself if necessary, but violent by nature? No. The opposite, I would say..."

"Thank you for your help. I've nothing more to ask you."

"I hope that in helping you I shall be helping him," she replied, "and now I must get his address for you."

He watched her leave the coffee shop and disappear into the throng of shoppers. Within ten minutes she was back. She handed him a piece of paper on which a name, Sylvester Manley, and an address in Streatham was written.

He realised how out of touch with the area he had become when, in a part he believed to be predominantly white, the door was opened by a woman of obviously Afro-Caribbean descent.

"Is this the home of Sylvester Manley?" he asked.

"This is his home, yes. You must be from the police. Come in, please."

She led the way to a front parlour which was redolent with the fragrance of cooking which had staled from spicy dishes. Every window was tightly shut and the central heating oppressively high. Each shelf, nook and cranny was filled with wood carvings, objects and ornaments, except where there were vases filled with orchids. He was invited to sit on a scuffed leather settee while the woman sat on a nearby cane chair. "You have come about my son, Sylvester?"

Aware that his easy access was due to mistaken identity, Samson decided to take advantage of an unforced error and, until he was sure of his ground, not to mention Paul.

"Yes, I have come about Sylvester."

"You are from the police? I wasn't expecting anyone to come so soon. Have you any news?"

"No news of Sylvester, I'm afraid. I've come to ask some questions. Incidentally, I should point out that although I have frequently worked with the police who might be referred to as public investigators, I am a private investigator. In the present case, both the police's and my aims are identical. We want to find Sylvester."

In saying this Samson felt that, if not strictly accurate at the moment, it would certainly be true once the police had caught up with, and managed to link, a murder inquiry with a missing-person case.

"What are your questions, Mister...er...?"

"Samson. I want details of your son's disappearance. When did he go missing, how long has he been away, where might he have gone, things like that."

"But I have already given the police those details when his father and I went to the police station early this morning."

"This is a double check. My questions might jog your memory about something important."

She looked slightly bewildered by this statement and said, "I must admit, Mr Samson, that I am confused. At the station they didn't seem to show very much interest. They said something about contacting the Salvation Army, but I must be wrong. Anyway, the more people who are trying to find my boy, the better it is. Shall I tell you what we told them?"

"Please do."

"When Sylvester didn't come down for breakfast yesterday morning I thought he must have overslept. They work him very hard at that place. I went to his room to wake him up. The door was closed and this was unusual. When I went into the room I saw at once that his bed had not been slept in and, lying on top of it, was his passport. Luckily his daddy had not yet left for the pharmacy and I called for him to come up. Little Coral came too although I didn't want her to. I didn't want her upset, you see. We went through his wardrobe and some clothes were missing, and a big leather bag. We didn't know what to do. In the end, Mr

Manley said, 'Let's leave it one more night and if he doesn't come home we will report it to the police'. Coral said we should report it at once in case he tried to leave the country. But how could he, without a passport?" She paused as if a thought had suddenly stuck. "I have just realised. Sylvester can be so forgetful, so absent-minded; maybe he got his passport out, meant to take it with him, and then at the last minute he forgot it and left it on his bed."

"Where would he have gone if he'd got his passport?"

"Why, Jamaica, of course. We have folks there and he loves it."

"Is there anywhere in England he might have gone to?"

"Only somewhere round about here. There's nowhere else he knows except we went once to Blackpool which he didn't like."

"Most youngsters like the place. How old was he?"

"Twelve or thirteen. One day he was out on his own and a gang of white boys surrounded him and drove him into a corner. They told him blacks weren't wanted in Blackpool and that the place had got its name on account of a pool, like a swimming pool, where blacks were thrown in and drowned. They said that if he didn't give them all the money he had on him they'd take him to the pool and drown him. When one of them tried to lay hands on him he fought back. I reckon he must have fought like a tiger because he got away and came running back to the boarding house where we were staying."

"How old is he now?"

"Eighteen, coming up nineteen."

"Has he got a violent nature?"

For the first time Mrs Manley threw back her head and gave a full-throated laugh displaying two rows of dazzling white teeth. "Violent! You must be joking, sir. My boy wouldn't hurt a fly. I'm his momma and I know. But –" she held up a finger as if to claim silence from a vociferous listener "– but if driven to it, he can look after himself. He's no coward. He would never look for trouble, and would go out of his way to stay clear of trouble, but if there's no way out of trouble except by using his fists, then his fists he'll use."

"Does he carry a knife?"

The residues of laughter lines disappeared from her face. "I don't know nothing about knives," she said, slipping back into the vernacular of her early years. "Why you want to know that, mister?"

"Idle curiosity, nothing more."

"Them Yardies give us good God-fearin' folk a bad name." With an effort she pulled herself together. "Is that all, Mr Samson. I *am* busy. I've got work to do."

Samson stood up. "I won't detain you any longer. Thank you very much. You've been most helpful."

As she went with him to the front door, Mrs Manley said, "I didn't mean to be rude to you just then, but I'm worried stiff about Sylvester. You'll do your best to find him and bring him home where he belongs?"

"Of course I will. And I understand how worried you must be. I feel sure the police will let you know of any developments."

"The police. Yes." She sounded uncertain despite the 'yes' and after a moment's pause went on, "And you, you'll let me know too?"

As yet she didn't know her son might be a rapist who was probably involved in the death by knifing of the man whose daughter had been raped, and that the dead man had been married to Samson's business partner. Looking two or three moves ahead as if in a game of chess, Samson could foresee a danger of conflict of interest if he became too accommodating to Mrs Manley; but, on the other hand, both he and Shandy would want to be kept *au fait* with any developments on the Manley front. On balance it seemed expedient to maintain, even encourage, mutual contact with the rider that sooner or later he ought to disclose a special interest in the case. After all, if the case should come to court it wouldn't do much for his reputation if he was seen to have been running with the hare and hunting with the hounds.

These pros and cons passed through his mind with lightning speed before he answered her question with, "Yes, I'll let you know of any developments, but I shall need your phone number." He took out his wallet and extracted a card. "This gives my office number if you want to get in touch."

As he was fairly near her home, Samson went to see Shandy. Much had happened since he had responded to her telephone call on the previous evening, and he wanted to bring her up to date with events before returning to the West End. Having left her and Kimberley comforting each other he was dismayed to find that circumstances had changed for the worse. Kimberley was in bed under heavy sedation prescribed by a doctor. She had suddenly cracked and, according to Shandy, "gone half-demented with guilt over her father's death".

"She blames herself for having been raped in the first place," Shandy continued, "and now she blames herself for his obsessive behaviour. She was so distraught I had to call in our GP. He'll come again this evening and if she's no better she'll have to go somewhere she can get profession nursing care. She saw me through my bad patch earlier on; I can't leave her now."

"You stay with her for as long as you need. Don't worry about the office, I can handle that. In fact, I'll be glad to. I'm beginning to think I retired prematurely."

"I'd be very grateful. I should be back next week."

"Take your time. I'm glad I dropped in. I was going to tell you what's developed in the last couple of hours but you won't want to hear that now."

"Yes, I do. Tell me. I can cope again. I can always cope when I have to."

Before he left, Samson outlined details of his meetings with Madhu at the SupaSava store and with Mrs Manley at her home.

That evening, while Mrs Manley was preparing supper the kitchen door opened and Sylvester walked in. "Hello Mom," he said. "I'm back."

Eighteen

Although the wind had been knocked out of her normally billowing sails, Christabel Manley was no stereotyped black momma likely to go saucer-eyed and exclaim 'Lawks a-mercy' at a sudden shock, it was nevertheless as much as she could do to control her emotions and her breathing, but she managed to respond to her son's dramatic announcement with, "And about time too."

She then turned off the oven and went to the kitchen door. "Josiah," she called out. "He's back."

"Mom, I can explain—" Sylvester began but was cut short by his mother.

"You can hold your explanations till your daddy is here."

After wiping her hands on her apron she sat down at a partially laid table. Sylvester shifted uneasily from foot to foot. He too would have liked to sit down but when he made a movement towards a chair he received a petrifying glare which seemed to glue him to the kitchen floor.

Josiah Manley and sister Coral arrived simultaneously at the door.

"You go straight to your room," Mrs Manley ordered and for a moment it seemed that Josiah thought she was speaking to him and he would gladly have turned to go away; but Coral whined, "Why must I?" and he remained.

"Because I say so. That's why. Now, off with you."

Complaining that it wasn't fair, Coral retreated and Josiah moved forward.

"Close the door, Daddy, and come and sit down."

Josiah shut the door on his daughter, who clearly felt that being excluded from the anticipated fun of seeing Sylvester in deep trouble wasn't fair, but did as she was told.

However, no sooner was his wife seated than Josiah had to rise again.

"Daddy, go fetch the Holy Book, will you, please."

He disappeared on his mission and the kitchen became silent except for the faint sound made by shuffling shoes as Sylvester fidgeted nervously under his mother's basilisk stare.

"Put it on the table," said Mrs Manley when her husband returned carrying a large family bible. "Now then, Sylvester, I want you to put both hands on the Holy Book and say after me – 'I swear by Almighty God I will tell the truth and nothing but the truth and, if I don't, may I be punished by eternal damnation.'"

Trembling, Sylvester repeated the fearsome oath. Standing in front of his parents who were seated at the table he was not unlike a soldier on court martial for having gone AWOL in the face of the enemy.

His mother, in the role of prosecuting officer, spoke. "You are in trouble, boy. Not just with us but with the police who are searching for you, and you know what happens to people who waste police time. So I want to hear why you wanted to run away from the beginning, do you understand? Right from the beginning. I want to know how it started; I don't want no shortcuts, no excuses, only facts. Now, get started. We're listening."

Of all the ordeals he had faced – witnessing a rape, detention by a madman in a freezing cold house, the death of the madman through a wound caused by his knife, and his subsequent disori-entated and abortive flight – Sylvester sensed that he was about to undergo the worst ordeal of all, an unremitting interrogation by his mother. He opened his mouth and an unintelligible sound emerged.

"Speak up, boy. I can't hear you."

"I don't know where to start." Normally he would have added the word 'Mom' but was no longer sure he would be allowed to use this familiar mode of address to his terrifying inquisitor.

Christabel Manley heaved a sigh. "Troubles are like proper books," she said, "they have a beginning, a middle and an end. I want you to start at the very beginning of the trouble you are now in."

In an attempt to bring saliva to his dry mouth Sylvester began to make masticating noises. The clucking sound annoyed his mother who demanded to know if he was chewing gum. He could only shake his head, which action did nothing to dislodge the vivid image which dominated his mind, that of a pair of white panties. He had sworn on the Bible to tell the whole truth, but how could he mention the panties which were the beginning of his troubles? As he tried to find speech, he felt that an after-life of damnation and hell-fire was preferable to a confession of theft of such a garment.

"I'm waiting, boy. Don't aggravate me."

"Going to work one day about a month ago I needed to pee and I was going through the little wood and I though I'd do it there..."

Avoiding mention of the panties Sylvester told of the rape of the girl and of how when the rapists had gone he was about to leave when the girl shone a torch on him. He now realised she must have thought he had taken part but at the time it didn't occur to him. He simply didn't want to be late for work.

Josiah made his first comment. "Quite right," he said. "Work comes first."

His mother was less understanding. "You didn't help the girl, you didn't report what you'd seen to the police, you didn't tell us about it. You shame us all, boy."

"I'm sorry. I truly am."

"Your sorrow hasn't ended yet, I'll be bound. But go on."

Stumbling over words and leaving incomplete half-sentences hanging like never-drying laundry on an ever-expanding washing line, contradicting himself, losing thread of the story, ignorant of how he came to be found by a madman who alleged he was one of the rapists, constantly being interrupted to clarify a point, interrupted also by his mother suddenly springing up and going to the door which she flung open to reveal little Coral who had been eavesdropping, Sylvester, who hadn't eaten properly that day and who had been standing almost motionless for more than an hour being periodically bombarded by relentless questioning, began to see the walls of the kitchen start to shift, to spin around, before he fell to the floor in a dead faint.

He came to with his mother kneeling on one side of him sponging his forehead with a cold damp cloth and his father, who stood on the other side, looking anxiously down at him. To his surprise, and with a sneaking sense of gratification, he heard what sounded like an apology from his mother for putting him through the ordeal. But, best of all, he'd got through most of his story without any mention of the accursed white panties. All that remained was to tell of the time he'd spent after ridding himself of the bloodstained coat.

On their previous visit to Kingston, Jamaica, they had flown from Heathrow by British West Indian Airways on a Tristar 500. *En route* it had stopped at Barbados. Although he had no passport, he had gone to Heathrow in the hope of somehow getting on a flight. Time had been wasted because although he knew the type of aircraft flown by BWIA, and that a stop on the way to Kingston to change aircraft might be either at Barbados or Port of Spain, he was unsure of which terminal the departure was from. When he discovered that Terminal 3, area G, was the place to aim for, he was so tired that he sat down to rest and immediately fell asleep.

He woke at dawn with a clearer mind and realised it was stupid to try to get on a flight without a passport. He had left Heathrow mid-morning by bus, couldn't remember where he had alighted, caught another bus, or was it two buses, and found himself at Marlow in Buckinghamshire. Although hungry, he was afraid of going into a restaurant of cafe, all of which looked too high class anyway, didn't dare to go into the local SupaSava store in case a security man recognised him, or any other supermarket, as he felt the police might by now be looking for him. So great was his sense of guilt even though, as he took pains to stress, the man's death had been accidental, in the end, desperate for his home and family, he had somehow got there. "And here I am," he concluded.

By this time his mother had resumed cooking and under her more kindly gaze he tucked in ravenously to a meal of sirloin steak with four types of fresh vegetables, followed by a huge quantity of his favourite ice cream.

As he ate, his mother and father discussed what should be done. Josiah Manley who usually deferred to his wife on everything was adamant. The police must be informed on the morrow after Sylvester had enjoyed a good night's sleep. He and Mrs Manley would go to the police station together and – an enormous concession for him – he would telephone the pharmacy and for the first time ever be late for work, if he went at all that day. For once, family would take precedence over employment.

Little Coral who had been allowed to join the others for a meal had tried to interject a viewpoint on Silly Sylly and had received such a blast of disapproval from her mother for her unsolicited interruption that she had remained quiet, contenting herself with trying to kick Sylvester's legs under the table.

His mother had tucked him into bed with a hot-water bottle and before switching off the light had said, "You've been a fool, boy, but you are our boy and we'll fight to clear your name, provided you've told the truth."

"I have, Mom. I have."

"Good boy. Now go to sleep and remember, in spite of your fool behaviour, we all love you."

With these comforting words Sylvester was soon in a deep sleep, but not before he had thanked God, and the Lord Jesus, for bringing him safely back to his home. He hadn't forgotten the silent sacred pledge made at the playing field at North Dulwich that if the Lord saw fit to see him home he would faithfully serve the Lord for the rest of his life. This was now the second time he'd come back home and he was so grateful...

Sleep blanketed out the rest of his vague prayer of affirmation and thanksgiving.

Samson who had been listening to the local weather forecast on BBC 1 ('rain and hail moving in from the east') switched off the TV and reached for a phone. He keyed a number which would connect with the office answerphone to see if there were any urgent messages which would need his attention in the morning. He was glad to be back in the saddle, or in harness; contradictory equine metaphors which for him were interchangeable and meant he enjoyed working as the head of a successful private inquiry agency.

The first two items were of little importance, but the third gripped his attention. "This is Mrs Christabel Manley speaking. Sylvester is back home. But he is in great trouble. Tomorrow Mr Manley and me are taking him to the police, but before we go we should like to know what could happen to him. We don't want friends or neighbours to know about Sylvester's problems yet and we wondered if we could speak to you about it as you told me you and the police had the same aims. Can you please let me know what you think." The message ended with her telephone number which Samson immediately keyed.

When Mrs Manley had finished giving resume of Sylvester's confession she asked what would happen to him once he was in police custody.

"Before giving you advice I should like to meet your son and hear the facts from him. I'm willing to come and see you early tomorrow morning before you go to the police, which you must do, and you can ask any questions then."

She asked him to hold on while she discussed the matter with her husband. On her return she said, "We thank you for what you say but we wonder how much you visiting us will cost."

"Nothing."

"You mean it's for free?" she queried incredulously.

"There'll be absolutely no charge for my visit."

It was arranged that he would try to be at the Manley's house by eight o'clock the next morning.

He was taken to the front parlour where the windows were tightly shut against the elements and the smell of recently sprayed air-freshener lingered. He was introduced to Josiah and Sylvester Manley, both of whom occupied the leather settee. Samson was invited to sit down on an armchair which was positioned directly opposite them. A small occasional table had been placed equidistantly between Samson and the two Manleys. Mrs Manley put her cane chair in a neutral spot which gave the curious appearance the she was proposing to act as umpire in some game to be played between the home team and the visitor. Verisimilitude of this impression was enhanced a pad of paper and a pencil lying on the table-top.

Samson initiated proceedings by asking Sylvester to tell him right from the beginning, as his mother had on the previous day, and to omit no detail however trivial it might seem.

When Sylvester had finished narrating events from the rape to the flight from the empty house to Heathrow and Marlow, finally coming to a stop at his home Samson said, "There's just one thing I find puzzling. You said it was soon after you entered the wood that you heard someone behind you. You turned and saw a man holding a gun in one hand and a bag from the store where you work in the other. He ordered you to leave the path which runs through the wood and with the gun pressed against your back, and carrying a bunch of carnations, you were guided through the wood to the place where you were held captive. Is that correct?"

"Yes, sir, it is."

"And the man still had the bag when you arrived at the house?"

Sylvester thought for a moment. "Yes, sir."

"And on your journey through the wood you didn't stop anywhere?"

"That is correct, sir."

"On your way did you pass through the small clearing where the rape took place?"

"We might have done."

"Surely you know for certain whether or not you did?"

"Yes, I think we did."

"Are you sure that it wasn't in this clearing that the man accosted you? It wasn't on the path, was it? I'm not trying to trap you, Sylvester, but I must tell you there is circumstantial evidence that the confrontation between him and you took place in the clearing. What do you say to that?"

Sylvester's eye swivelled wildly round the room as if seeking help from its walls of the plethora of objects, finally coming to rest on a bronze statue of Sir Garfield Sobers executing a sweep shot to leg. But the inspirational West Indian cricketer had no inspiration to pass on to Sylvester who would sooner have died than confess he was in the clearing to see if the rape victim's white panties were still visible.

Mrs Manley, impartial as any Wimbledon umpire said, "Speak up, Sylvester, don't keep the gentleman waiting."

"Er…"

"C'mon, boy, you lost your tongue?"

"You're right, sir. Now I come to think of it. I went there for a pee."

"What's the matter with you, boy? You trying to say you only have to go into the wood and it affects your waterworks?"

"No. Mom."

Samson intervened. "It's not important, Mrs Manley."

Sylvester shot him a look of gratitude.

"Before I go on." Samson said, "there is something I should tell you." He went on to explain his special interest in the case. The man who, according to Sylvester, had been accidentally killed was the husband of his business partner and had been convinced that Sylvester's appearance immediately after the rape had been due to his intent to retrieve a scarf left by himself, a rapist. He looked directly at Sylvester. "Was the scarf yours?"

On safe ground at last Sylvester replied, "No, sir. It belonged to the look-out guy."

"I believe you." Samson said. "And I'm inclined to believe the rest of your story. You strike me as one of these unfortunates who is liable to be in the wrong place at the wrong time." He turned to Mrs Manley. "I've told you of my interest in the matter and I shall quite understand if you wish me to leave. On the other hand, I'm happy to stay and tell you what your son may expect after reporting to the police which is something he must do, and as soon as possible."

It was Josiah who replied. "You've been straight with us, mister. We'd appreciate you staying."

Samson proceeded to explain that it was virtually certain that Sylvester would be arrested and charged, possibly with murder. It would be necessary for an inquest to be opened by the coroner but this would, if a charge had been made, be indefinitely adjourned. Next would be committal proceedings in front of magistrates and, assuming that they committed Sylvester for trial at a higher court, it would be for the solicitor representing Sylvester to ask for bail. At some stage the Crown Prosecution Service would be consulted and, provided they thought the case strong enough to warrant a hearing, there would be a formal trial with judge and jury. For this, Sylvester's solicitor would instruct a barrister to defend him. There might even be two barristers, a Queen's Counsel and a junior.

An awed silence followed this exposition. It was broken by Mrs Manley.

"We can't pay for all this."

"Sylvester will apply for legal aid. His solicitor will do this for him."

Samson was asked if he could recommend a solicitor as they didn't have one.

"If I were in Sylvester's shoes I'd want Helen Phillips of Phillips and Lyall. She's first class on criminal law. I'll have a word with her if you like."

When he left the Manleys to visit Shandy on his way back to town, Samson departed with their heartfelt gratitude ringing in his ears. It was from the bells he liked best when it came from a disadvantaged source.

Nineteen

Accompanied by his parents, Sylvester went to the police station to explain his part in the death of Paul Bullivant. The interview was conducted by Detective Inspector Tapsell and a detective sergeant who, conscious of the prevailing public mood which favoured reverse discrimination, treated Sylvester, a black youth, more gently than if his skin had been white, to the point of parody of the role they had to play when questioning a black. Whereas a white youth might have expected to feel the bristles of a besom broom, a light feather duster was used to clear up any ambiguities in Sylvester's statement. The detectives' task wasn't made easier by the watchfulness of Helen Phillips.

Although he was charged with causing unlawful death, he could have been excused for thinking this was nothing more serious than stealing sweets from a confectioner. He was granted police bail on condition that he surrendered his passport. Assured by Helen Phillips that he could expect a fair trail and be defended by an expert team of lawyers, Mrs Manley behaved as though her son were already a free man. Sylvester, however, knew differently. He had seen films on television where backward prisoners were cruelly mocked by inmates and warders alike, and heard from boys at school whose fathers were doing a stretch that the weak went to the wall in prison.

His inchoate fears increased when at the magistrates court hearing he was committed for trial at the Crown Court, this time charged with murder. He was still allowed bail on condition that he reported each week to the police station. None of the Manleys understood how the change of charge came about, although there were due formalities. Helen Phillips continued to assure them that all would end well, but Mrs Manley was less sanguine about the outcome. Strangely it seemed as though somehow Sylvester's fears had been transferred to his mother; the more worried she became the less he seemed to care. It may have been through some protective mechanism of the mind that he began to feel as if the trial which lay ahead concerned someone else. In a curious way he became detached from reality and appeared to accept whatever the future might hold. Christabel Manley, aware of his fatalistic attitude, was afraid he would accept any accusation thrown at him, right or wrong, and through lack of fighting spirit would end up with a life sentence in prison. Josiah was equally concerned, but more practical. "He is what he is," he told his wife. "You won't change him, only confuse him."

The mills of the law, like those of God, can grind slowly, and as the months passed by it seemed that the grinding had come to a halt. In the interim between committal proceedings and the trial, Sylvester's detachment, the feeling that what lay ahead and what had happened in the past was not his problem, increased, as did his religious beliefs. He was in daily communication with his God and, during his prayers, occasionally received encouraging messages from the Almighty – which crystallised into simple language were: 'No need for worry, boy, I'm with you.'

His withdrawal from reality was not so total as to verge on a psychotic state such as schizophrenia or full-blown paranoia; he remained aware that some sort of ordeal lay ahead but was confident that with God's help any difficulties would be surmounted, provided – and this was important – that he honoured his pledge to serve the Lord in whatever way the Lord should require, even if this would mean leaving his family and wandering the face of the earth. Behind a number of complex mental processes stood a little sentinel of which Sylvester himself was unaware. This sentry had the cunning of the most cunning of all foxes and guarded something which, in essence, was nothing more or less than a keen sense of self-preservation.

The coroner's inquest was adjourned *sine die*. Sylvester asked what this odd expression meant and was told it was Latin for 'without a day being appointed for continuance'. "Those two small words mean all that," he marvelled.

And then came the news that a thirty-year-old man from Leeds had been arrested for the rape of a teenager. When arrested, he had confessed to eleven other similar offences including the rape of Kimberley. He had chosen to plead guilty to the eleven rapes as by doing so, once sentenced, the slate would be wiped clean and he could begin life afresh. He had little option but plead guilty to the final rape as he had been caught *in flagrante delicto*. The Latin tag intrigued Sylvester and he repeated it to himself over and over again. He was told that literally it meant 'while the crime is blazing', or more colloquially, 'being caught in the act'.

Incredibly the two well-worn legal terms of art were the beginning of a love affair between a poorly educated black youth of negligible academic ability and a dead language. Sylvester was greatly impressed by the concision of Latin and its terse, no-nonsense factual approach to life's problems. The ancient Romans evidently didn't bullshit around; they gave it to you straight.

His mother wondered if the strain of awaiting trail had caused Sylvester to go a bit off his rocker, but Josiah Manley who knew some Latin was more understanding and encouraged the youth in his quest to learn more. He explained that a number of words in the English language owed their origin to Latin and very many medical terms were Latin based. "You catch a bad cold and you have *rhinitis*," he said by way of illustration, "which means inflammation of the nose, or *rhinus*." And, warming to the subject of nasal extremities he went on to say that the word 'rhinoceros' was literally 'hard nose,' and then that 'arteriosclerosis' was "hardening of the arteries'.

Sylvester listened in awed fascination and made up his mind to become a Latin scholar. He managed to purchase a dog-eared copy of *Kennedy's Latin Primer* and what had begun as a love affair became a lifelong marriage. The bond between father and son grew stronger and Christabel Manley could only look on disapprovingly as over the kitchen table they began a translation with the help of a crib of Virgil's *Aeneid* – '*arma virumque cano*' – an opening which neatly encapsulated much of what was to follow.

The prospect of being found guilty at the trial held no dread for Sylvester. A spell of quiet in prison would give him the opportunity to study and take a correspondence course in Latin. He gave in his notice at the SupaSava store, but to escape the nagging of his mother was obliged to take on casual work as a labourer or in distributing leaflets from door to door. These employments held up his studies, but when possible he persevered in what at first had seemed a hopeless task. The one snag was in pronunciation, not that this was necessary at present, but he didn't know whether, when in the seclusion of his room, to speak the words as if in English or to adopt the modern the modern mode which turned '*virumque*' into '*wirumque*'.

The self-induced compulsion to master the Latin language increased his detachment from reality. When a date for the trial was fixed he had no fears. His apparent lack of interest in whether or not he was found guilty was an attitude which made his mother start calling him Mr Cool – "Mr Cool, come down, your dinner's ready," and "Wake up, Mr Cool, breakfast's ready."

Sylvester's solicitor, Helen Phillips, had been born and brought up in Wales and her softly lilting accent reminded him of the way some Caribbean women spoke, a melodious sound which sang out for a composer to transcribe it to notations on a sheet of music. He felt a rapport with her, and for her part she understood he didn't wish to identify himself as someone accused of murder.

The date for the trial was set down for November, by coincidence almost a year to the day after Kimberley's rape. Jonathan Holmes-Whittingley, a Queen's Counsel, was briefed for the defence and it was agreed at a conference in chambers that Shandy should be called as a witness to testify on Paul Bullivant's obsession. It was legally well established that in many actions a wife was a competent but not compellable witness, but whether the same held for a widow was largely *obiter dicta*. The question of compellability would be irrelevant if Shandy agreed of her own volition to testify, and Helen Phillips decided to approach her on the matter.

First, she had a word with Samson, whom she knew far better than Shandy. He agreed that it would strengthen the defence's case if she could testify that Paul's obsession in hunting down an innocent man had indirectly contributed to his death. A meeting was arranged to take place one evening in Samson's flat. Samson, a late-developing sybarite, had decanters of wine and canapés for the occasion, but neither these nor the blandishments of Helen Phillips were necessary to induce Shandy into co-operating. Her willingness to give evidence in support of Sylvester was based on a reason extremely personal and private. She had worked out that Paul had gone straight from a session of fierce and satisfying love-making to a place where a guiltless captive was – or so he thought – awaiting torment, mutilation or death. This was a terrible blow to her self-esteem, and it had accentuated the sense of shock at Paul's death. She had gone to sleep in the belief that their marital difficulties were over and an hour or two after waking had found they were indeed over, everlastingly over, due to the death of her partner in marriage. She had yet to come to terms with what she regarded as a betrayal.

The only snag from a legal point of view in calling Shandy as a witness was that the prosecution might object on the grounds that her evidence was partly hearsay. It would be for Mr Holmes-Whittingley to counter this argument and for the judge to rule on whether certain evidence was admissible.

Of the twelve jurors, three were white women, two were Asians, two were black, and the remaining five were white men. Helen Phillips had found out that one of the blacks was from Nigeria and the origins of the other were Jamaican. The latter was a professor of economics at London University. He was always immaculately dressed and would wear a red rose in the button-hole of a dark grey pinstripe suit. Sylvester regarded him as a likely friend on the jury, someone of his own country and race who would be prejudiced, if only a little, in his favour.

Prosecution counsel opened the case of *Regina v. Manley* and more than once used the term *mens rea*. Helen Phillips turned round to Sylvester in the dock behind her. "It means guilty intention," she whispered. "He is going to try to prove you intended to murder Mr Bullivant."

By his admission to the police it was clear Sylvester had sprung out at Paul Bullivant with a knife in his hand. It would be for the defence to show that the knife was intended as a weapon of self-preservation against someone who had left him tied up and had shown no mercy.

The opening speech was followed by police evidence during which Sylvester saw his flick-knife, now in a cellophane wrapper, produced as an exhibit. Its function was explained for the benefit of the jury. Defence counsel, who up to this point hadn't said much, pressed the policeman giving evidence to admit that most Jamaicans of the defendant's age carried knives; but the policeman refused to make a generalisation. He was pressed some more until the prosecution counsel stood up and protested that, "Surely this is all *de minimis*?"

Helen Phillips turned round. "*De minimis non curat lex*," she whispered, "The law doesn't concern itself with trifles."

An adjournment was requested so that a conference on the issue might take place between opposing counsel, to which the judge after a prodigious yawn said, "Very well then."

Half an hour later, when the hearing was resumed, it was obvious that Sylvester's counsel had won the argument because the prosecution were willing to accept that most Jamaican youths carried a knife as a sign of manhood. The judge suddenly showed interest in the matter. He asked, "What if the police should stop and search a young West Indian and find a knife of his person. It not this *prima facie* evidence of carrying an offensive weapon?"

A three-cornered discussion between the judge and two counsel followed which had no relevance to the trial as it concerned the clash between the English legal system and foreign cultures. How can the two be reconciled without appearing to be biased? A newspaper reporter sensed that he had a story here and began writing feverishly in shorthand. His effort wasn't wasted. On the following morning a national newspaper gave prominence on page five to the headline 'Judge speaks out on racial issue'.

As yet unaware that his case would receive such attention, Sylvester waited for the discussion to end, as it did soon after the reporter left the court to make telephone calls. The judge stood up, as did everyone else. The hearing was adjourned until the following day and Sylvester was led down to a cell in the basement of the court house.

It was a bleak sparsely furnished hutch with a neon light in the ceiling but no means to switch it off inside the cell. Josiah Manley was allowed a short visit. He told Sylvester, "Your momma sends all her love, but is too distressed to come and see you."

Shortly after his departure, Helen Phillips arrived with the junior counsel. "Mr Holmes-Whittingley sends his apologies but he's had to rush back to chambers on an urgent case," Helen explained. "Mr Wisdell here just wants to sound you on something."

The gist of a long and tortuous talk on tactics was that if Sylvester were called to give evidence, the prosecution could question him and possibly inflict much unwarranted damage on his case. Moreover, by calling him, defence counsel would lose the right to speak last when closing speeches were made. On the other hand, if he were not called, the jury might conclude that his evidence was so suspect that the defence didn't dare risk putting him in a position where he could be cross-examined by the prosecuting counsel. Did Sylvester have any views on the matter?

"Yes. I don't want to hide away. I want to tell my side of the story."

"You may feel differently tomorrow."

"I don't think I shall, but tomorrow is another day."

Mr Wisdell gave him a searching look. "Your solicitor tells me you are interested in learning Latin. I'm a bit of a Latin buff. Do you know Horace?"

"I know he was a Roman poet."

"He was something of a philosopher too. *Carpe diem*, make the most of today, enjoy the present, was his guiding precept. I recommend him to you."

With that quotation Mr Wisdell departed. Helen Phillips remained a while to make sure Sylvester was as settled as possible in a strange environment.

He pondered the day's events in court, but didn't ponder long because his concentration had been limited and his attention had frequently wandered. He had no doubt he would be found not guilty at the end, particularly with someone like the elegant black professor on the jury. But most of all he believed God was on his side. Each night before he fell asleep he prayed to his heavenly Father and renewed his sacred pledge of service when he was once more a free man. Tonight was no exception.

During the following day the remaining Crown witnesses filed in and out, including a fingerprint expert who was savaged by Mr Holmes-Whittingley, who would later produce his own witness with diametrically opposite expertise. When the prosecution case was closed Mr Holmes-Whittingley opened with his fingerprint expert so that the jury might remember the contrast.

Sylvester, who easily lost interest unless facts were expressed with the terseness of Latin phrases, did pay sufficient attention to the nub of the expert disagreement. This was that the handle of the knife bore the imprint of the dead man's palm, which indicated that he had grabbed the knife before Sylvester, and in struggling to prevent him from making the wound worse Sylvester had done exactly the opposite. At least, this was what Mr Holmes-Whittingley was arguing.

Shandy was the next witness to be called. Newspaper reporters (for three were now five) gripped pencils in anticipation of headlines which read 'Widow Gives Evidence Against

Dead Husband' or 'Widow Fights to Clear Accused of Husband's Murder'. They weren't to be disappointed. Shandy spoke of Paul's obsession with the rape of his daughter, which he had wrongly attributed to the accused in the dock. Of the two men who had committed the rape, one was dead and the other in prison for that and other rapes. Sylvester Manley was entirely innocent. She was unshaken by prosecution counsel's cross-questioning and when she stood down there were one or two handclaps from the public gallery for her courage in testifying on oath in the manner she had. No one in the well of the court realised that the handclaps had come from Mrs Christabel Manley and a close friend seated beside her.

Two more defence witnesses followed. Neither added much substance to the case, although Sylvester was pleasingly gratified that Mr Cartright, the manager of the SupaSava store where he worked, was willing to turn up and give a glowing reference to Sylvester's honesty and his popularity as a hard worker – he had even returned to work after a severe bout of influenza although his sick note had not expired. He had never shown the slightest sign of violence even when racially provoked by another employee. Mr Cartright had seen the incident in question and heard the words expressed and was amazed at the way in which Sylvester had without backing off retained control of his temper. The employee who had tried to bait him had been dismissed on the spot.

And then it was Sylvester's turn to enter the witness box.

Avoiding leading questions, Mr Holmes-Wittingley led him skilfully through events from the moment when he had gone to a spot in a nearby wood to urinate up to the point when he had managed to cut himself free from a tightly bound cord around his wrists. He made much of the fact that the skin had been painfully burned by the bonds and when the two men had fought on the floor, with Sylvester on top, so great was the pain that he was forced to drop the knife. It fell, accidentally piercing an artery in Mr Bullivant's neck. The truth of what happened next would never be known, but Mr Holmes-Whittingley submitted to the jury that both men had attempted to pull out the knife but their combined efforts had simply driven it deeper...

"Mr Holmes-Whittingley, kindly save such statements for your closing speech. They are not appropriate now," the judge intervened, stern of voice and mien.

"As you lordship pleases."

Continuing his examination-in-chief Mr Holmes-Whittingley concluded by praising the honesty of the defendant in coming forward to inform the police of what had happened.

"I think that'll be enough for today," said the judge gathering up his papers. Court is adjourned until tomorrow."

It was a matter for debate whether an adjournment at this point favoured defence or prosecution, but on the whole it was considered to benefit the defending team, provided prosecution counsel couldn't unsettle the accused and create a fog of uncertainty in the minds of jurors, who may have forgotten some of the previous day's evidence.

Sylvester, spending his second night in the cell, had no opinions on the problem. He simply wanted to get home to start the rest of his life. He knew his parents, particularly his mother, would object to what he intended; but it was his life, not hers, and he wouldn't be dominated by her.

Once again his father paid him a short visit which was followed by Helen Phillips with whom he was now on first-name terms.

"Only one more day," she said. "All that remains is the cross-examination of you by the prosecution, the two closing speeches and the judge's summing-up. Then the jury will retire to consider the verdict."

"I shall be glad to be home again. The food here isn't a patch on my mother's cooking."

She smiled. "You're a cool customer, Sylvester. I've never met anyone quite so cool in such adverse circumstances."

"That's what my mother calls me, Helen. Mr Cool."

"No worries about being questioned by the silk leading the prosecution tomorrow?"

He shrugged. "Why should I worry? I've told the truth. You know, Helen, I've been thinking. I wouldn't be here now if I hadn't stopped one morning on my way to work to have a pee. Isn't it strange that having a pee can lead to all this? All the thousands of pounds spent on a trial, to say nothing of other expenses."

"That's a thought. Mind you, you were very unlucky to be an eyewitness to a rape on account of relieving yourself."

"That's true, but you never know. It might all work out for the best." He paused. "Is there a Latin saying for that?"

She laughed. "I expect so, but I don't know it."

She stayed a few minutes more before leaving with, "Good-night, Mr Cool. Sleep well."

Sylvester's cross-examination the next day went well, in spite of efforts to trip him up by contradicting evidence given in the examination-in-chief. He scored especially well when prosecuting counsel said, apropos his denial that he had intended to kill the man who had tormented him, left him bound and helpless in a strange place and then returned to torment him some more before possibly maiming him for life, "May I remind you that you are on oath."

"I don't need reminding," replied Sylvester calmly. "The good Lord is my shepherd. He knows, and I know, I am speaking the truth."

When he realised he was getting nowhere with protracted questioning and might alienate the jury by continuing, counsel sat down and Mr Holmes-Whittingley began his speech for the defence. It was an eloquent and emotional plea on behalf of Sylvester which concluded, "The patent innocence of the accused has shone like a beacon of light throughout the murky depths of this trial and there can be only one verdict, that of not guilty."

In contrast, the prosecution's closing speech appealed to reason rather than emotion and concentrated on the fact that two men had fought to the death and the survivor's story was only one side of the case. What might the dead man have said? Would he have agreed that the accused had shone like a beacon of innocence? "I doubt it. I very much doubt it, and I invite you to doubt it too, so much so that you find the accused guilty as charged."

The judge's summing-up was succinct and Sylvester heard the words 'reasonable doubt' uttered many times, but he lost the thread of the summing-up and just wished the judge would finish, the jury would retire, find him not guilty and he could go home to sleep in his own bed. But it was not to be. The jury couldn't reach agreement and were sent away to spend the night at a hotel, and they were warned not to discuss the case with anyone else on pain of punishment for contempt of court.

Sylvester's faith wasn't shaken but he prayed most earnestly that if it was God's will – and only if it was His will – that he be found not guilty, let it be as early as possible the next day as the weekend was nigh and he didn't fancy being banged up in a cell until Monday.

For a long while the following day, it seemed that the Lord's hearing aid hadn't been switched on. Half-way through the afternoon, the judge was told by the jury's foreman that agreement couldn't be reached on a verdict. The judge sent back a message that he would accept a majority verdict of ten to two.

When, twenty minutes later, the jury filed back into court, a silence fell that almost screamed to be broken by a dropped pin.

To the well-established formula which begins, 'How do you find the defendant?', by a majority verdict of ten to two Sylvester was found not guilty of murder and also not guilty on a second count of manslaughter. These verdicts were greeted by a cheer from the public gallery.

The judge turned to him and said, "You are free to go."

The jury were formally discharged, the prosecution and defence teams gathered up reams of paper and legal textbooks, and Sylvester found himself being congratulated by family, friends, and some people he didn't know. He felt like saying, 'Don't congratulate me, give thanks to my Father in Heaven.' Later, he wished he had done so, as he was certain that it was God's will that he should be free.

*   *   *

No one had eaten lunch that day and Sylvester went to a nearby restaurant for a celebratory meal with his parents and little Coral. They had hardly sat down when the black professor of economics walked in and took a table at the far side of the room.

"Excuse me," said Sylvester, "there's someone I want to speak to."

He hurried across to where the juror was seated.

"I just want to thank you for voting for me—" he began but got no further as the professor interrupted him.

"Save your gratitude. My vote went against you, not for you. I think you had guilty intent. You meant to kill. That was my belief, and it still is, *man*." A cruel emphasis on the word 'man' denoted contempt for what the juror saw Sylvester to be, a young semi-literate Jamaican tearaway who was a disgrace to his native country and his race.

Sylvester returned to his table, a look of hurt disbelief on his face.

Josiah used all his powers of persuasion in an effort to find out the reason for the mood-swing from celebratory joy to unhappy silence, but without success. In the end he said, "Don't let it bug you, son. Whatever was said is his problem, not yours. Forget it."

But Sylvester couldn't forget, and in the peace and quiet of his room when he went to bed, the truth crashed through barriers of self-deception in a hurricane which swept away the spurious sense of a different identity and the protective withdrawal from reality. The professor had been right; he did have guilty intent when he thrust the knife in the direction of Paul Bullivant's throat. He had intended to kill. Had he wished, he could have let the knife drop harmlessly to the floor, but he hadn't. As it was, he had borne false witness and got away with murder and, thanks to God, was at liberty once more. But in exchange for mercifully granting him freedom God would exact a price which, *inter alia*, would include a heavy, lifelong burden on his conscience, and from this there would be no escape.

Epilogue

In the twelve months between November and November, John Samson, accepting that full retirement had been a mistake, came back to work three days a week. The problem of accommodation was solved when he took on the tenancy of a room on the floor above that occupied by Samson Associates. He continued to be, on the firm's notepaper, a consultant.

Shandy, although saddened by what had happened, soon recovered her poise, as did Kimberley. From an early age, she had been attracted by fragrances and perfumes, and liked the idea of one day becoming an aromatherapist, earning a good income by giving aromatherapy massage. However, first she would have to take a course in beauty treatment.

As for Sylvester, acquittal at the trial seemed to change his character. Never an extravert, he became reclusive and spent much spare time either at the local library or in his room at home. In casual work he avoided becoming too friendly with anyone. The change in his demeanour worried his mother, who summed up her feeling by saying to Josiah, "Mr Cool has become Mr Cold-Shoulder."

To this observation Josiah gave his standard reply: "He is what he is, you won't change him."

Unknown to his parents, Sylvester had come to the

conclusion that the best way to give service to the Lord in atonement for the sin of denying, under oath, that he had committed murder, was by becoming first a convert to Roman Catholicism and then a novice monk. He continued to study Latin and took a correspondence course on the subject. He read everything available through the public library on Roman Catholicism, including information on various monastic orders.

One night he had a vivid dream in which he was following a hooded figure who wore a black gown. Suddenly the figure turned and under the cowl Sylvester was shaken to see the face of the professor of economics. The professor gave him a friendly smile and Sylvester awoke convinced that the dream contained a message from God. It didn't take long to decode what the Lord intended for him.

The Benedictine Order of monks were also known as the Black Monks. The figure in his dream had been that of a black man, and he, Sylvester, was black. He already knew that one of the Order's aims was the performance of divine office in choir. He possessed a resonant tenor voice and enjoyed singing hymns as did the contralto Christabel and the basso profundo Josiah. He knew too that Benedictine monks tried to attain 'personal sanctification compatible with living in community' and although he wasn't clear what was meant by 'personal sanctification' he felt sure the monks would guide him towards it.

It would be a wrench parting from his family who would greatly disapprove of his change of religious persuasion, but his mind was made up. The time for thought was over; it was time for action.

He left his bedroom to go downstairs to break the news to his parents.

Newport Libraries

THIS ITEM SHOULD BE RETURNED OR
RENEWED BY THE LAST DATE
STAMPED BELOW.

Newport
COUNTY BOROUGH
BWRDEISTREF SIROL
Casnewydd

Please return this item to the library from which it
was borrowed